WEB OF DOMINATION

She had thought, when they began to fasten it on her, that there might be some way out. Gemma might be persuaded to undo the straitjacket and give her temporary freedom. But even this possibility was denied for, too late, Amber realised that this restraint was not equipped with a row of straps at the rear, but a heavy-duty zip fastener secured by a small padlock at the back of the neck. The straitjacket was tight and both pairs of hands were employed to raise the zip. Its ascent coincided well with Amber's rising excitement. An excitement which was at last punctuated by the soft, terminal click of the padlock.

Other titles by the author

HOUSE OF ANGELS
HOUSE OF INTRIGUE
HOUSE OF TEMPTATIONS

WEB OF DOMINATION

Yvonne Strickland

This book is a work of fiction.
In real life, make sure you practise safe sex.

First published in 1997 by
Nexus
332 Ladbroke Grove
London W10 5AH

Copyright © Yvonne Strickland 1997

The right of Yvonne Strickland to be identified as the
Author of this Work has been asserted by her in
accordance with the Copyright Designs and Patents Act
1988.

Typeset by TW Typesetting, Plymouth, Devon

Printed and bound by
Caledonian Books Ltd, Glasgow

ISBN 0 352 33154 2

Contents

1

Villa Raffaello

The red Fiat slowed and Gareth looked up at the driver's mirror. Sophie was screened from view in the back seat by an outspread and well-worn road map.

'Well?' he said as they approached the small cross-roads.

Victoria, sitting by his side, stared ahead saying nothing as she had for much of the time since they left Arezzo around mid-morning. True, she had conversed when they stopped for lunch at an ancient town with the odd name of Poppi, but only to discuss superficialities with little more than polite indifference. The town had occupied them for longer than intended. Even so, Gareth had taken his time. The wooded hills of the Casentino offered some of the most attractive scenery in Tuscany and had tempted them away from the main routes.

The car slowed further, pulled on to the grass edge and stopped. Victoria gazed across the peaceful treescape, falling away and rising again in the distance, basking under the late afternoon sun. Gareth had not looked directly at her for some time but her image was fixed in his mind. Sharp brown eyes set in soft, high cheek-boned face with full and sensual lips. A face framed in rich brown hair, pinned up in rolling swirls. He twisted about and addressed the expanse of billowing white paper to the rear. 'Well?'

The wall of paper descended and an anxious face appeared. Her hazel eyes were softer than Victoria's but her lips just as sensual. A hand appeared and pushed long, flaxen hair away from her cheek. 'Well what?'

Gareth's mouth broadened into a smile of contrived

good humour, though he hoped his frustration was being imparted sufficiently to elicit a meaningful response. 'Well, where d'you reckon we are? There isn't a signpost.'

Sophie pushed aside one of the carrier bags which occupied part of the back seat and tilted her head. 'Look, since we turned off the main road, I can't follow anything on this map. It shows the entire country, Gareth. There isn't enough detail. I don't think this road is even on it. We should turn around and go back if you ask me.' She glanced down and shrugged. 'I'm totally lost.'

'Join the club,' muttered Gareth.

Without turning, Victoria said, 'Well I am surprised, dear. You didn't have any trouble navigating yesterday afternoon.'

Gareth gritted his teeth, 'Okay, Vicky, what do you think?'

Her eyes fixed hard on his. 'Why ask me? I haven't got a map.'

Gareth tapped fingers on the steering wheel. 'We don't have much petrol left. It might be a good idea to go down rather than up.'

'According to the dial,' said Victoria, 'we don't have any petrol left at all.'

Gareth looked wistfully at the fuel gauge. The needle was firmly in the red section. It had been there for some considerable time. 'There's always a bit more than you think. It's not as empty as it looks.'

'You hope,' added Victoria.

'Well you could have kept your eyes open for a garage! These aren't the easiest roads to get around.'

'I did.' Victoria smiled triumphantly. 'I kept them open when I shouldn't have. Remember?'

'How could I forget,' sighed Gareth, beginning to turn the car around. He hesitated and took the right hand turn. 'We might as well let the crossroads decide our fate.'

Sophie remarked, 'I think we should have gone left,' and busied herself in unsuccessfully attempting to fold the map. But her mind was on yesterday, and the events of that fateful afternoon flashed through her mind again.

* * *

2

They were to stay overnight in Arezzo. The hotel, a few minutes stroll from the Piazza Grande, had seemed ideal and Victoria, with a working knowledge of Italian, had negotiated a couple of rooms. One for herself and Gareth, and one, with some difficulty, for Sophie, who had travelled over with them and had remained attached ever since their leaving Rome. Sophie, oddly enough, had been Victoria's idea. 'Why don't the three of us travel together?' she had said. 'Sophie is going on to a hostel near Viareggio once we're there.' What had occurred to no one until too late, was the fact that Viareggio was close to the end of their trip. So it had seemed only fair that Sophie should stay with them until they reached Lucca or Pisa, where she would catch the bus and go on alone.

They had sat for lunch at a little bar off the Corso Italia, Arezzo's main shopping street. Victoria wanted to visit the Casa del Vasari but Sophie was much more inclined to explore the sprawling antiques market in the Piazza Grande. Gareth, in preferring to stay outdoors, had opted to stay with Sophie.

There had been no ulterior motive. His relationship with Victoria had been going steadily for six months. The firm of London accountants he worked for was on the same street as the firm of solicitors where Victoria worked. He had met Sophie through Victoria but she had always appeared to him preoccupied and not especially communicative. That day though, in her short white skirt and blue top, she would have easily turned his head had they passed in the street.

They had arranged to meet Victoria at five-o-clock. That had left well over over two hours of free time but the market was hot and crowded. Sophie had said, 'I think I'll pop back to the hotel. I could do with the sun cream.' Gareth had returned with her, but instead of setting out again, they had gone to the small shaded garden at the rear of the hotel and shared a bottle of chilled Vernaccia.

'I didn't think students could afford to swig wine,' Gareth remarked. Sophie always paid her share of everything and this bottle of wine was no exception.

3

Tree-filtered light sparkled in her eyes. 'We're not all paupers you know. All right, I couldn't survive on my grant but dad gives me a decent allowance. I wouldn't be over here otherwise.'

The Vernaccia had gradually diminished and neither seemed in any hurry to go back to the antiques market. With the final glass gone, Sophie said, 'I've got to go to the loo and I think I'll have a shower while I'm up there. It's so hot today, isn't it?'

Gareth agreed, watching the hair fall across her cheek. 'I wouldn't mind freshening up either.'

They entered the gloomy hallway and collected their room keys from the board. On climbing the narrow stairs it was only natural that he should gaze at her slim body, the curve of her swaying behind and her long legs. Her alluring physique was on a par with Victoria's and that was no mean comparison. As for her being uncommunicative and reserved, well perhaps his judgement had been premature. Perhaps Victoria's more assertive manner tended to eclipse Sophie when they were together. On the landing, Gareth smiled, 'Give us a shout if you want someone to soap your back.'

It was the sort of typical male remark which it was hoped would lead on to something further but seldom did. Gareth was quite taken aback when she smiled up at him and brushed the wisp of fair hair away from his ear with her finger. 'I'd better not shout. But you could come and ask.'

Then she was gone, leaving him with mouth slightly ajar and heart beating a little harder. But she was only teasing. That's the way most people were.

Gareth entered his and Victoria's room and undressed, his mind full of Sophie's words and Sophie's smile. Instead of entering the small bathroom, he stopped to contemplate. There were distant sounds from the town: a shout, the occasional car horn. Little else. His eye moved to the door. It was no use. Gareth stepped into the bathroom, seized a towel and hitched it about his waist. In a moment, he was pulling open the bedroom door to glance along the dimly lit landing.

4

There was only stillness and utter quiet. Sophie's room was directly opposite, just two steps away. He twisted the handle of her door slowly. The door was unlocked. A surge of excitement ran through him as the door opened with a soft creak and he slipped inside. But had she really intended to leave it unlocked? The blinds were part closed but he could see that the room was empty. There was her skirt and top laid neatly on the bed. To his left stood the bathroom. Gareth stepped forwards and cleared his throat. 'Hello! Er – anybody home?' From around the bathroom door appeared a face. 'Oh, there you are.'

'Sorry, I, er, I wasn't sure if . . .' He felt his face redden.

Sophie broke into a wide grin. 'I never thought of you as being shy, Gareth.'

'Shy? No, I'm not usually shy. It's just that – well, I wasn't sure.'

She gave a little laugh and vanished back into the small bathroom. He hesitated at the doorway, glimpsing her naked by the bath, flaxen hair clipped up and fastened in a bun above her head. She had her back to him and was turning on the creaking shower taps. Pipes rattled and clanged as water spluttered forth and began to drum into the old enamel bath. When she turned towards him, Gareth waived any pretence about not regarding her form, even though he'd found ample opportunity to assess it before by the poolside at the hotel near Rome. He had already seen how full and firm were her breasts: a little fuller, perhaps, than Victoria's. His eyes fell momentarily upon the fine down of pale straw pubic hair. The effect she was having upon him could hardly go unnoticed by Sophie, for his arousal beneath the white bath towel was impossible to conceal.

Behind Sophie, the shower continued to hiss and chuckle down the plughole. Still smiling, she moved forwards and, as if sensing his residual uneasiness, put her arms about his neck and kissed him. At the taste of her perfumed breath and warm lips upon his, at her thigh pushing against the aching hardness, all doubts evaporated, all thoughts of caution were eclipsed by the stirring within his loins. Then

5

she said, 'The hot water is running away. Let's get in there first.'

He helped her over the edge and both attempted to position themselves under the shower, only to find it almost impossible because of the meagre dimensions of the bath. They took turns under the spray, Sophie saying, 'Careful! I don't want to get my hair wet,' as each liberally soaped and rinsed the other, hands and fingers caressing bodies with uninhibited intimacy so that instead of speech there were soft moans and sighs. Several times a lubricated hand slipped beneath his testicles, making his pelvis tighten and his engorged penis quiver.

At one point, Gareth turned her to face away from him and passed his arms about her body to cup and squeeze her breasts and kiss her long neck. His penis slipped easily under the wet softness of her behind as his hand slid down her stomach to find and stroke the lips of her sex. He instinctively began to move his pelvis back and forth and it was when his penis head butted against her anus that Sophie stiffened and let out a soft, 'Oh!'

Gareth hesitated and held her tightly. 'Is that where you'd like to have it?'

Sophie twisted about to look into his eyes. 'I – sometimes I – No. Not now. Let's dry off and get out of this grotty little bathtub.'

'Yes, let's do that,' he agreed, thinking how much easier their lovemaking might be elsewhere. He turned off the shower but it continued to dribble feebly as he rubbed himself dry hurriedly, his penis swaggering and impatient.

It was he who made the next move in this voluptuous game. Sophie, standing by the sink, bent forwards to dry her lower legs and placed one foot upon a padded stool. The sight was too much for Gareth, who stepped over and fell to his knees behind her, whispering, 'Stay where you are.'

Sophie glanced about with a smile, leaning further forwards as his thumbs eased apart the cheeks of her behind. She felt the slight roughness of his face upon her soft flesh and tensed as his tongue invaded her sex from the rear to find the pearl of pleasure nestled within. It was

6

evident that her arousal was increasing as she leant further forwards still to spread her legs wider, and that this position was one which pleased her considerably. He suppressed the urge to rise up and enter her for full intercourse, though his own need had become almost unbearable and his penis ached to thrust and revel within her body. But this situation was a novelty he found exciting also, and there seemed no reason why the final act should not be deferred for a time. Sophie began to moan and grip hard on the sides of the sink. Gareth continued to tease her clitoris and taste the nectar of her passion, but at a whim, let his tongue dart back a little and flicker about her puckered anus. Sophie stiffened and let out a yearning sigh and he knew he must continue as he was driving her close to crisis point by arousing her in this manner. His tongue danced back and forth, darting lizard-like about her front and rear in equal measure until she began to gasp loudly, her head rocking from side to side in ecstacy. Suddenly, she stopped moving and her body set rigid. Then there came a long, sobbing cry as she shivered uncontrollably in the fever of climax.

Gareth determined to fulfil the last act and, holding her by the thighs, stood up with swaggering shaft poised to strike. To his surprise, Sophie spun about to face him and moved them both away from the sink. She fell to her knees before him. Her left hand, cool and electrifying, slipped under and cupped his scrotum, while the other encircled his shaft. Without hesitating, she ran her tongue about the quivering and expectant organ, licking it eagerly, twirling about the glistening head with exquisite skill. Gareth found her actions as much torment as pleasure, desperate as he was for release. But Sophie knew very well what she was doing, and as though hearing his thoughts, took the distended head and ample shaft as deeply into her mouth as anatomy would permit, her lips forming a full circle about the swollen flesh whilst her fingers closed about the root. Gareth leant forwards, pelvis jerking involuntarily back and forth while his penis was held and suckled with an eagerness which convinced him she desired nothing else.

7

The effervescence in his loins rose quickly as both mouth and hand played their lustful game. Gareth cared for nothing other than the riot of pleasure that was boiling up out of control and rapidly approaching the point of no return. Sophie's enthusiasm had, if anything, increased as a white heat spread through his body and the currents began to surge.

It was Sophie who saw the bathroom door swing open. In a panic she withdrew him, but too late. Gareth, with eyes closed tightly, clasped her head, cried out and began to ejaculate. A horrified Sophie seized the quivering, spurting organ in her hands and attempted to stem the copious flow as she might have tried to contain the frothing of an agitated champagne bottle.

Victoria stood by the door, coolly regarding them both.

Blissfully unaware of her prescence, Gareth, eyes still closed, sighed loudly. Sophie remained kneeling, hands and face streaked with semen, a glistening strand of which swung between her mouth and the head of the wet and still erect penis.

The voice had been a peal of doom. 'Well, what a pretty picture. You'd have done us all a favour if you'd locked the door, wouldn't you! But I suppose you were in too much of a bloody hurry to think about the obvious!'

With that she had slammed the bathroom door and left. Gareth's face had remained a mask of shock and disbelief for some time afterwards.

The image faded from Sophie's mind, but the echo of the slamming door lived on like the beat of a distant war-drum.

Gareth changed gear as they crested the rise of a shallow hill and began to descend. It was then that the engine coughed, began to splutter and, with a final protest, stopped. Victoria glanced sharply at him, her expression one of ill-disguised exasperation. Through her mind passed the words, 'I told you we ought to get petrol before we left the main road, but you wouldn't bloody well listen!' She wanted to shout at him but the words would not come, even though it ought to be part of his punishment.

On the other hand, perhaps her refusal to communicate last night and her offhandedness during today had been enough. Even in their present situation, freewheeling down a nameless country lane in an unknown part of Tuscany, it occurred to Victoria that she had no rights over Gareth. They were not engaged, although with Gareth at 24 and herself at 21 years old, it might well have been considered a natural development. Their relationship had been one of convenience. Perhaps it had been too convenient. Victoria's resentment was born not of jealousy but from the indignity of being duped.

As the car rolled along with only a quiet rumble of tyres on pitted asphalt, Gareth seemed rather vulnerable. And what if she had been driving the car? Might they not have ended up in exactly the same situation? 'Pull over as soon as you can and let's think about it,' suggested Victoria.

'Okay,' responded a sullen Gareth, breaking gently as the car picked up speed under its own momentum. A bend in the narrow road loomed and as he steered around it, a large gateway appeared, set back to their left. At that point the road widened and Gareth steered off it, bringing the car to rest, crunching gravel on the open area before the gate. 'Looks like the end of someone's driveway. Maybe they can help us out.'

'It looks a bit posh to me,' remarked Sophie, peering through the side window.

They found themselves overlooked by two large stone gateposts, each surmounted by a stern looking granite eagle, perched as if to lift off and swoop upon the unsuspecting passer-by. The gates, a convoluted rococo fantasy in scrolled iron, each contained an oval cartouche, within which was set an elaborately wrought and gilded letter 'R'. One of the gates stood part open. Victoria wound her window down to let in the breeze. Without the cooling system, the interior of the car was becoming unbearably hot. The sound of insects nearby and of birds in the distance only served to emphasise the silence of the engine.

'This drive must lead somewhere,' said Gareth. 'Maybe we could buy some petrol from them.' He released his safety belt. 'I'll take a walk and see what's up there. We might be lucky.'

'You'll be lucky to find anyone who speaks English,' said Victoria as Gareth swung open the door. 'I'll come with you.'

'Then I'm coming, too,' added Sophie. 'I don't want to be sitting in here on my own with some old fart going on at me because we're blocking the driveway!'

'Now, hang on,' put in Victoria as Sophie's door swung open, 'one of us has to stay here to keep an eye on our things.'

Both looked at Sophie. Sophie fell back into the seat. 'Oh, all right, it'll have to be me, I suppose. But don't be long.'

The gravel path appeared well kept, as did the surrounding bushes. Climbing away up the hills were well tended vineyards. After a minute's walking, they rounded a small group of trees and Victoria glanced over her shoulder. The car was out of sight. As though it was all of a sudden safe to speak, she said, 'I was bloody embarrassed yesterday, you ought to know!'

Gareth stopped. 'Vicky, the last thing I wanted to do was upset you, or her for that matter. But – but, oh, Christ! I never set out to do anything. What I'm saying is that it's not all my fault. And remember whose idea it was to bring her with us? Not mine!'

'Look, Gareth, I've decided I'm willing to let it go. I suppose I made more of a fuss than I need have done. I should have known better than to blunder into the room like that when you'd both gone up together. We all like our bit of fun now and again and I think perhaps I took our relationship too seriously. That was my fault.'

Gareth thrust his hands into his trouser pockets. 'Then you and I are pals again, Vicky, yes?'

Victoria smiled and squeezed his arm. 'Actually Gareth, I think I'm beginning to see the funny side of it now. Somebody should have been there to record your expression, let alone the rest! Come on, let's find this place.'

The villa nestled on a gentle, wooded rise, its façade glowing ochre-grey in the afternoon sun. Square headed windows of inconsistent dimension told of renovations and additions in earlier times. Two thirds of the building, under a terracotta roof, rose to a first floor only. But the remainder, of heavier masonry, continued up to a higher level, forming a squat tower, with small, semi-circular arched windows below the parapet. It was at this end, beneath a rusticated stone arch, that the main entrance stood. Two steps led up to imposing, heavily panelled oak doors, to one side of which there hung an iron bell-pull. A short way from the steps, something caught Gareth's eye. He stopped and glanced up at the window to the left of the door.

'What is it?' asked Victoria.

'There was someone watching us just now. Looked like a girl.'

'Well I can't see anyone. We can stand here and wait if you like but I suggest we ring the bell. Are you volunteering or shall I?'

'I'll give it a go,' offered Gareth, and advanced up the steps to grasp the iron handle. He pulled once, released it and stepped back. Both waited.

'Did you hear it ring?' asked Victoria. 'I didn't.'

'Didn't hear anything. I'll have another – hang on, I think . . .'

A bolt rattled and the left hand door of the pair opened with a squeak which belied its size and weight. A woman appeared, looking down at them with questioning green eyes. Her face was that of a gentle, well-mannered person. She appeared to be in her mid-twenties. Her long black hair was swept back at the front and fell in a shining swathe over her shoulders. From her ears hung gold pendants in the form of slender, delicately engraved cylinders. The velvet black dress which clothed her slim form was long-sleeved and close fitting at the bodice, flowing loosely from her waist to her ankles. At the scooped neck, over the cleavage of her breasts, was fixed a gold-edged black cameo.

11

Victoria regarded the smooth, fresh complexion and considered her pale but attractive. To Gareth the term 'attractive' would simply not do at all. He thought her intensely beautiful. When she spoke, her voice was altogether in keeping with her gentle features. '*Buongiorno. Desidera?*'

Victoria smiled, hands slightly raised. Gareth sensed a hint of nervousness in her voice. '*Si, Buongiorno,* er – *abbiamo un problema con la macchina. Per piacere –*'

'Oh,' cut in the figure in black. 'You are English!'

'We are,' put in Gareth with some enthusiasm. 'We're sorry to bother you but we seem to have got ourselves lost and we need a garage.'

'He means we're in a bit of a mess, actually,' added Victoria. 'We've run out of petrol. We were wondering if we might buy some. Or phone somewhere for help, maybe. We're stuck right outside your gate.'

'Petrol,' said the woman, thoughtfully. 'We have diesel, I know. The nearest garage is five or six kilometres from here. Perhaps Sebastiano . . . Look, I will make a couple of phone calls. You had better step inside.'

'Please,' said Victoria, 'we don't want to cause you any trouble but we've left someone waiting in the car. She'll be worried if we don't go back soon.'

The woman's expression did not alter. 'Then you should go and tell her. This might take some time. Better still, bring her back here. Your car will be perfectly safe where it is for now.'

'English!' said Sophie for the second time on the way to the house. 'Out here in the middle of nowhere?'

'Well, she sounded English to me,' Gareth replied. 'And this isn't exactly the middle of nowhere is it? Just feels that way. Even so, we're dead lucky to find anyone willing to give us a hand.'

They rounded the curve in the path and Sophie exclaimed, 'Oh, what a lovely old place!'

'Yes, isn't it. And so is the woman who answered the door – but not old, if you see what I mean. Looked very elegant as well. I don't think our jeans and T-shirts are quite the right image around here unless she's just off to a party.'

To the west, a warm sun hovered above rounded hills. The oak door stood ajar as it had done when Gareth left. There was still no one in evidence. Gareth and Sophie stopped before the entrance. Inside, the house looked dark. Then the figure reappeared, regarded Sophie for a moment, smiled and pulled the door wide. 'Please come through.'

Inside the entrance hall, where Victoria stood, they found themselves beneath a timber-beamed ceiling and surrounded by white plaster walls with stone arched doors, narrow windows and glass globe lamps perched on ornate iron brackets. A plain but imposing flight of red carpeted wooden stairs led up to the next floor, which appeared to be better lit. The woman turned to them and said with an almost disconcerting calm, 'I fear you won't be going anywhere for a time. The garage is closed. It is run by a local family. Sometimes they are open, sometimes they are not. Sebastiano, our estate manager, has no petrol either.'

Gareth, Victoria and Sophie each glanced at the other, none of them knowing how, or indeed if, they should reply. But the woman in black continued, 'As it appears you will be staying here for the night, I think it a good idea that we introduce ourselves. I am –'

'Staying?' interrupted Sophie. 'I didn't know we . . .' she trailed off and Victoria gave her a 'keep quiet!' glance.

The woman continued calmly, holding a hand out to Gareth. 'I have introduced myself to Victoria but not to you both. I am Barbara – Barbara Deveraux. This house is the Villa Raffaello.' Gareth and Sophie took her hand in turn. Gareth noted that whilst the hand appeared delicate and well manicured, their new-found hostess displayed the quiet confidence of one whose authority was undisputed.

Victoria glanced at Gareth and back to Barbara. 'Look, this is awkward for us. We can't just stroll in like this and expect to be put up for the night; it isn't fair. Obviously, we'll pay you for the trouble and inconvenience.'

'That's right. We'll have to,' added Gareth.

13

'We need not concern ourselves with that for the time being,' answered Barbara. 'This is a rather large property and there are only four of us living here at present. It is not as inconvenient as you may think, so you need not worry on that account. If you are in agreement, I will phone Sebastiano again. He will organise one of the men to bring the tractor around. They will tow your car up to the house and you may bring your luggage inside. In the morning, Sebastiano will get the petrol and you can be on your way. In the meantime, I will show you a couple of spare rooms and while you are refreshing yourselves, I will organise a little food and drink.'

'It's quite lovely,' said Victoria, buttoning the white dress. 'The view from here over the gardens and hills. Quite wonderful.'

'They must be loaded,' added Sophie, in cream top and navy slacks, bouncing gently on the bed to test the mattress. 'There must be six or seven rooms on this floor and there's that tower thing.'

'Well, if all the rooms are as well furnished as this, you're right – loaded. I wonder what Gareth's room is like.' No one had considered it appropriate to question the fact that Barbara had allocated to Gareth a room on his own, while putting Victoria and Sophie together.

'Gareth's room is fine,' came a voice from the doorway. Gareth, in pale blue trousers and denim shirt, gestured over his shoulder. 'It looks out over an old courtyard and stables at the back. Christ, this place is streets ahead of any hotel we've seen so far. And it's air conditioned.'

'That's not surprising,' responded Victoria. 'We've not actually been staying in luxury accommodation have we?'

'No, but we all agreed we wouldn't go over the top. I don't think we've done too badly.'

'No, nor me,' agreed Sophie, 'but then I used to go back-packing most of the time so I –'

A tapping on the open bedroom door interrupted her. 'Excuse me,' came the voice. 'Miss Barbara would like to know if you'll all be coming down soon.'

The girl who stood framed in the doorway was, in Gareth's practised estimation, little more than eighteen. Shoulder length blond hair curled out at the edges to frame a soft round face with wide blue eyes and turned-up nose. Her full lips remained slightly parted. Her deep blue dress was short sleeved and fell loosely to just above her knees. Stirred by her looks, an eager but ill-prepared Gareth began. 'Oh, er, yes, I think we're all about ready, aren't we?' He glanced at the others for confirmation.

'Yes, I think we are,' replied an amused Victoria.

'Ooh, definitely!' put in a grinning Sophie, jumping up from the bed.

'Then,' said the girl, 'if you go to the bottom of the stairs and turn left, you'll see a door with a pointed arch. They're in there, waiting.' With that, she was gone.

As the three left the room, Gareth muttered, 'God, what is this place?'

'Never mind, dear,' replied Victoria. 'I'll ask if they have something to calm your nerves!'

The sun had dropped below the hills but the entrance hall, almost devoid now of natural light, was illuminated by the soft glow of the wall lamps. Ahead, the heavy wooden doors were shut. From the left there came voices and, as the girl had said, a pointed arch opened into a dimly lit room. None of the three had paid attention to the arch earlier but Gareth, a casual student of medieval architecture, assessed it as belonging to the early fourteenth century.

Victoria entered first, followed by Sophie and Gareth. Daylight still filtered through the narrow, stone-mullioned windows but was augmented by an iron-cage lamp which hung by a chain above the main feature of the room, a long, narrow and apparently very old table in dark, heavy timber with about ten equally venerable chairs set about it. Had Gareth's academic interests been allowed full rein, he might have let his eye wander upwards to admire the finely proportioned rib and panel vaulting which sprang from the walls at shoulder height to enclose the space above. A glance at the room's occupants, however, was sufficient to curtail further musings.

At the head of the table stood Barbara. The other figure, sitting at right angles to her, pushed her chair back on the stone flagged floor. 'My sister, Elaine,' said Barbara. Elaine offered her hand to each in turn with a clear, 'Hello.' Both wore black, as Barbara had earlier, but these dresses, with gold embroidered edges were lower scooped at the neck to reveal more of their breasts. Victoria and Sophie noted their antique gold filigree earrings. Gareth was as little concerned with these as he was with the antiquity of their surroundings. If he had been taken aback by the sight of Barbara, and of the girl who had addressed them upstairs, he was equally moved by the appearance of Barbara's younger sister, whom he guessed to be little older than Victoria – perhaps twenty-two. Her hair, long, shining and straight like Barbara's, was a deep brown, similar to Victoria's, and her eyes, under fine arched brows, appeared grey. She had the conservative approach to make-up exhibited by her sister, her full and sensual lips being a muted red, as were her fingernails. And though her features were not as sharp as Victoria's, her eyes were those of one whose intellect was not to be underestimated.

Victoria was invited to sit at Elaine's side; Gareth and Sophie were placed opposite. Barbara asked, 'Are your rooms comfortable? Do you have everything you need?'

'Couldn't wish for more,' offered a smiling Gareth.

'Our room is really lovely,' answered Victoria. 'This whole house is quite beautiful, really it is.'

'Fantastic!' added Sophie, escalating the superlatives.

'You're our first foreign visitors since we moved into the house,' said Elaine. 'By foreign I mean not Italian, of course. I suppose we're all foreign as far as they're concerned. Anyhow, if Barbie thinks it's okay for us to put you three up for the night then I'm sure it is.'

'Well I could hardly turn them away,' said Barbara. 'They would have been cooped up in their car all night outside the main gate.'

'It's more than we could ever have expected,' said Victoria.

16

At that moment, the girl who had spoken to them earlier entered and stood a short distance from the table. Barbara glanced at her and said to the guests, 'I thought we might have a light meal now, cold meats and salad, then something later on in the evening if you so wish.'

'Whatever you think,' answered Gareth.

'I could eat a whole cow!' grinned Sophie. Victoria eyed her as one marked for a lingering death.

From a chest of drawers, having the same antique appearance as the table, the blonde girl produced ornate, silver knives and forks, then red serviettes, and began to lay the table. Gareth was careful to suppress any visible reaction, sensing the warmth of her slim and perfumed body as she stood by his side. He was aware of Elaine's eyes upon him and, when the girl left the room, she said, 'I hope Gemma introduced herself properly before you came down.'

'Er, well,' replied Gareth, 'she didn't actually say who she was.'

'She didn't really get the chance,' put in Victoria.

'She's always a little reticent,' added Barbara, trying to put them at their ease.

'You'll want something to drink,' said Elaine, changing the subject. 'We have soft drinks but you must be aware that this region is famous for its wines, unless you don't touch alcohol, that is.'

'We all enjoy Chianti,' smiled Victoria. 'That would be wonderful.'

Gareth, by now feeling a little less reserved, smiled at Elaine and added, 'I've never been too strong on self-denial.'

'That's true,' agreed Victoria, 'he hasn't. It's the only thing he gives up at Lent.'

Sophie was about to say, 'God, I could down a gallon of the stuff,' until she noticed Victoria eyeing her once more and merely replied, 'Yes, we all like a glass now and again.'

When the food arrived, another woman entered behind Gemma, pushing a wheeled trolley and smiling with

17

greater familiarity than any of the others had upon their first meeting. She was around twenty, and distinguished in attire from the rest by her dark blue, close fitting dress which was cut well above the knee to show her slender black-stockinged legs. Gareth, attempting not to stare, nevertheless awarded her full marks on his scale of assessment. Her high heel sandals clicked loudly on the stone floor as she proceeded, with Gemma, to serve the food.

'You have not met Amber yet,' said Barbara. 'She is the fourth member of our little household.'

Amber smiled back. 'Hi everyone!'

Her bright copper hair curled in abundance over her shoulders and fell in wisps about her ears and forehead. High cheekbones, long eyelashes, foxy, mischievous brown eyes and an impish smile gave her an appearance some would describe as sly. Gareth thought she was one of the sexiest women he had ever seen.

While they ate, Victoria questioned Barbara and Elaine about their surroundings. 'Please tell us about this house won't you, and how you came to be here.'

'Yes, we'd love to know!' enthused Sophie.

'It was left to us by an uncle,' answered Barbara. 'Our father's brother. He died in a yachting accident last year, together with our parents. He had no children of his own and no other family left alive so it came to us as a working estate. It is quite self-sufficient.'

'Was that by any chance Wallace Devereaux?' asked Gareth.

'Yes, the very same,' answered Elaine. 'I suppose you remember it from the newspapers do you?'

'Oh, more than that,' answered Gareth, 'one of his offices was close to ours. We undertook some work for him.'

'And so did the solicitor's I work for,' added Victoria. 'Though I wasn't involved myself. It was all very confidential.'

'Well, what a small world it is,' murmured Elaine.

'This house is quite old,' said Barbara in a soft voice which, nevertheless, held everyone's attention. 'Some of it

18

goes back to the early 1300's – this wing in fact. It was part of a fortified manor. We think this room was once a chapel.'

Victoria felt instinctively that Barbara held no desire to dwell upon their uncle's business affairs.

'What's above it, I mean inside the tower?' asked Gareth.

Barbara eyed him calmly. 'Just storage space, nothing more.'

'I'd love to explore it,' put in Sophie, hoping her expressed interest might bring forth permission to do so.

'After 1500,' continued Barbara, 'much of the house was rebuilt and extended for greater comfort. It is now part of a wine producing consortium. Wallace spent a great deal of money in updating production techniques as well as bringing the house into the twentieth century. There are two satellite dishes on the top of the tower but you cannot see them from ground level.'

Barbara and Elaine proceeded to talk about the area and its wines. It was good enough reason for Gareth to keep his eyes fixed upon them as he ate. He wanted to impress their beauty on his mind and capture their images forever. He tried in vain to imagine them naked and amorous but was wary of both, almost believing that the quietly perceptive Barbara or the sharp-eyed Elaine might read his thoughts.

When the table was cleared by Amber and Gemma, it had long been dark outside. Elaine suggested the three might take a stroll around the gardens as the night air was warm, and they agreed, returning later to sit under the stars by the swimming pool. Small lamps on slender poles were illuminated as Amber and Gemma brought out evening snacks and more wine. Was it his imagination, or did Amber deliberately brush a leg against his as she set down the tray? Deliberate or not, she certainly brought her head close and glanced into his face with a brief smile, the poolside lamps sparkling in her eyes as brightly as the stars reflected in the pool.

'What time d'you think we ought to be down in the morning?' asked Victoria.

'Oh,' answered Amber with a shrug, 'Sebastiano won't be going for the petrol until around nine o' clock, so be down for breakfast by then. Where are you planning to visit next?'

'Siena,' answered Gareth. 'We'll find somewhere to put up for a couple of nights.'

'You'll get there easily in an hour,' said Amber. 'You should take it slowly and go by the back roads.'

'I'd rather stay here,' sighed Sophie. 'It really is the most gorgeous place.'

Moonlight filtered through the blinds to fall across Sophie's face. Her eyes were wide open. At her side, a sleeping Victoria breathed softly. Careful not to disturb her, Sophie slipped quietly from the bed. To cover her nakedness she reached for her bathrobe draped over a nearby chair. There was enough light by which to find her wristwatch and ascertain the time. It was not yet one o' clock. She crept around the bed in silence. The door opened with a faint click and Sophie gazed down the landing. The dim illumination from a small nightlight on a wall bracket at the far end was enough to confirm that the passage was deserted. Opposite was Gareth's room. Sophie closed the door and hesitated. A thin strip of light shone from beneath his door. She moved forwards and listened. There was total silence. Sophie took a deep breath and tapped. The door opened so quickly that she cried out in surprise. There was Gareth in his bathrobe. Sophie whispered, 'I can't sleep. I was going for a walk when I saw your light. I wondered if . . .'

'I can't sleep either. Want to go down to the garden or are you coming in here?'

'Maybe later. Look, want a dare?'

'It all depends,' he whispered.

Sophie moved closer and glanced about. 'Well I don't know about you, but I wouldn't mind seeing inside the tower.'

'That's a bit cheeky. I doubt if they'd like it. But I know what you mean.'

'She said it was only for storage,' hissed Sophie. 'It's not as though we're out to pinch anything.'

Gareth looked along the landing. At the far end the staircase led up into darkness. 'Yeah, right,' he grinned. 'Just a quick look, then back here. Okay?'

'Okay,' repeated Sophie, taking his hand as they moved quietly along the passage.

The staircase was solid stone, narrow and uncarpeted. It sloped up and passed out of sight between coarse masonry walls, turning abruptly at right angles as they ascended. 'It's pitch dark up here,' whispered Gareth to the figure clutching at his bathrobe close behind, 'We'll never see anything.'

'Oh, go on,' insisted Sophie. 'There must be a light somewhere.'

Gareth continued up into the blackness, hand outstretched and feeling along the stone. 'We probably walked right past the damn switch at the bottom of the stairs. Ah! Here's the top step I think, and –' His fumbling hand found the switch. Suddenly they could see. Sophie joined him in what appeared to be a narrow gallery. On the left were the small, round-arched windows they had noticed from outside. In the plain stone wall to the right were set two doors under Gothic arches. The warm light in the gallery came from four illuminated glass globes, one positioned either side of each arch. 'Right,' said Gareth, 'you choose which door we try.'

'The one furthest away. And let's hurry. I'll get bloody chilblains walking on this cold floor!'

At the far door they stopped and Gareth pushed slowly down on the old iron handle. The heavy wooden door, set with iron bands and large bolt heads, did not budge. Gareth noted the large keyhole beneath the handle. 'Waste of time. It's locked.'

'Oh, bugger,' breathed Sophie. 'I suppose that means the other will be, too.'

'Right then, back we go.'

The first door appeared no different than the second, but Gareth gave it a try. There was a creak, and the door

21

moved. Sophie's face lit up as Gareth put a finger to his lips. The door swung quietly inwards but revealed only darkness. Gareth moved part way inside. Sophie's hand gripped his shoulder. 'Let me have a look!'

'Give me a second,' he whispered, fumbling about the wall inside the doorway. A click, and the room flooded with a soft glow from lamps high in the walls. Sophie followed him inside. For a minute, neither spoke, but gazed about the beamed chamber in wonderment. 'Bloody hell!' whispered Gareth, at last.

The room was not more than six metres by nine and their bare feet confirmed the floor to be heavily carpeted. Various items of furniture were to be seen; several chairs, some obviously intended for comfort, and two in black upholstered leather of somewhat sinister aspect. A black upholstered bench stood near one wall, while the corner to the left was occupied by a large cupboard with panelled doors. In the far corner to the right stood a shower suite, partially obscured by a half-open maroon curtain. Nearby, like a child's paddling pool set into the floor, was a circular pit, lined and upholstered with a smooth black material carrying a dull sheen.

But that which demanded their full attention stood half-way along and a short way from the wall to their right, like a monument in black timber to a forbidden and sinister religion. A large wooden X loomed some two metres high, each of its solid limbs equipped with two straps in polished black leather, with another, wider strap hanging where the timbers crossed. Its purpose was quite unambiguous, even to those beholding it for the first time. The heavy curtain which might have concealed it was pushed back against the wall at one end of a semi-circular track. Slowly, without speaking, Gareth and Sophie moved forwards until they stood in awe before it.

'Well, what do you make of that?' asked Gareth softly.

Sophie glanced anxiously about the room and at the open door. 'I don't think we should stay in here any longer, Gareth.'

Gareth continued to consider the ominous form. 'Well,

it was your idea to explore the place. They'll all be in bed by now and I'm sure no one could possibly hear anything on the floor below if we're quiet. Far more likely to hear us in my room, don't you reckon? Anyway, I think it's all quite fascinating.'

Sophie put her arms about his neck and they kissed. 'I suppose you're right. But we're very naughty, aren't we?'

Gareth pulled her closer. 'Tell you what, I bet Vicky doesn't show up this time.'

Sophie eased back from him. 'I hope nobody else does either, Gareth. I think you should close the door.'

Gareth hurried to do as she wished and at once returned. 'There, happier now?'

'A bit,' answered Sophie, fingering the collar of his bathrobe. 'But there isn't anywhere proper to – I mean there's nowhere to lay down.'

'Never mind,' he whispered, holding her tightly. Their kisses became feverish and Sophie could feel his arousal through both bathrobes. Gareth released the belt at her waist and felt the perfumed warmth of her nakedness. Sophie dropped her arms, letting the bathrobe fall to the floor about her ankles. Gareth began to ease her backwards, his lips fast upon hers as their feet stepped over the discarded garment. Sophie returned his kisses with added enthusiasm, their presence in this forbidden place conspiring to fuel her passion. Gareth held her firmly, almost lifting her from her feet and rocking gently from side to side.

'Ah! Christ, Gareth, that's bloody cold!' Her back was pushed against the wooden cross. Sophie's eyes widened in alarm as he took firm hold upon her wrist. 'Gareth! What are you doing?'

He laughed and kissed her ear. 'Only a bit of fun.' She felt him pull her right arm upwards. 'Gareth! No! You're not going to –! No, don't you dare!'

'I said it's only a bit of fun,' he whispered hoarsely, lifting her arm higher. 'I'm not going to hurt you.'

She gripped his shoulder with her free hand. Her heart beat rapidly and she said in a low voice, 'Gareth, I'll scream.'

23

'You'll wake everyone up if you do – then what?' By now, her arm was stretched out at an angle above her head and pushed against the wooden limb.

'Gareth, you sod! Why?' But Sophie knew why and her heart beat faster still as he raised his free hand to take the leather strap and pass it around her wrist.

'I want to see you helpless. Just for a few minutes, totally helpless.' The strap rasped through its buckle and was fixed securely. Gareth quickly lifted her other hand from his shoulder and Sophie caught her breath and closed her eyes as the second strap circled her left wrist. She knew, as the strap tightened, that it was too late to struggle. But it was Gareth, after all, not some unknown assailant. Her eyes remained closed as cool leather fitted and constricted about her waist. Gareth fell to his knees, took hold of her right ankle and pulled it aside. She offered no objection, no resistance.

Had they not been so engrossed, they might still have been unaware of the slowly opening door, for the lights in the gallery outside had been switched off. The shadowy figure which glided into the room quickly vanished in silence behind a wide black curtain which covered the section of wall opposite.

With the remaining ankle fixed, Sophie hoped that Gareth would be satisfied with his efforts. 'What are you doing now?' she hissed. In moments the question was answered as the four remaining straps were fastened about her elbows and thighs. Gareth stepped back to regard her, secured to the timber contraption and spread out in helpless rigidity. He folded his arms and smiled. 'Wow!'

'I feel like a mounted specimen,' said Sophie. 'Now what?'

'Now what? D'you think you'll be okay there until the morning?'

Sophie's mouth fell open and her eyes widened as though a spectre had materialised in his place. She attempted to twist against the straps, only to confirm the futility of such an effort. 'Gareth – no! Don't you dare leave me like this – Gareth, please!'

24

For a time he gazed at her: flaxen hair tumbled about her shoulders and lay in wisps over her firm breasts; her shapely legs were held wide apart with her sex awaiting his attentions. If he had wanted to fool her into thinking his interest had waned, he had not succeeded, for the material of the bathrobe was insufficient to stay his erection. At last he returned to her and they kissed, his hands ran feverishly from her waist to her breasts, as did his mouth, teasing and arousing her swelling nipples. Sophie closed her eyes in blissful resignation as Gareth sucked the teats to protuberant redness before he began his long slow descent to her secret place.

His lips moved from side to side down her chest and stomach with the delicacy of a butterfly. She stiffened and relaxed in turn against the restraints, moaning her pleasure. Only recently had he learned how easily Sophie was aroused and he was not about to hurry her, in spite of his own need for fulfilment. His hands moved down to her thighs and Sophie caught her breath as his tongue plied the fine down above her moistened sex. Her body tensed in voluptuous expectation.

The hidden watcher breathed deeply and heard the beating of her own heart. At her back, running flush along the wall, ran a row of mirrors. Her hand touched the cold glass and she was certain that if Gareth had known of their existence, he would have pulled aside the curtain to give Sophie a full view of themselves.

Sophie gave a soft moan as the searching tongue finally alighted at her sex and slipped eel-like between her lips to seek the focus of pleasure. The lustful intruder had a companion, for his finger entered, too, and slid inside to assist in the incitement of her passions. But it was his tongue, caressing the pearl within its shell, which raised the flames higher and it made little difference when the finger slipped from her. Until, that is, it found a new passage, and, well-lubricated from its previous sport, pushed easily into her anus, for he remembered how sensitive she was in that place. Her body set hard and her moans increased as the finger moved upwards, firm and hard. Coils of burning pleasure spread as the tongue and finger drove her out of control. Her moans became louder and, long past caring who might hear, Sophie let her head fall back and wailed as one in torment.

In the darkness, behind the curtain, the hidden watcher's fingers performed their own lustful solo.

When Sophie was released and stood by the cross, Gareth let slip the bathrobe and positioned himself behind her with arms about her middle. She felt the head of the engorged and eager penis slip beneath the cheeks of her behind to butt impatiently against her sex. Neither spoke, for the movement of their bodies said all that was needed. Both sank to their knees, with Sophie falling forwards until she rested on all fours. Gareth, hands clamped upon her thighs, thrust home the head of his erection, and with little effort found it sheathed within the heat of her body. Sophie spread her legs wider to allow him deeper entry, whilst Gareth arched his back above her. The final act began as stroke followed stroke in rapid, urgent rhythm.

Michievous brown eyes gleamed through the gap. Gareth's frantic motions reached a pulsing climax and his groans echoed around the walls of the stone chamber. The gap closed and the hidden figure fell back against the mirrored wall, choking gasps suppressed and contained within the intimate space of the heavy curtains.

2

Theatres of Passion

'Of all the places to end up,' said Victoria. 'Who would have believed it.'

'Sure,' agreed Gareth, steering slowly around a sharp bend in the narrow road, 'and from now on we'll be spoiled wherever we go.'

'I thought it was fabulous,' came Sophie's voice from behind. 'I hope we paid them enough.'

Gareth glanced at her in the driver's mirror. 'I had to insist. In the end they took it as if they were doing me a favour, you know – almost taking pity on us!'

'They probably did take pity on us,' commented Victoria.

'They're obviously loaded,' continued Sophie. 'You could tell by the way they dressed. People like that don't need to show off. I wouldn't mind dropping in on a few more like that.'

'When we get home,' said Victoria, 'we must write and thank them for all the help they gave us.'

Gareth said nothing and kept his eyes fixed steadily on the road. Victoria sensed the aura of guilt. 'Gareth, you did take their address, didn't you?'

He gripped the steering wheel. 'No, as it happens, I forgot.'

Victoria's eyes widened in anger. 'Gareth! How could you forget something so simple?'

'It was all that arguing over money. If you two had hung around longer, one of you could have got it.'

Victoria nodded in despair. 'Men! Bloody hopeless.'

'Er, Vicky,' came the voice from behind. 'He isn't the only one who's hopeless I'm afraid.'

'What d'you mean?'

'Well, it's my watch – I've just realised I don't have it. What I'm saying is, I left it behind at the house, I think.'

Victoria looked back at the downcast face. 'Don't tell me, Sophie – it's incredibly valuable and there isn't another one like it anywhere.'

'There probably isn't, unfortunately. It was my grandmother's, so it really is precious, I'm afraid.'

Gareth groaned, 'Okay, okay, so we have to go back, but not now, it's too late. We'll sort out what to do once we're in Siena, then go and make bloody nuisances of ourselves again!'

'I'm sure you can't face the thought of seeing Barbara and Elaine, or the two maids,' smiled Victoria sardonically. 'But I've got an idea to get you out of disgrace.'

'Oh, really?'

'Yes, really. We buy them a thank you present. We call in on our way to somewhere else and pick up madam's watch at the same time. That will tidy things up nicely, won't it.'

'What should we get for them?' asked Sophie. 'I can't imagine anything they'd want.'

'I don't know off-hand. We'll find something in Siena.'

'And where would we be heading if we passed that way again?' queried Gareth.

'Ask Sophie, she's got the map.'

From the rear of the car came a rustling of paper. A minute passed before Sophie spoke. 'There isn't anywhere else except for Arezzo. It goes up into the Alps if we carry on in that direction. It looks like the opposite way to almost everywhere.'

'Well, let's decide later,' suggested Gareth. 'Vicky, can you see what that roadsign says?'

'Colonna di Grillo,' replied Victoria.

'Sounds like a restaurant,' mumbled Gareth.

'Oh, I've found that!' exclaimed Sophie. 'We drive right through then turn right at the main road. It goes straight to Siena.'

* * *

Explain to Barbara exactly where you found it.' Elaine stood aside from the office desk, where Barbara sat. Amber looked down at the object resting by the telephone. 'It was on one of the chairs in the tower. Near the wooden cross.'

'And what were you doing in the tower?' asked Barbara, calmly. 'Gemma is doing the cleaning this week.'

'I saw the top stairs lights were on. I was up and dressed first, you see. I just went up to check if anyone was there, then I found it.'

Elaine looked hard at Amber. 'And did you see anyone else?'

'No, course not. I would have told you if I had, wouldn't I?'

Barbara remained impassive. A ripple of doubt passed over Elaine's features. A doubt which ran deeper than Amber might have cared to know.

'I'm sure I saw the younger of those two girls wearing it,' said Barbara, lifting up the small, octagonal gold watch. 'It looks quite an old and valuable watch to me. I really would be surprised if they don't return sooner or later.'

'They'll have to if they want it back,' said Elaine. 'I can't imagine they have a clue as to our postal address and we haven't got theirs.'

'We could find out where Gareth and Victoria work,' said Barbara. 'if their employers' addresses are amongst Wallace's papers.'

'Maybe,' agreed Elaine, 'but I suggest we give it a couple of weeks before we bother to look.' She turned to Amber. 'Go and tell Gemma to come here – now!' Amber hurried from the office, the hint of a smile touching her lips.

'Gemma will have to be punished if this is true,' continued Elaine. 'It was her duty to ensure that the door was locked, even if Amber didn't actually find the watch in that room. You know as well as I do what a little liar she is!'

'Quite, but if she is telling the truth and one or more of them did find their way up there last night, they may talk when they're back in England. It could be difficult if they come into contact with any of the people Wallace entertained here.'

'Assuming they return, what are you suggesting we do about it?'

Barbara gave a subtle smile. 'You know, even after the briefest of acquaintances with people you can often see the direction in which they might be led, sometimes rather willingly. Sometimes with a little persuasion.'

'Persuasion?'

'We might consider that as a possibility if the occasion presents itself, although manipulation might be a more appropriate word under the circumstances. They must be given good reason to keep the secrets of this house to themselves. We have the means to ensure that, do we not?'

'I think I see what you're getting at,' said Elaine, 'and I'm more than happy to go along with it. But it is possible they never –'

She was interrupted by a tapping. Gemma entered in white nylon satin blouse and loose blue cotton skirt. Barbara allowed her to close the door and step forwards before asking, 'Where are the upstairs keys?'

'The keys?' replied Gemma nervously. 'They're in the kitchen. In the usual place. Why?'

'Did you use them yesterday?' asked Elaine.

Gemma shivered when Elaine looked at her that way. There was something wrong. There would be consequences. 'Use them? Well, no. No, I didn't use them.'

'Should you not have done so?' asked Barbara.

Gemma folded her arms in a gesture of self-protection. 'I'm sorry. I'm not sure what you mean.'

'We had visitors,' said Elaine with a mearest hint of anger. 'What are you supposed to do, either of you, when you're on room duty and we have people in this house?'

Gemma closed her eyes. 'Oh, yes. The tower room. I forgot to lock it. I didn't think about it at all because –'

'Well you should have thought about it, shouldn't you!' cut in Elaine, gesturing towards the watch. 'This was found in the tower earlier today. It belonged to one of those girls. That means they were most likely up there nosing about, and all because you didn't lock the door!'

'I – I'm sorry! But with them turning up all of a sudden, there was a lot to do. We were both –'

'Too busy!' interrupted Elaine. 'Too busy to spend less than a minute in locking the one room which you know full well has to be kept private!' Elaine gestured to the door. 'Go and wait up there whilst we discuss this matter further. Go now!'

Gemma left quietly, passing across the deserted entrance hall and up the stairs to the first floor. There she paused to look at the afternoon sunlight spilling through the mullioned windows on the landing before continuing up the unlit stone steps to the tower.

She waited in silence for what seemed an eternity. Even though she knew the chamber and its sinister trappings well enough, she never felt at ease within its dark walls. Now there was the added feeling of expectancy which stirred her in an emotion not entirely born of fear.

She was standing a short way from the mirrored wall when the door opened. Two figures were silhouetted against the daylight which illuminated the gallery outside. Barbara approached first, then Elaine, in whose arms rested an amorphous black form. She moved past Gemma, who did not turn, and placed the object down on the chair to her side with a muffled, metallic click. Barbara stood before Gemma and said, 'You really have been a silly girl, haven't you.'

'Get this off,' ordered Elaine, tugging at the loose collar of Gemma's blouse. Gemma looked at her questioningly. 'Now!' snapped Elaine. Gemma's fingers sprang to the collar and began to twist open the buttons. Barbara reached across to pick up the object from the chair and let it fall open with a delicate wind-chime tinkle. Brass buckles and eyelets glinted against black leather. Straps swung loose, imparting a rich dark odour. She examined the garment thoughtfully. 'So beautifully made. These things must have cost a fortune.'

'Beautifully made and totally secure. Such an asset at times like this,' added Elaine, taking the limp, warm blouse. 'And the rest,' she ordered, snapping open the

31

hook on Gemma's black lace brassière. The brassière slipped over Gemma's shoulders, down her arms, and she obediently unbuttoned her skirt. Throughout the ritual of undressing, Gemma gazed ahead in silence, her expression a mask of indifference. Within, blood pulsed through her veins and her thoughts skipped back and forth like a dragonfly.

In a short time she stood all but naked, wearing only small, black lace briefs and shadow-black nylon stockings held up by garter tops. Barbara held the sinister garment open and spoke softly. 'Put your arms inside.'

Elaine took her arms from behind and helped Gemma's hands push through each end of the internal sleeve. Barbara lifted the jacket about her shoulders. Now Elaine seized the edges and quickly pulled them to almost meet at the girl's back so that her arms were held contained within and folded across her chest. Gemma swayed on her feet, feeling the jacket constrict to the swish and click of straps and buckles. Still she said nothing, though cocooned in beetle black from neck to waist, for she was no stranger to physical restraint, nor to what might occur afterwards. This was a role she had accepted when Wallace held sway at the villa. But then it had been a charade, a game with a beginning and an end, often predetermined. With Barbara and Elaine, but especially with Elaine, things were far less certain. Barbara's voice drifted by. 'I take it you no longer require my presence.'

'No, you can leave it to me,' replied Elaine.

Gemma watched the heavy door swing shut to an echoing thump and Barbara was gone.

'Aren't you wondering what they must have thought when they entered this room?' asked Elaine. 'What they might have done?' Gemma did not answer. 'Perhaps that sense of adventure and discovery awaits us again when we find the key to the next room – don't you think? Or are you familiar with its contents from past times? I sometimes wonder.' Elaine often reflected on the other chamber. The heavy, iron-banded door had never revealed its secrets.

All this time Gemma had remained silent. The straitjacket was her punishment and more must follow for her error was too serious without a doubt to be rectified by a mere hour or so in restraint. A hand fell upon her shoulder. 'Over here!'

Gemma moved in the direction of the wooden cross. She glanced at Elaine but the grip tightened and two more steps found her almost touching the sinister apparatus. Elaine reached about her and took the hanging ends of the black straps at the centre of the cross. Gemma breathed in sharply as cool leather enclosed her slim waist and quickly tightened.

'Legs apart!' snapped Elaine.

Again Gemma hesitated. 'Elaine, please – what are you –'

'Just do it! You're not here to ask questions!'

Gemma shuffled her legs apart awkwardly until her feet touched the lower members of the cross where they joined the floor. A hand seized her left ankle and pulled it further so that Gemma had to turn her foot aside to avoid stubbing stockinged toes against the hard timber. An ankle strap was quickly but not tightly applied, though the next strap, about her thigh, was fastened much more firmly. The other leg was likewise soon fastened.

'Good,' breathed Elaine. 'I hope we're nice and comfortable.'

Only a few steps separated the bound figure from the large cupboard set into the corner. Elaine reached it in silence and Gemma heard the door creak open. She was unable to see Elaine, but could hear the sounds of objects being moved about. After a while, the sounds stopped. Perhaps it was a stirring in the air which told her that Elaine was close behind. Gemma tensed as fingers reached inside her lace briefs and the elastic suddenly tightened. There was something strange about the feel of the hands upon her flesh. The warmth, the texture – Elaine was wearing latex gloves. A sharp rip and the briefs gave way. Another rip and they were pulled off and thrown to the carpet. Gemma looked down to find a small stool had appeared on the floor between her legs. Something cool and hard touched the inside of her thighs. She leant forwards and glimpsed with dismay the rim of a large white chamber pot. 'What are you doing? Why is –'

'Why do you think? Don't tell me you've forgotten what used to go on in here!'

'But that was when, when . . .'

Elaine walked around the cross and appeared before her. Gemma's eyes widened at the sight of the riding crop. Elaine held it before the frightened eyes, flexing it in pink-gloved hands. 'D'you know, I find this room ever more fascinating. When I think what delights we might have next door, I tingle in anticipation. We really must chance getting in a locksmith, mustn't we?' She moved to the side of the cross, slapping the riding crop against her long dress. 'Ah, well, back to business. Are you ready, Gemma? Are you tingling in anticipation, too? Are you going to use the piss pot now or do you need a little help?'

From the corner of her eye, Gemma saw the crop raised and cried out, twisting with frantic futility against the straitjacket and straps. The first blow fell with a crack which rang about the dim room. Gemma shrieked, 'I won't do it in front of you! I won't! I'll tell Barbara!'

Elaine studied the trembling behind for a moment and raised the crop again. 'I really wouldn't put it to the test, dear, if I were you!' Gemma shrieked again as the crop struck her bare flesh. The crop swished again, then a fourth and fifth time. Gemma's cries became continuous though her struggles had ceased. Elaine moved further behind her. The strokes continued, more measured and somewhat harder. The cries became screams, echoing about the stone walls of the chamber. Elaine stopped and examined the reddened behind. Gemma shook her head, wailing in despair, eyes and cheeks glistening with tears, hair wet and streaked across a woeful face. Then Elaine was back before her and placing a hand beneath her chin. She lifted Gemma's head up and gazed into her hurt and reproachful eyes. 'Well, I am getting into the swing of things, aren't I? Literally, you could say!'

'If you hurt me any more,' wailed Gemma, 'I'm going to

tell what I know – what went on over the years! Believe me I will! The police, the papers – the whole bloody lot!'

Elaine gripped her jaw and pushed her head back further. 'Are you, you little slut! Well let me remind you of what I said last time you made your silly threats. Wallace left a lot of records in his private safe. Quite detailed and very intimate. And remember the photographs? Do you? And the videotapes? It's all there. You and that other randy little whore performing with his pals, male and female.' A rubber gloved hand flashed and caught Gemma hard across the mouth. 'And you with this very same piss pot. Quite bloody charming! I bet he enjoyed going through the family album in his spare time. I'm sure the police and the papers would love all that. And remember, it was nothing to do with Barbara or me. Nothing at all. So do it! Go to whoever you fancy and see where it gets you.' Elaine stepped out of sight. 'Now, I said I'd got into the swing, didn't I, and I meant it.'

Gemma's mouth fell open as she reappeared and a crack split the air. Elaine lifted the whip and coiled it like a vicious, glistening black snake. A vindictive smile crossed her face. 'You'll think the riding crop was just a toy after this! And it bloody well is! This,' she said, shaking the coils before Gemma's horrified eyes, 'this is the real thing!'

Gemma screamed as Elaine circled about to the rear. 'No! Oh, no! No, please!'

'Are we ready?' came the voice. 'I'm going to begin!' The whip was raised, but did not fall.

Gemma was urinating. Pissing copiously and uncontrollably into the ceramic pot. She continued for several seconds, her body releasing its liquid contents, head held back, eyes closed, a long moan rising from her open mouth.

She did not react as the hand touched her shoulder. But when the voice said, 'Now that wasn't difficult, was it?' she began to weep again, quietly. Elaine pulled the stool and chamber pot away, slipped off the straps which held her legs akimbo on the cross and guided her backwards.

Gemma was shaking. 'I – I can't walk. My legs, they're –'

'Oh, yes you can. Just give it a few seconds.'

Gemma looked into the cool grey eyes and Elaine kissed her on the forehead. She closed her eyes and moved forwards to kiss Elaine on the lips. They began to walk away from the cross, towards the shower suite. Still trembling, Gemma said, 'You wouldn't use that on me would you?'

'That rather depends on you, doesn't it?' Elaine pulled aside the curtain and they both entered the tiled area. Gemma was turned around and eased slowly down astride the white porcelain bidet, situated between the shower cubicle and toilet bowl. 'For all our sakes you must never forget to lock up this room again when strangers are in the house.' Water began to swirl about the bowl between Gemma's widespread legs. 'Though perhaps you should become acquainted with the whip. Perhaps it's what you really need.'

Gemma shook her head. 'No, not that. It would be too much.'

A latex hand reached for the soap behind the bidet, carried it between Gemma's legs and dipped into the hot water. Gemma tensed as soap and fingers caressed her groin. One hand reaching about her hairless sex from the front, the other from the rear. Smooth and lubricated fingers played a voluptuous game, teasing the clitoris, slithering against the anus. She who had such a short time ago driven her into a turmoil of dread and physical anguish, now uncoiled plumes of lust within her belly. A lust which the attentions of the riding crop had already awakened. Elaine had punished her a little more severely than usual this time. But the punishment had been as a total eclipse so that the sun of pleasure might blaze all the brighter afterwards, banishing the shades of fear with the promise of delight.

As the gloved fingers entered her Gemma let out a little cry. One slipped deeply into her sex to explore the grotto of pleasure, while its companion pushed firmly up the rear to enter her rectum. She writhed and gripped the fingers with her muscles, willing them deeper. Elaine had total control of her body, pain and passion alike, and Gemma was unable to resist either. Elaine felt the girl stiffen, watched her head fall backwards as she braced her legs against the bowl. Gemma heaved against the straitjacket and cried out as loudly as when the riding crop had assailed her. This cry, too, might have been one of torment but it was not, for her body sang to the wild and abandoned drums of orgasm.

Still wearing the restraint, Gemma waited as Elaine rinsed out the chamber pot and began to wash and powder the gloves. Walking to the centre of the room, she stood before the device which had held her; looked at the empty straps and lost herself in thought for a time, wondering about the three departed guests. Then Elaine was at her side. 'It's not over yet, Gemma.'

'Oh, but I thought . . .'

'And what was it you thought?' replied Elaine, walking to the black curtain and swishing it aside to reveal the range of mirrors. Gemma eyed Elaine's dark reflection. 'I thought I could go now.'

Elaine did not reply but remained still for a moment, gazing down at the floor. At the base of the mirror lay a white object which she reached for and picked up. It was a small handkerchief with an embroidered edge. Unfolding the handkerchief, she examined it closely. In one corner, embroidered in blue, was the letter A. Elaine slipped the handkerchief into her sleeve. 'Oh, you thought you could go, did you? Well, there's another little mistake I'm afraid. You can remain as you are until it's time for you and Amber to prepare dinner.' She returned to Gemma and placed a hand on her cheek. 'You'll be alone for a time with your thoughts. I suggest you stand before that mirror. Look at yourself wearing the restraint. See the guilty person you are and remember it could happen again. Because it could, couldn't it?' Her lips touched Gemma's like the ghost of a flame. 'Retribution is never far away, my sweet.' Her fingers pushed the bedraggled hair from Gemma's eyes. 'And because of your negligence, they will come back, perhaps tomorrow, perhaps the day after, who knows?' Elaine moved towards the door. 'Tomorrow, you'll carry on with your duties as normal. There will be no confinement, no locked doors. But you will not venture out of the house, not even for a minute: I'll make sure of that!'

Within the time it took Gemma to consider these veiled threats, the door had closed and she was alone. The mirror drew her close and for a minute she stood before it. Turning sideways she jerked her enclosed arms, as if that might somehow disclose some way of getting free of the leather cocoon. It did not. With quiet resignation, she walked to one of the upright chairs and sat down. Her behind smouldered but the cool leather was soothing. Leaning back against the padded headrest she closed her eyes. In her mind lingered the tantalising image of Elaine and the soft touch of her lips. After a few minutes, she drifted into sleep.

'You're going to have to learn some Italian aren't you, dear?'

Gareth eyed Victoria over the table. The sun glistened on rich sepia hair held by a large clip at the back. A smile floated on her lips. Across the sweep of the busy Piazza del Campo, and against a clear blue sky, rose Siena's medieval Palazzo Pubblico and imposing bell tower, their red brick facades glowing mellow in the hot afternoon sun.

Gareth, eyes narrowed against the light, considered the proposition.

'I think he should,' remarked Sophie. 'He'd be much more useful to us.'

'As it happens,' said Gareth smugly, 'I have picked up a few words: *vino*, *birra* and *gelato*.'

'Well you're bound to if you spend so much time boozing and stuffing your face with ice cream. I think you need a little more than that if you intend to get about on your own.' She pushed back her chair. 'But never mind, for the time being I'll make sure we don't accidentally poison ourselves. What's it to be?'

Gareth breathed in. '*Una birra grande, per* – er, please.'

'Wow!' responded Victoria.

'*Una birra*, not *grande*,' added Sophie.

Victoria edged through the cluster of tables and disappeared into the overflowing bar. 'Vicky's still sore at us isn't she?' said Sophie, leaning closer to him. 'I can tell by the way she talks.'

'I don't think so. It's just her style.'

'When we were in that room,' said Sophie almost in a whisper, 'what d'you think happened?'

'You mean the lights in the gallery? I keep thinking about that, too. I doubt if it was Vicky. Maybe someone was passing by downstairs and switched them off, otherwise we'd have known about it, wouldn't we?'

'Imagine,' whispered Sophie. 'Just imagine if somebody had come up – if we'd been caught. Christ, how embarrassing! Much worse than Arezzo.'

'Well we weren't,' responded Gareth.

Sophie relaxed back in the chair. 'But it was such a gorgeous old house. What wouldn't I give to live in a place like that.'

Victoria returned, holding aloft a tray bearing three glasses, sparkling with condensation.

'We were just talking about the villa,' smiled Sophie. 'How well off those two sisters are. Don't you think?'

'Yes,' agreed Victoria. 'And we'll see how well off they are again in a day or two.'

'It was probably a figment of our imagination,' remarked Sophie, lifting the glass to her lips. 'I bet we never find it again.'

'Then bang goes your watch,' said Gareth.

'Oh, it's most likely jammed down the side of the car seat. I never looked, you know.'

'Well, I did,' said Gareth. 'I had a good look around the car when we got to the hotel. I don't reckon it's there, unfortunately.'

'I think we should go straight back from here,' put in Victoria. 'Wherever else we go is bound to be further away, and remember, Sophie's going to Viareggio and we're flying home from Bologna.'

39

'Okay, then,' agreed Gareth, 'we'll shoot off back there tomorrow.'

'No, stupid!' said Victoria in despair. 'I've booked our hotel for two nights, haven't I!'

'And we've only the one room, haven't we,' added Sophie, taking care to avoid any hint of innuendo.

'Well, it's an extremely popular town,' responded Victoria. 'I think we were dead lucky to get anything close to the centre in the tourist season.' She reached up, adjusted the clip to keep the hair from her eyes and looked at Sophie. 'Anyway, there's no point in you paying the same as the two of us again just for a room on your own when there's a convertible settee in ours. I don't think we're too bothered about modesty any more.'

'Quite,' agreed Gareth, savouring the cool beer.

Victoria eyed him with mild but undisguised reproof. Gareth appeared not to notice, but clasped his hands behind his head and leant back with eyes closed to bask in the warm sun.

There was room for only four tables, each with four basketwork chairs, in the little garden at the rear of the hotel. The night air was pleasantly cool, and the ornate lamps set in the wall by the door cast shadows behind potted plants and shrubs.

'This is just the kind of evening I like,' said Gareth, pouring the wine.

'We could have our breakfasts here in the morning,' said Victoria. 'If some of us don't get up too late, that is.'

'Oh, don't worry about that,' he replied, 'I'll claim the table while you two are still admiring yourselves in the bathroom.'

'You up first!' responded Victoria. 'When that happens, I'll write to *Time* magazine. They'll give you a double page spread.'

'Someone will have to be last,' said Sophie. 'There's only the one bathroom.'

'It won't be a problem,' replied Victoria as Gareth looked poker-faced from one to the other. 'He'll still be snoring away like an old sewing machine long after we're finished. He'll never get down here first.'

'He might if we don't go to bed too late,' consoled Sophie. 'What time is it now?'

'Just after nine-thirty.   uch too early to think about that.'

'Sorry to interrupt,' put in Gareth, 'but there's another bottle of wine waiting for us before we quit.'

'We're only halfway through this one,' said Sophie.

'Well, there you are,' replied Gareth. 'We'll stand no chance at all if you both keep chattering.'

'I'll hang about down here so you can get changed,' Gareth had offered. Victoria and Sophie left him to contemplate the empty glasses. Behind the counter of the small reception area a round-faced man with receding black hair and a tenor voice, smiled broadly. '*Ciao!*' he called.

'*Ciao!*' returned Victoria as they climbed the narrow, dim stairs, rather less steadily than they might have cared to admit. Sophie was reminded of the stairs leading to the tower at the Villa Raffaello. She wondered again what Victoria might have made of it as she watched her turn the key in the door to their room and said, 'We'd better leave the latch off so his lordship can get in.'

'A dangerous practice,' muttered Victoria as they entered. 'But I suppose you're right.'

Fresh from the bathroom, in blue cotton pyjamas, Sophie sat on the bed next to the open suitcase. In the room next door, the shower had stopped running and Victoria was humming to herself. Sophie rummaged through the case absent-mindedly. It contained much she had not used since their arrival in Italy. Here was an unopened paperback book, extra items of clothing, a small jar of instant coffee tumbled in with her make-up collection and, secreted under folded blue jeans, the most important travel accessory of all. Slowly, she lifted the secret object out into the light and ran her fingers along the pink shaft. It had remained in her case, its services not yet required. She

41

wondered about Victoria. Did she give herself pleasure this way? Perhaps not, with Gareth around.

She liked Victoria a great deal and, behind the mildly cynical manner, felt Victoria liked her, notwithstanding the complications of the last few days. She was lost in thought, telling herself they could remain true friends, given the chance, when that familiar voice cut in. 'Okay! I'm finished!' There was Victoria in maroon pyjamas.

Sophie, shocked out of her reverie attempted to conceal the vibrator inside the case. 'Oh! I didn't mean to . . .'

But as Sophie's face reddened, Victoria broke into a smile and flopped down on to the bed beside her. 'Oh, you silly girl! Get it out. Let's have a proper look!'

'Vicky, really! It doesn't matter does it? It's just something I thought I'd – Look, just forget about it, won't you?'

Victoria squeezed her hand. 'Come along, dear, it's not like you to be shy. We all have one. Personally, I've got several, but that's another story.'

'If you must,' sighed Sophie. She revealed once more the gleaming object, light reflecting from its polished hardness. Victoria took the hand that held it and raised it up until the vibrator stood poised between them. The mist of shyness and guilt had not quite lifted from Sophie. Victoria reached out and pulled her closer until the vibrator was next to their faces and their eyes met. 'If – no, when we get the chance,' whispered Victoria, 'when we have a bit of privacy, just the two of us, we could play a little game. What do you say?'

Sophie regarded her sharp brown eyes. A smile fluttered across her face. 'I wouldn't mind, Vicky. I just wasn't sure about – you know, if you were into that kind of thing.'

'Who knows what people are into, dear. Life can be full of surprises when you peep behind the net curtains.'

Considering her remark, Sophie could no longer be certain if Victoria was unaware of her exploits in the tower. But it seemed not to matter, for Victoria pulled her closer still and whispered, 'Let's make a promise on it, shall we?'

Sophie nodded and each put her lips to the instrument of carnal pleasure. Without warning, the door rattled and sprang open. 'Ta-raaaah! Hope I'm not too . . .'

'Oh, bloody hell,' groaned Sophie.

Victoria jumped up and glared at him sternly. 'I don't suppose your mother ever taught you to knock before entering a lady's bedroom!' Gareth remained fixed in the doorway, mouth ajar. 'Well?' snapped Victoria. 'Are you going to stand there gawping all night or d'you think it might be worth coming right inside and closing the door?'

Gareth did as Victoria suggested and as his back was momentarily to them, Sophie let the vibrator fall back into the case. 'I'll just get showered and changed, then,' he offered with contrived nonchalance. The two girls continued to watch in silence as he awkwardly stripped down to his briefs and, avoiding eye contact with either of them, delved into his case to retrieve his electric shaver and pale blue shorts.

As the shaver began to whine, Victoria and Sophie spluttered into laughter. 'That's got him wondering,' said Victoria. 'He'll think he's being made sexually redundant by new technology!'

'Oh, dear,' said Sophie, swaying back and wiping an eye on her sleeve, 'poor Gareth.'

'Poor Gareth?' echoed Victoria. 'Poor Gareth my arse! He's been screwing both of us, hasn't he? It's about time we got something out of him on our own terms, lovey. What do you say?'

Sophie fixed her gaze on Victoria and considered for a moment before breaking into a wide smile of approval. When the sound of running water reached them, Victoria glanced at the bathroom door and said, 'Okay, let's get all this stuff off the bed! But first . . .'

Enveloped by the warm intimacy of the shower, Gareth had wondered about the two girls. If there was something going on between them it might be just as well if he pretended not to have seen the vibrator.

As he dried himself, Gareth was consumed in thought. Phrases and sentences rushed through his mind. Things to say which might give some semblance of normality to the conversation when he rejoined them. It was unnaturally quiet. Maybe they had gone to bed and were already asleep. They had all consumed more wine than usual that evening. Gareth reached for the stool by the bathroom door. His shorts had vanished. He peered at the tiled floor and up at the door hooks. 'No,' he muttered, 'they've got to be in here somewhere.'

They were not, though it took him another half-minute of searching about the tiny room to convince himself that the shorts were definitely gone. His briefs hung washed and dripping over the sink, so he pulled the damp towel from the rail and hitched it about his waist.

The bathroom door swung open. 'Have either of you seen –'

On the bed sat Victoria and Sophie, arms about each other, humming quietly and rocking gently from side to side. They were quite naked. Victoria looked up at the bewildered face, reached behind and produced the blue shorts, swinging them for a moment on the end of her finger. 'Weren't looking for these were we?' With that, she tossed the shorts over her shoulder. Gareth watched them slip down and vanish between the bed and the wall. Victoria and Sophie resumed their positions, Sophie licking the nipple of Victoria's breast before each squeezed the other and began to laugh.

'Okay,' said Gareth, propping himself against the door frame, 'what's going on?'

'Going on?' replied Victoria with sudden innocence. 'Sophie and I were just chatting, or should I say chattering – you know, the way we girls do.' She turned her face to Sophie's and kissed her. 'Weren't we, dear?'

'That's right,' agreed Sophie, 'just a little quiet conversation, until he barged in again as usual.'

'Shall we make a bit of space for him?' purred Victoria, aware of his eyes roving, trying to assimilate every aspect of their nakedness.

'Oh, I suppose we could,' agreed Sophie. Both bounced aside on the creaking bed until there was sufficient space between them, then sat leaning back with legs crossed to stare at the hesitant figure in the doorway.

'Yeah, all right then,' smiled Gareth, still harbouring a degree of uncertainty. Uncertain or no, he was aware of a stirring beneath the towel.

Sitting between their warm and perfumed bodies, Gareth adjusted the towel, hiding the fact that he was falling into their trap, if trap it was. But a soft arm slipped about his waist from each side and electric lips touched his cheeks, sending ripples of ecstasy down his neck and spine. Thoughts of caution evaporated and the stirring in his loins increased, the skirt-like encumberance of the bath towel proving ever less effective in the containment of his burgeoning erection. He flung an arm about each of their shoulders, giving and receiving kisses with increasing fervour.

'Are we comfortable?' came Victoria's voice as Gareth's and Sophie's tongues entwined. He might have turned to reply but suddenly his eyes sprang open and his body jolted as though touched by a hot knife. A hand had pushed under the hem of the towel and brushed between his thighs, reaching with cool fingers to close about his penis. Sophie grasped the front of the towel and wrenched it away to expose the engorged shaft, held firmly by the smiling Victoria. Sophie, too, joined in the voluptuous game, encircling the root of his ample penis with finger and thumb as Victoria, with agonising slowness, worked the soft skin beneath the head back and forth. Gareth closed his eyes and sighed.

'He's got to earn his pleasures, hasn't he, dear?' chimed Victoria.

Sophie's fingers pushed under the testicles. 'Oh, yes, Vicky,' she cooed, 'he's got to work for his pleasures. He can't leave it all to us. Dear me, no!'

'Yeah, right,' groaned Gareth, from a distant land of glittering colours and soaring passions. 'Whatever you say. Anything!'

Victoria pulled away her hand. Sophie did likewise. Gareth returned to the here and now, gazing with despair upon the abandoned organ. But Victoria was scrambling up, to the groan and twang of protesting springs, and tugging at Gareth to swing him about so that he fell unresisting into the middle of the bed. For a little while, Victoria and Sophie knelt over him, running fingers about his chest and stomach, ignoring altogether the aching and neglected penis.

Victoria, with a mischievous laugh, swung over his head and, gripping the wooden headboard for support, lowered herself down on to his face. Gareth, with instinctive alacrity seized her thighs and pushed out his tongue to greet and spread the lips of her sex: an art which Victoria had, during their months together, encouraged him to develop with considerable skill. While Victoria, with her back to Sophie, was enjoying the attentions of the darting and penetrating tongue, Sophie gave full expression to one of her own inclinations. Taking the warm, ceramic-hard shaft in her hand, she coursed a feather-flame tongue about the bulbous head with exquisite delicacy before allowing her lips to enclose it and take the burning lance into her mouth. This act fuelled Gareth's lust to the point where he pleasured Victoria with an ardour to which even she was rarely accustomed, hands grasping her ever tighter whilst his tongue engaged in fervent and passionate play with the clitoris.

But if Gareth considered that this act might run its frenzied course to the final climax, he was mistaken, for the endgame had not yet begun. His surprise was evident when Victoria suddenly lifted herself out of his tongue's reach. Sophie, too, curtailed her actions to leave his flushed penis glistening wet and Gareth once more beset by frustration. Victoria and Sophie moved to change places, to the further protestations of the bedstead, though it was not to be an exact reversal of roles. Sophie positioned herself as Victoria had done, but facing down the bed and not towards the wall, giving Gareth full access to her vulva and anus. Victoria faced Sophie and straddled the lower part of his body, poised over the rearing shaft, moving back and forth to let the head furrow between the moistened lips it so yearned to penetrate. But Victoria was impatient, too, and dropped suddenly, squirming down to accept his full length and driving him in to the root. Each leant forwards to embrace and support the other above his prostrate form and the final joust commenced to the groanings of the ancient bed.

Together they established a rhythm, Victoria and Sophie rocking back and forth, mouths joining in voluptuous combat with one another, kissing, biting and sucking as the fires began to rage. Gareth flexed his pelvis and his tongue played frantically within Sophie's honeyed sex. Soon enough, all were losing control and careering towards the precipice. The bedstead shook with a rhythmic clanging, and in their swaying abandonment to passion, seemed on the verge of collapse. But it was too late! For had it done so at that moment, it would have made no difference. Victoria, writhing violently, threw back her head to let out an anguished cry. Gareth, feeling the crisis upon him, thrust his tongue alternately into Sophie's front and rear passages, so that her moans joined the clamour of sounds. His fingers gripped and dug hard into Sophie's behind, his pelvis shivered and the loud groan signalled his own copious release as Victoria's body set rigid in burning climax.

With the tides of pleasure receding, they relaxed and sighed in unison. Victoria rose up and withdrew the glistening shaft from her body. As Sophie disengaged herself the bedstead squealed like a rusted iron gate. Red faced, Gareth let out an exhausted sigh and struggled upright amidst disordered bedclothes. 'God, I don't remember locking the door!' The metallic creaking and twanging resumed as he heaved himself to the floor.

'That's nothing new,' Victoria remarked sardonically, heading for the bathroom.

Sophie half sat, half fell on to the side of the bed. Barely had she relinquished the weight on her legs when a sharp ping issued from underneath the mattress. The section on which she rested gave way and fell by several inches. Another ping followed and it settled further as the entire frame groaned in weary capitulation. Sophie, struggling upright, clapped a hand over her mouth. 'Oh, Christ! We've busted it!'

Gareth stared at the bed then covered his face with his hands. Maybe none of this was true.

3

The Trials of Gemma

Behind them in intricately carved white marble arose the
triple-arched façade of Siena's cathedral. Gareth eased
himself down on to the steps between Victoria and Sophie
with a sigh.

'Don't tell me you're suffering cultural overload,' said
Victoria. 'You were so keen before we left England.'

'It would be easier if we lived here,' answered Gareth.
'It's all too much.'

'I like that tower on the side,' put in Sophie, 'the
campanolo.'

'*Campanile*, dear,' offered Victoria.

'Yes, that as well,' agreed Sophie, pushing her sun-
burnished hair from her cheek and returning to the rapidly
melting ice-cream, 'It looks like one of those black and
white striped liquorice allsorts. If you ask me, the whole
thing looks like a gigantic cake from the side.'

From the corner of his eye, Gareth watched Sophie with
the ice-cream cornet. She had licked the softening ice-
cream into a pink dome and twirled her tongue about it in
a way which fascinated him. While Victoria seemed absorbed by the milling crowds in the piazza and the to-ing
and fro-ing of tourists up and down the cathedral steps, he
continued to study Sophie as her tongue, with exquisite
and sensual skill, circled the diminishing mound. She
closed her eyes as though her thoughts were far away as
her lips circled the cornet. He blinked and turned away,
not wishing either of them to notice his preoccupation and
began to gaze nonchalantly at the crowds, his mind savou-

ring the delights of the previous evening. Like a sudden eclipse, a hand passed back and forth over his eyes and Sophie's voice shattered the silence. 'Are you all right Gareth?'

'I think he's passed away,' remarked Victoria wryly.

'I hope not. Who's going to fix the bed?'

'Oh, we'll manage. We could shove the cases underneath. No one will notice it's broken until we've left. The whole thing was due to collapse anyway.'

'I'm still here,' put in Gareth, vainly trying to attract their attention.

'Can you imagine if the manager had barged in the way a certain person does,' continued Sophie.

'I daren't,' replied Victoria. 'I'm only glad he wasn't around this morning. He'll be there tonight though, you'll see. We'll have to walk by the reception desk and smile.'

'He'll be listening,' said Sophie. 'I bet he was last night. He'll have his ear to the wall outside.' She pondered for a moment at the way Victoria's attitude had changed. Victoria had always been rather correct. She was glad, excited still, at the thought of what they had done together. And what if they had been caught the way Victoria had caught her and Gareth that afternoon in Arezzo? What if someone had discovered them in the tower at the villa? Barbara or Elaine perhaps? They might have walked in while she was spread naked and helpless to the cross. Sophie felt a stirring in her belly.

The big mirror in which she saw herself reflected was of another time: the heavy, gilded rococo frame a riot of twisting scrollwork with, at the top corners, plump little cherubs bearing oddly knowing expressions. Gemma sat on an old upholstered stool and observed Barbara and Elaine through finely crazed glass, standing at either side.

The room lay at the far end of the landing and nothing within it except the electric light seemed to belong to the present day. Gemma was used to it, as was Amber, for it had to be kept in order as a part of their duties. But when inside this room alone, she always wanted to stand and listen to the silence. A silence as heavy as the gold and maroon brocade-draped four-poster bed and the thick brocade curtains which were pulled aside with tasselled cords to allow the northern light grudging admittance. It was a room of pensive, almost melancholy atmosphere. A twilight room where no one ought to raise their voice above a whisper and sound was stifled as in a deeply buried vault. Amber sometimes called it the Vampire's room. She said it reminded her of a scene from a Dracula movie. To Barbara and Elaine it was simply the 'end room.' In Wallace's day the room had been used by visitors, including one special guest of whom Gemma would not speak. Since then it had remained unoccupied.

Gemma knew perfectly well why she was here. It was part of her punishment. Not that she would be obliged to remain in the room, for there was work to be done. But this was an appropriate place to start.

'Sit up straight,' said Elaine, passing the onyx hairbrush firmly through Gemma's shining blonde hair.

Gemma obeyed, adjusting her position and stiffening her back. A metallic click sounded but the steel handcuffs, which held her wrists together behind her back, were quite secure.

'She has nice hair,' said Barbara quietly.

Elaine glanced up. 'Yes. One of these days she'll do something really stupid and I'll cut the lot off, you'll see.'

Gemma's lips parted to form the word 'No,' but the protest was stillborn. Her eyes returned to contemplate her reflection in its soft black gown of lined silk. She was all but naked under the gown, wearing only garter top stockings in sheerest black, and the shoes. The shoes, too, were a punishment. Some might consider the patent leather, open-toe style most attractive, the daringly high stiletto heels very glamorous, if hardly practical. But the little brass padlocks, which swung from snug straps about her slim ankles, said they could not be removed.

'That's enough for the moment,' said Elaine.

Gemma was disappointed when Elaine stopped and lowered the brush on to the delicately carved chest of

50

drawers which stood darkly to one side of the mirror. She had found the brushing soothing and very sensual. Barbara's hand stroked her neck and, at the same time, the top drawer of the chest whispered open and Elaine's fingers entered the secret realms. Gemma was tempted to glance sideways to see what Elaine had taken out of the drawer. Then came the words which told her. Elaine said simply, 'Open', and lifted the glossy pink rubber ball up to her lips. It was Gemma's instinct to recoil and protest. The first reaction was forestalled by the tightening hand on her neck. The second was a mistake, for the ball was at once pushed firmly into her mouth, while her hair was pulled back and unseen hands manipulated the straps which quickly tightened. Barbara's fingers and thumb held the gag in position until a smooth click ensured its security. Gemma felt the cool metal of the small lock against her neck. In the mirror she saw her face reflected, with lips forming a full circle about the implanted pink ball and the thin strap tight about her cheeks.

Elaine picked up the onyx brush once more and said, 'A little tidying up and she can get on with her work,' then brushed the hair over cheeks to partly conceal the pink strap. Only the ball was obvious, sitting below wide blue eyes. Elaine reached down behind Gemma and moments later her arms were free. Gemma's fingers rose up inquisitively to touch the gag, gliding over both strap and ball.

'She'll need to have it out at lunch time,' said Barbara.

'Fine by me,' answered Elaine, 'but she'll wear ankle cuffs during that time.'

Elaine looked into Gemma's eyes. 'Take it easy in those shoes and you won't have too much of a problem. You'll help to prepare lunch as usual then report to the office at one o'clock unless you intend to go hungry. I wouldn't risk going outside if I were you.'

'I doubt if she will in those shoes,' remarked Barbara. 'She wouldn't get very far and neither will we if we don't go soon.'

'All right,' answered Elaine. 'It won't take me ten minutes. Anyway, I don't expect the wine importer's rep is

51

in any great hurry. He never has been before!' As they were about to leave the room, Elaine remarked to Gemma, 'I hope you're not going to sit there admiring yourself for too long.'

Gemma did remain by the mirror for some time. She heard Barbara and Elaine on the landing outside, their voices fading as they descended the stairs. The dull thump of the heavy wooden entrance door told her they had departed the house and that she was quite alone. Amber had left for the village market at eight thirty that morning and would not be back for at least an hour. Everyone knew it did not take the time she spent there to do the shopping. There was talk of an assignation. With whom, no one knew nor cared, provided she said nothing out of place about the house. If she did, she knew what to expect, and it might be worse than anything she cared to imagine.

Her fingers moved again to the rubber ball. Silence closed as invisible shrouds and moved as a dreaming presence. And there, a short step away, the four-poster bed, solid and immovable as a monumental tomb. Sometimes, as now, she had thought of climbing naked on to it and pulling the curtains about to engulf herself entirely in its musty interior. Would she dream in there? Would she awaken to find that the one who sometimes came to the house and used this room had returned? The one whose image still called and made her shiver even more than did the gaze of Elaine.

Gemma breathed in, nostrils flaring, air hissing past the rubber ball. In the mirror she saw it was wet at the sides. She rubbed the saliva away with her fingers and stood up. There was work to be done.

It was almost ten thirty when Gemma, at the top of the stairs, saw Amber cross the hall with two bulging carrier bags and disappear towards the kitchen. Gemma saw no reason to make her presence obvious and so continued with mundane chores. Amber must know of her continuing punishment. She certainly would when it came to her going down to the kitchen, but it wouldn't be the first time. As for the ball gag, it had caused some small discomfort at first, but not now. It had, as she put it to herself, settled down, almost become a part of her, like wearing a hat or gloves.

If anything mattered, it was the shoes. She had stopped her work from time to time to sit down, finding her legs had begun to ache. Gemma worked on with her private thoughts, and was about to enter Barbara's room with fresh bedding when Amber appeared on the landing. She regarded Gemma with amused silence before approaching. 'Oh, dear! Haven't we been a naughty girl!' Amber stopped before her, glanced at the ball gag and up into her eyes. 'Aren't you tall in those shoes? I must say I do like them, though. Brings back a few memories, don't you think?'

'Mmmm,' came Gemma's muffled response.

Amber circled around as Gemma, clutching the bed sheets, turned to remain facing her. 'You know, I think you look awfully sweet like that. Still, I bet you wouldn't mind if it was off until they come back, would you? They'd never know.' She moved to her own bedroom door and opened it as she turned to see Gemma still watching. 'As it happens, I might just know where there's a key. There's more than one key for most things – there has to be hasn't there? Tell you what, lovey, give us ten minutes to shower and change then I'll see you in the Vampire's room – yes?'

Amber was devious. Gemma had better reason than anyone to appreciate that. In the time it took her to strip the bed and tidy the room though, she concluded that it might just be worth taking Amber at her word and that, in any case, there couldn't be much to lose. Leaving Barbara's room she stopped to place the used sheets in the Aladdin basket by the window. Outside, the sunlit landscape lay at ease under a clear blue sky. Yes, she wished she could leave the house for a time and stroll through the gardens, perhaps into the vineyards, for if Amber really did have keys, she might have one for the shoes as well. Just to feel the sun, if for only half an hour.

The door of the end room was ajar. Amber was already there.

When Gemma entered, Amber was seated on the edge of the four-poster, waiting. She stood up and smiled. Gemma suspected she had little or nothing on beneath the white bathrobe. Her rich, copper-brown hair fell unkempt about her shoulders. Her hands were pushed deep into the big pockets of the robe and Gemma glanced down at them, wondering if she might produce the key. Gemma pointed at the pink ball.

'Oh, yes, that. We'll sort it out in a while. Wait until you see what I've found.' She squeezed Gemma's arm and, with a glance which could only mean mischief, stepped over to the chest of drawers where the handcuffs still lay. Gemma anticipated that Amber might pick them up. She did not. Instead, she pulled open the lower drawer and stooped over it. Gemma recalled that neither were meant to pry into drawers and cupboards which did not concern them. She suspected that Amber had long ago delved into the chest, as well as everywhere else. Amber left the chest and, concealing that which she had lifted out, closed the bedroom door and leant back against it with her arms behind. The ball gag really had become an impediment, for Gemma was desperate to ask what Amber intended.

Amber returned to her side. A soft thud sounded on the bed but before Gemma could look around, Amber's arms were about her waist and holding her tightly. 'I should have put high-heels on, too, then we'd both be the same height.'

Gemma found the backs of her legs against the rock-like frame of the bed. Amber placed a kiss on the pink ball, then on her neck. 'Look, precious, they're not due back till around one o'clock. We've got time for a bit of fun, the way we used to.'

Hands tugged at the belt on Gemma's gown and it fell open before she could prevent it. Arms at once slipped inside and closed coolly about her body. Kisses fell upon the nipples of her exposed breasts. Gemma tried to push Amber away but only succeeded in falling backwards on to the bed to land with her behind on something hard. Amber began to laugh and, in a flurry, removed the bathrobe to reveal her own nakedness. Gemma had seen her sex often enough before, so its total lack of hair, making it as smooth as her own, was no surprise. That, like much else, was a legacy of the old days.

Gemma raised herself up to see what it was she had inadvertently sat on but did not attempt to stop Amber from pulling the black gown away entirely. And there it was – an implement of lust the like of which neither had experienced for some considerable time. Two amply proportioned penises, in realistically veined pink latex, lay joined end to end. They met at a disc shaped cushion, studded with rubber teats and intended to allow flexibility between the two organs as well as ensuring that both users received the generous proportions in equal measure.

'One of the best I've ever seen,' cooed Amber as Gemma, too, stared at it.

Amber might have been uncertain of Gemma's reaction for the gag denied facial expression as well as speech, but the fact that she did not attempt to retreat from the bed was enough. She tugged at Gemma's arm and said, 'Let's get on here and pull down the curtains. Let's shut the whole bloody world out. Let's get this up and fuck ourselves silly!'

Amber shuffled on her knees on to the heavy maroon bedspread and, seeing Gemma do likewise, unhooked the brown velvet sashes to let the drapes fall with a dull swish about the bed. In moments they faced each other in near darkness, enclosed and isolated. They might have been adrift on a vast sea of night or in the shrine beneath some great, unopened pyramid. Amber moved closer. 'Better be careful with those shoes, dearest,' she whispered as each slipped her arms about the other.

Gemma sighed gently, nuzzling the rubber ball against Amber's cheek and neck. Amber spread her lips about the ball until they met Gemma's and both shared it for long seconds. Hands scurried about bodies like furtive creatures of the night. Exploring fingers found breasts firm and teats hard in expectation. Amber tongued and sucked though Gemma could not respond in like manner. But it was

Gemma whose fingers began the game in earnest, for her hand slipped quickly down the smooth warmth beneath Amber's stomach to spread and caress within the lips of her sex. Amber caught her breath but was not to be left behind, for her fingers at once found their goal and Gemma let out a deep sigh as her own sanctum of pleasure was entered.

For a time they remained locked together, cheek to cheek, each fuelling the passions and stoking the flames higher within the other, for such intimacy was far from unknown between them. In one of their own rooms, they might have continued as they were, but despite the growing urgency, Amber stopped her play and quickly reached down. She lifted up the double organ, wanton mischief shining in her eyes. 'Lie down,' she breathed, pushing Gemma by the shoulder.

Gemma obeyed, falling aside and back, struggling to spread her legs either side of Amber without snagging stiletto heels on the bedspread. Amber placed the double-ended dildo by her side and assisted by lifting up and steadying Gemma's knees. Gemma relaxed and closed her eyes, then tensed, air whistling about the gag. Something cool and firm had furrowed between the lips of her sex. It stroked back and forth, pushing ever harder, spreading her wider but meeting little resistance, bathed and lubricated by her own arousal. Gemma moaned quietly as the bulbous head and thick shaft invaded and penetrated fully. Amber placed a hand quickly under each of her knees and lifted them higher so that the identical twin of the implanted organ protruded at an angle. She lifted herself up on to all fours and moved forwards, almost doubling back Gemma's legs under her own arms until she found herself poised above the waiting shaft. She, too, was moist with passion and had no inclination to tarry. Feeling the head against her own sex, Amber arched her back and spread her legs wider to allow it easy entry. Once the gates were breached, there was no hesitation. A long sigh and her body welcomed the full length of the rubber penis in expectation of ecstacy, every nerve and fibre gratified at its arrival. Gemma embraced its twin with fervour, gripping the thick lance with her vaginal muscles, working her pelvis rhythmically and squeezing her clitoris against the protruding teats on the disc. Amber matched her rhythm, each working to reinforce the carnal striving of the other. Red heat surged through their bodies, locked as in mortal combat, and fingers gripped flesh as though in agony as they united in a gasping, sweating struggle for fulfilment in this secret enclave of passion.

Both felt the crisis approaching, each tried to match the impending surge of climax with the other. Gemma's cry, a long loud wail began and she attempted to cross her ankles behind Amber's neck. Then Amber threw back her head and, with body squirming hard about the dildo, gasped and sobbed in the grip of orgasm whilst Gemma writhed and shook beneath.

At last they were still, though Gemma still moaned quietly through the gag. Amber lifted up and withdrew the double organ from them both, seeing it glisten even in the near darkness. 'Let's get ourselves sorted out,' she said, pushing aside the drapes. Gemma, aware once more of the stiletto heels, turned on her side and eased herself up, aching and feeling a wetness about her mouth and cheek. The rubber ball! Amber was supposed to remove it. But Amber was in the bathroom. Gemma at once began to hitch back the drapes and straighten the bedspread. Barbara and Elaine must not find out.

When Amber appeared, wearing her bathrobe, Gemma watched her replace the rubber implement, washed and shining dry, back inside the chest. Gemma never would have guessed the drawer to contain such a thing. She had begun to wonder what else might be hidden there when it slipped shut and Amber turned to face her. Gemma started forwards, a finger pointing at the rubber ball. 'A he!' she gasped.

An amused Amber tilted her head to one side. 'A he?'

Gemma nodded and pointed at the back of her neck. 'A he!'

'Oh, the key. You want the key.'

Gemma nodded frantically. 'Mmmm!'

Amber folded her arms. 'Sorry lovey, I made a mistake, there isn't one. Not that I know of anyhow.'

Gemma, realising she had been tricked, would have screamed if only she could.

Amber moved towards the door. 'It wouldn't do you any good now, anyway. Have you seen the time?'

Gemma knew there was a clock in the room but no, she had not seen the time. Suddenly, it seemed as though she ought to consider it.

The glass-domed clock rose above a fussy and over-worked ormolu base. It rested on a brocade-shrouded table away from the window, shadowed by the four-poster. The gilded ball pendulum rotated slowly in utter silence. Little of that mattered to Gemma, however, for her eyes fell upon the scalloped dial and saw the time. It said twelve thirty! With a moan of consternation, she grabbed the black silk gown and hurried to the bathroom.

'Have you been upstairs?' asked Elaine coldly, from the part opened office door.

Barbara stood by the window, hands raised, unclipping her hair to let it cascade, shimmering over her shoulders. Barbara knew from the way Elaine had entered the room and from the clear and even tone of her voice and the brightness of her eyes that Elaine was simmering beneath with anger. 'No, I haven't been upstairs yet. Is there something wrong?'

'Yes Barbie, you could say that. You could say there's something wrong. I've just been up to my room and seen her finishing off the bed. At this time, at a quarter to one, when she is supposed to be in the kitchen.' Elaine placed one hand on the door frame, the other on her waist. 'She didn't notice me looking so I went to check the other rooms. I thought everything was more or less all right until I got to the end room. And d'you know what I found?'

'No dear, I do not know what you found. I may look psychic but I think you will have to tell me.'

Elaine lowered her voice. 'There are stains on the bed-spread, still damp.'

'Stains? What sort of stains?'

Elaine hesitated. 'Well, not the sort of stains people talk about. What I mean is, the little bitch has been bringing herself off in there when she should have been working. Those sort of stains. I'm quite sure of it.'

'I see,' murmured Barbara. 'And what about Amber? Have you spoken to her?'

'Yes, just now in the kitchen. That one's playing innocent as usual. Claims she's been out all morning.'

'She has been out, we both know that. Still, I know what you mean, though I do not think either of them would admit to anything.'

'No,' said Elaine, 'that's why I'm not going to ask, though I'm convinced it's Gemma. The other one's too crafty to get caught out so easily. I'll teach her a little lesson this afternoon while you're out, see if I don't. As for her pal, I'm going to watch her very carefully from now on. She'll slip up sooner or later, you'll see. And when she does –'

'Yes, well,' said Barbara, 'I don't think she is quite as attuned to your methods of correction as Gemma. It might not achieve the results you, or we, would wish.'

'Do I sense a hint of disapproval?'

'Oh, no, the last thing I want to do is spoil your fun and games. You have developed such a rapport with those two, especially Gemma. It's all a matter of personality, I feel. They respect me for different reasons so I do not propose to interfere with the status quo just yet.'

'Then I'll let her – both of them – have lunch in the usual way,' said Elaine. 'After that Gemma can come in here for questioning and the other one – well, I'll send her out for something. What time are you back?'

Barbara glanced at her watch. 'The way things are going, with lunch it looks as if it will be around four o'clock.'

'Right,' said Elaine, 'I'll go and see what they're up to.'

'If she finds out I'm bloody well for it,' Gemma protested.

'She won't though will she?' Amber replied, fingers

groping inside the wall cupboard. 'Where's the salad dressing?'

'It's here on the tray. Look, when I came out of the bedroom, I saw her going into where we'd been. I just hope she didn't notice anything out of place, that's all.'

'For Christ's sake Gemma, we just had a bit of fun. What's the harm?'

'That's not the point. You always seem to get away with things. I don't.'

Amber's eyes narrowed. 'Perhaps you're one of life's victims, lovey. Perhaps it's what you really want. Look, everything's about ready. Are you taking the salads in or the drinks?'

'It's awkward. I daren't carry too much in case I . . .' She pulled open the silk gown below her knees. Amber regarded Gemma's feet for a moment. She saw it was not only the precariously high heels which caused concern, for the sandals remained securely fastened as they had been all morning. About each of Gemma's slim ankles was fitted a smooth steel band, both joined by a short bright chain.

'Oh, yes, quite,' commented Amber. 'Still, at least you can talk and have something to eat now. Just think, if you'd been wearing those earlier on' – Amber turned to leave with the salad tray – 'we wouldn't have –'

A figure stood in the kitchen doorway. 'Don't let me interrupt, will you,' said Elaine, tersely.

'Oh, er, just on our way,' chirped Amber with a quick smile.

Elaine stood aside as Amber passed. A sharp clicking of metal tipped heels on ceramic floor tiles, and the chink of a metal chain, muffled by the black gown, accompanied Gemma, who followed close behind, clutching a bottle of chilled white wine. A hand descended on to her shoulder and Gemma stopped to face two cool grey eyes.

'When you've had your lunch and cleared up in here, come to the office. Be there by two o'clock.'

Gemma's heart quickened. 'Two o'clock – yes.'

Early afternoon sunlight spilled part way across the landing. Gemma glanced through the nearest window and by chance observed Amber walking away along the gravel path. She continued along the landing with careful, measured steps, feeling the hard tug of the bracelets on her ankles if she attempted to walk normally. The stairs were going to be difficult. Coming up, she had partly walked, partly hauled herself on the heavy wooden banister, using the toes of her sandals to gain purchase on the stairs. Going to the toilet and using the bidet had, thankfully, not been a problem. But if only the chain had been a little shorter. The ball gag, she considered, had been far less of a problem. At the top of the stairs she halted, clutched the banister and lowered herself to the floor. Placing a hand on the carpet at each side, she began to ease herself down on her behind step by step. It was going to take a little time, and it was almost two o'clock, but at least the descent would be accomplished without mishap.

The gloomy entrance was silent, the doors leading off it closed, with the exception of the kitchen door which stood ajar to allow in a little more light. Gemma walked with an almost mechanical step across to the office door. She raised a hand and tapped three times. The voice that bid her enter was matter-of-fact, but Gemma was not reassured by its tone.

Elaine stood silhouetted against the window. She remained looking out even when the soft click of the closing door reached her ears. Gemma found the room unduly bright after the relative darkness of the entrance, for the office was modern and entirely out of keeping with the rest of the house. Elaine turned with a suddenness which made Gemma blink and for a moment, stand transfixed. But at that moment, time seemed to freeze and fix Elaine's image. Here was not the Elaine of this morning, nor of yesterday. This was not the Elaine of ever before, and the image crowded all else from Gemma's mind.

Her rich brown hair was gathered up at the top of her head by a band of red silk and swung down at the back in a pony-tail. Her fine arched eyebrows and long eyelashes were darkened to emphasise the fairness of her skin and her sensual lips matched the silk hairband in colour. The blouse, in shining black satin, had flounced sleeves buttoning closely at the wrists and at the high, flared collar. Pencil-slim, cut just above the knees and fitting her lithe body to measured perfection, the crimson satin skirt was split up one thigh to contrast with the sheerest shadow-nylon on her legs and the gleaming patent black of spike heel ankle boots. But it was the all too familiar riding crop Elaine held curved across her chest with black, kid gloved hands which caused Gemma to step back and all but trip because of the fetters.

'Stay where you are!' Elaine's voice cut the air.

Gemma froze.

Elaine moved with a swish around the large desk and stopped to face her. 'It's good of you to keep our appointment my pet. I wouldn't have been at all pleased if I'd had to come and find you. Not pleased at all.'

Gemma was trembling but could not take her eyes from Elaine. She wanted to ask why, but deep down she knew and dared not speak. Elaine raised the riding crop to Gemma's mouth and ordered, 'Open!'

Gemma opened her mouth and the crop was pushed between her teeth. She inhaled the strong odour of leather.

'Now hold it there!'

Hands at once fell to Gemma's belt and the gown was loosened and pulled open. In a moment, it had been tugged from her and cast over an empty chair. 'Turn around and face the wall!'

Gemma turned, gritting her teeth on the riding crop. There came a swish of nylon on satin as Elaine stepped quickly back across the room. A drawer opened and closed. There were other sounds, unidentifiable sounds, and once more Elaine was close. Gemma felt her wrists seized and pulled back. It was one of those moments when she might have tried to resist Elaine, one of those moments when she never did. Cool leather enclosed both wrists and tightened as it passed through the buckle.

She was not sure what might come next, though she did not expect Elaine to kneel down behind and unlock the ankle cuffs. With these gone, Gemma felt a little steadier on her high heels. In the silence, the swishing of Elaine's movements and her own breathing seemed to fill the room. Soft leather gloves touched her back and pushed behind her upper arms. Gemma half knew, caught her breath and glanced about, feeling the braided leather wet in her mouth.

'Keep still!' snapped Elaine.

The short leather strap had part encircled her limbs just above the elbows. Elaine gripped the brass buckle and free end, drawing them closer, pulling back Gemma's arms and shoulders and forcing out her breasts. At last the strap ends met and Elaine threaded the buckle. Gemma let out a sharp groan as the buckle rasped and her elbows were forcibly drawn in to be pinned strictly and securely together at the middle of her back.

'Good. Now turn around!' ordered Elaine.

Gemma's breasts might have been considered only a little larger than average but were firm and the nipples prominent. These assets were now, with her arms trussed back, particularly well emphasised. Elaine tugged the riding crop from her mouth, slipped a hand about her waist and guided her to a chair on the opposite side of the room. Gemma saw what caught the light on the seat but at first did not understand. Elaine positioned her close to the chair, placed a foot on the seat with her thigh against Gemma's behind, and an arm about her shoulder.

With their heads so close together, Gemma turned her face to gaze into Elaine's eyes. Neither would have predicted what happened next. In returning her gaze, Elaine tasted the scented warmth of Gemma's breath, as Gemma tasted hers. Drawn together like feathers in a gust of wind their lips met with sudden passion and Elaine's hand cupped her breast. Each closed her eyes and time seemed to slow as this brief, electrifying moment spread out and blossomed. Suddenly Elaine drew back, the words, 'You little bitch,' forming almost inaudibly on her mouth. Gemma, lips still parted and smeared red, saw the flicker of surprise in Elaine's sharp eyes. At once, Elaine stooped to pick up one of the two metal objects from the seat. To

Gemma, it appeared as a small, bright spring-loaded clamp, small enough to sit in the palm of a hand. From it, on a short, delicate chain, hung a grape sized steel ball. Elaine held up the shining clamp, squeezed the sides to open small jaws at the top. As Gemma watched, mesmerised, Elaine brought the object to her right breast and released her grip upon it so that the jaws closed and fastened with cold hardness on the swollen nipple. Gemma shivered as the sensation of its touch arced through her belly and limbs. For a moment, her eyes closed tightly, opening again to see the second clamp about to close upon her other nipple. Once more, the oddest of sensations passed through her loins.

'Trussed and clamped,' breathed Elaine, stepping back from Gemma. 'What a pretty picture you are! I think you should wear those more often.'

Gemma gasped and turned awkwardly to face her, the steel balls swinging at the ends of the chains and making her breasts quiver. A conflict of discomfort and brooding ecstasy simmered inside her, for the clamps tormented and stimulated in equal measure.

With a swish of skirt and stockings, Elaine turned quickly towards the desk. Gemma's eyes widened for she thought Elaine was about to take up the riding crop which sat there. Elaine did not, but swung about and part sat, part propped herself against the desk with fingers spread over the edge at either side. 'Now then, go to the middle of the room!'

Gemma moved from the chair in silence to stand before her in a position she judged half-way between Elaine and the office door.

'Turn around, slowly!'

Gemma began to turn until she was side on to Elaine. 'Stop!'

She knew how Elaine's eyes were feasting on the strap which squeezed into the flesh above her elbows, causing her shoulders and arms to sing with a dull and growing ache. In a wall mirror next to the filing cabinet, Gemma could see her mouth and cheek were smeared with Elaine's lipstick. There too was the teat-clamp at each out-thrust breast and the dancing steel balls which added to the exquisite torment whenever she moved.

'Keep turning!' came the voice.

Gemma continued in silence until she found herself facing the door and thought how odd it was that such a bizarre scene should take place in so mundane a setting. And there again was the chair where the nipple clamps had lain. In a moment she would face Elaine once more.

Elaine's eyes were on her once more. 'Walk to that chair, then over to the mirror. Keep on until I tell you to stop. And look only straight ahead!'

Gemma half turned but paused, making the steel balls swing about in circles and rock the clamps from side to side. 'Elaine, my arms! Please!'

'Move!'

Gemma began, taking short steps, attempting to walk and turn so as not to rock the silver clamps. But the steel balls danced and teased her swollen nipples regardless. At each turn, Gemma glimpsed Elaine from the corner of her eye and knew well what she was doing. Slowly and with studied deliberation she tugged at the fingers of one of her soft leather gloves until it slipped free of her hand. Without taking her eyes from Gemma, she let the glove drop, to land silently on the carpet before spike-heeled feet. Another turn and she noticed Elaine easing off the other glove. By this time, the ache in Gemma's arms was giving way to a numb warmth and the grip on her nipples had caused them to feel impossibly large. A rush of excitement swept through her mind at the thought of them appearing as they felt and she gazed hard as she once more approached the mirror. But Elaine's voice cut through her thoughts. 'Stop and come here!'

Gemma halted, turned to face the intimidating figure and stepped forwards. She stopped short, not wishing, not daring, to tread on the limp and discarded gloves. Elaine reached a hand towards her breast. Fingers closed upon the bright steel and squeezed the clamp open. Elaine placed it upon the table by the riding crop, then removed its companion. Gemma inwardly sighed. The relief was perfectly sensual.

Elaine pointed down with straightened arm and ordered, 'Pick them up, one at a time!'

Gemma took a step back, peered at the gloves and looked back into intense eyes. 'How can I – my arms – I can't –'

'Christ! Why d'you think you're not gagged?' shouted Elaine. 'Now do it!'

Gemma took a deep breath and sank awkwardly to her knees. Manoeuvring her face towards the gloves was not easy with her arms trussed so tightly and she almost toppled on to her side. But after a few seconds of gasping effort, during which time Elaine remained quite still and silent, Gemma found her eyes close to the gloves. Equally close were the spike-heel boots. Her teeth closed upon the first glove and an aroma, more delicate than that of the riding crop, entered her mouth and nose. Gemma tried to rise but in making the attempt, was obliged to shuffle forwards to maintain her balance, and found her cheek pushed against the glass-smooth nylon of Elaine's leg. Elaine did not move. Gemma raised herself to her knees and placed the glove into the waiting hand.

Shuffling back a little, Gemma sank to the floor a second time and had soon managed to obtain a hold on the other glove. But before she could rise, Elaine had reached down to seize and hold the strap about her wrists, pulling up her bound arms so that Gemma was held close to the floor with her face against the booted toes.

'You're really not trying are you!' Elaine shouted. Then a crack split the air as the riding crop fell with a shocking sting across her exposed behind. The sudden scream which flew from Gemma's throat also released the glove, and whether Elaine was aware of this or not seemed irrelevant, for the crop hissed a second time to find its all too easy target. The office rang to an unfamiliar sound as the riding crop fell again and again to the accompaniment of ever increasing howls – howls that became sobs as Gemma's tears sprang forth.

The whipping ceased. Gemma had not felt inclined to count the biting strokes but knew there had not been very many. That was unimportant, for her weeping at Elaine's feet was continuous and through wet eyes she saw dark stains on the carpet and on the glove close to her face.

'Now pick it up!' came the voice.

Gemma squirmed about with tears trickling over nose and cheeks, her behind a raging furnace. Teeth once more fastened on to the leather glove and with a determined effort she struggled to her knees before dropping it into the waiting hand. And as if having overcome the most gargantuan of tasks, Gemma moaned and sagged forwards, her head falling against the yielding warmth of Elaine's stomach, her cheek pushing into smooth, crimson satin. At that point, Gemma cared little whether or not Elaine might push her away or, indeed, apply the riding crop again. And in not caring, she was not at first surprised when a hand brushed her cheek and came to rest on the back of her head. Why she sank lower on her knees until her cheek rested against the relative hardness of the *mons veneris*, she could not have explained; nor why she turned her face inwards and bared her teeth to bite gently against the smooth, tight fabric where it stretched across Elaine's sex. The fact that the voice came in a harsh whisper, 'God! You little slut!' mattered not at all, for the hand caressed her head and pushed her face harder between the thighs, still tender nipples feeling the satin smooth and sensual. Gemma felt Elaine squirm against the table but the tightness of the skirt prevented further progress. Gemma looked up to find Elaine's eyes bright and her lips parted as though about to speak though she remained silent. Gemma begged softly, 'Please.'

Very slowly, Elaine's hand moved to the waistband. The snap of a button, the whirr of a zip down to the split thigh, and the crimson skirt fell aside. Before her eyes, the strictly bound Gemma found the lace tops of Elaine's stockings, held taut by elasticated, crimson-ruffle suspenders. Gemma at once pushed her nose and open lips against the heat of Elaine's sex, the only barrier now being small briefs in red nylon lace. The hand again touched Gemma's head and remained as though Elaine was hesitating. Then both hands moved over the tops of the stockings to quickly unclip the suspenders.

Gemma sank back, eyes closed, knowing she must allow Elaine to ease down the briefs, though her desire to go on was overwhelming. She sensed, rather than saw, when the briefs were gone and opened her eyes only for a moment. In that moment there was Elaine, leaning further back against the table with legs parted and eyes narrowed, arms propped behind to keep herself steady. In that moment, too, there was the smooth whiteness of the thighs and soft, short down of dark hair above her sex.

Gemma did not hesitate, but with the urgency and enthusiasm of a bee upon a nectar-laden flower, set lips and tongue to the focus of pleasure, worshipping the pearl within its shrine before pressing on to the inner sanctum. This unexpected delight fuelled Elaine's passions faster than either could have anticipated. The one upon whom Elaine had inflicted torment, who still knelt before her in helpless subjugation, was now the agent of irresistible voluptuousness, serving her in the most intimate manner of her own will. Elaine knew Gemma's inclinations better than anyone except for Amber, and might have considered what she was doing as a part of her humiliation. But such thoughts were fast evaporating in the fires which began to consume her body. Gemma tasted Elaine's excitement and rising heat, felt her vaginal muscles tighten and her body begin to tense; she knew that she was the one in control and that Elaine was at her mercy. She knew amidst the turmoil that she could cease her play and throw Elaine into despair. That was the power she had. But she wanted to serve and what better way than this!

Elaine leant further back and, gasping uncontrollably, glanced up at the ceiling before closing her eyes for the inevitable. And Gemma, knowing her to be already speeding towards the precipice, drove her on ever faster until Elaine came with an intensity which Gemma would not have considered her capable.

* * *

Only after the straps were gone did Gemma realise how numb and aching were her arms. Elaine had not spoken, but sat behind the desk, staring towards the wall as Gemma rubbed and flexed elbows and shoulders. She at last pulled on the black gown, and with hands clutching the collar, stood looking at Elaine, waiting. Summoning up courage she said, 'Elaine, I – I hope that was all right for you. I wanted to – I mean I –'

'Get out!' snapped Elaine, without moving. Gemma remained motionless. Then Elaine's eyes blazed at her. 'Did you hear me, you slut?' she yelled hoarsely. 'Get out of this room! Now!'

Something triggered inside Gemma and she rushed to open the door. Without another word, without a backward glance, she was gone. For a time Elaine sat still, her eyes fixed upon the door. After a minute she took a deep breath, leant back into the chair with eyes closed and whispered, 'Damn you, you little bitch! Why did I let you do that? Why?'

4

The Intrigues of Amber

Gareth toyed with the half-finished glass of orange juice and looked at Victoria. Both looked at Sophie. Sophie, who had said very little, was staring in silence at the bowl of breakfast cereal and swinging her spoon idly above it. The sun had not yet begun to filter into the little patio garden but the air was morning fresh and perfumed with flowers. An overtly dejected Sophie said, 'I was thinking about it before we came down. I'm really messing up your holiday aren't I? Maybe we should have split up in Rome. I seem to be getting in the way of things all the time. Look, let's forget the bloody watch. It's not as though it ever cost me anything.'

Glancing up at the sky in near disbelief, Gareth took a deep breath and leant back into the seat, a token move to distance himself from a delicate situation.

Victoria smiled with an expression which said that no one was kidding anyone. 'Now then dear, let's not complicate matters. Gareth knows we're going back, I know we're going back and you know we're going back, so let's forget the last-minute remorse. It's only a matter of whether we leave here straight away or in an hour or two. Personally, I favour setting off sooner.' Victoria wondered how, after the unbridled intimacies of the last few days, Sophie could so easily present herself as the disinterested party and opt to withdraw from plans which had been agreed solely for her benefit. Gareth reserved his opinion; it seemed the least perilous route to follow for the moment. Victoria turned to him, 'Well, when do you want to make a move?'

Gareth shrugged. 'Soon as you're both ready.'

Sophie glanced towards the hotel reception and placed a hand over her mouth. 'Before they find out what's happened to the bed, if you ask me.'

Victoria and Gareth agreed, considering the consequences which might accrue when the hotel owner found that one of his prized pieces of furniture had passed beyond a state of mere decrepitude.

'How long d'you expect those bits of string will hold it together?' asked a newly enthused Sophie as if in fear of being overheard.

'Until a couple of fat Germans or Americans get into it, I reckon,' replied Gareth. 'Then the whole bloody lot will go through the floor.'

'Oh, God!' breathed Victoria. 'Can you imagine the look on their faces?'

'Especially if they're hard at –' began Sophie.

'Yes, quite,' put in Gareth. 'If we clear off now, we'll have time to look at one or two old villages on the way. We shouldn't have any problems finding the villa this time.'

'Famous last words,' murmured Victoria.

'This map,' mumbled Sophie from the rear of the car, 'has more detail on it than the old one, but we still don't know the name of the area or the road where the villa is.'

'Okay,' said Gareth, 'but we can't be far from the road we came along on the way to Siena.'

'I wonder if we didn't take the wrong turning out of that last village,' said Sophie. 'These little back roads wander all over the place like strings of spaghetti. You just can't tell which is which.'

'I think what she's trying to say, dear,' sighed Victoria, 'is that we're lost. Lost again, that is.'

'Well, at least we're getting used to it,' remarked Sophie, with a hint of resignation. But her mind was full of distractions. When they had left Siena, her map reading talents not yet required, she had drifted into sleep amongst the carrier bags and other clutter. And once asleep, she had begun to dream.

In the dream she had found herself once more at the Villa Raffaello, in the secret room above the house where, surrounded by those sinister fittings and furnishings, she had indulged in such voluptuous sport with Gareth. As then, she was naked, and spread helpless upon the wooden cross, but there was no Gareth. Instead, there was Barbara and Elaine, swathed in darkness, and others she could not identify for they, too, were all but concealed in black. Figures moved about, laughing and touching her intimately, squeezing and sucking on her breasts until the nipples were reddened and swollen. All the time they were crowding in on her while the two sisters, heads pushed together, watched and smiled, faces bright against the darkness. Fingers played about her stomach and sex, whilst one entered, slipping inside like a lizard's tongue and making her cry out.

'There's no one to hear you,' cooed a voice from the darkness. 'No one to help, no one to help . . .'

She was transfixed with fear and shame but with it, her excitement was heightened and she knew they would drive her to a climax. One knelt before her bound form while another crouched below the cross at the rear. Two tongues converged and entered her most intimate places, playing their devilish game with her passions. Shadowed forms whirled about as the crisis approached. All of them breathed in unison, but the low moans which enveloped her in tangible sound she knew somehow to be her own. The orgasm seemed to be happening to another Sophie in another time and another place. She was gasping and shaking as though the earth itself trembled. Something was pushing her around and there was a glaring light!

She raised a hand to protect her eyes as the sunlight glared in through the window and the car swayed around the sharp curve of a badly made road.

'Wakey-wakey!' came Victoria's penetrating voice, dispelling the haze of semi-consciousness. Sophie looked at her in dazed confusion as Victoria asked, 'Who's been having a bad dream?'

It had taken Sophie some time to recover her senses but

the shame of her dream world had remained with her. Indeed it might have made itself obvious had not the part-opened map lain across her knees, for her own fingers, pushed down the front of her cotton slacks, had been fully engaged in the business of arousal performed in the dream by others. She had found herself wet and excited and only with some difficulty had she regained any composure, managing to extract her hand from her crotch unseen by maintaining the position of the map. Gareth had said, 'How about you try and figure out which direction we have to go.'

She had stared at the map and wondered: did Victoria know? Had Victoria watched her masturbating in the back of the car? The trees and countryside had rolled past her vision and she had glanced back down at the map. It had made no sense at all.

'What we should have,' said Gareth, 'is a car compass. I use one back home. It makes life easier when you get to a junction and there's no signpost.'

'What about the sun?' suggested Victoria. 'You usually can't see it at home but it seems to always be shining out here.'

'That would be okay if I could remember where it was last time.'

'Oh, that's easy,' said Sophie. 'When we turned right at that junction and ran out of petrol, it was shining in through the back window. And when we left in the morning and went straight over the junction, it was still shining in the back window. So, there you are.'

'There I am what?' answered Gareth. 'It does that east and west the entire length of Italy.'

'Well, I'm only telling you, aren't I?' responded Sophie. 'I can't see how you'd be any better off with a compass in that case.'

Gareth gripped the steering wheel. 'Fat lot of use you two are.'

'Dear me,' said Victoria, glancing back at Sophie. 'He didn't think that the other night did he? Tell you what, next likely looking place we pass through, I'll get out and ask. Someone around here might know.'

'A good idea,' muttered Gareth, as they slowed at an anonymous junction. 'It's getting a bit late.'

'What's the time?' chirped Sophie. 'I'm lost without my – oops, sorry!'

'A quarter to three,' answered Victoria. 'And if you really must know, we're never going to get to Florence in time to find a hotel unless we – look Gareth! Slow down!'

Lumbering towards them and crouching under the seemingly massive weight of an ordinary sized spade, there came a swarthy individual of rustic aspect, in open waistcoat and well-worn trousers. The car stopped as he drew near and Victoria wound down the window.

The man appeared not to notice them at all, until Victoria leant out and called, '*Scusi! Scusi! Mi può dire dove la Villa Raffaello?*'

The man stopped and peered at her with dark eyes set in a wrinkled, leathery face. A cigarette stub wobbled precariously on his lower lip but no hint of recognition appeared on his features.

'*La Villa Raffaello,*' repeated Victoria, '*per favore?*'

Still nothing. He did, however, stab the spade into the ground and push back the careworn flat cap which already resided at an unnatural angle on a mop of thick grey hair.

'He might not know them,' put in Sophie, 'with them being English and all that.'

The man's eyes lit up and he smiled benignly. '*Ah! Inglese! Si – Le sorelle Inglese!*'

'Yes,' smiled Victoria. 'The English sisters!'

Not only his face, but his entire upper body became animated. Words and gestures flowed in best operatic manner, arms and hands darting this way and that as Victoria punctuated his dialogue with a frequent, '*Si* – er, yes – *si!*'

The verbal cornucopia exhausted, he seized the spade and Victoria smiled. '*Mille grazie per l'aiuto!*'

The man lifted his hat with a crumpled grin. '*Prego, signorina! Prego!*'

'Bloody hell,' said Victoria, as the car gathered speed. 'I could barely keep up with most of it. We're actually near the estate but the house is on the other side. Take the next but one right turn – I think.'

Eventually, after further turns into narrow roads which might have been the same as those they had just left, Victoria cried, 'There, Gareth! There's the villa over to the right!'

'If we hadn't stopped that old bloke,' remarked Sophie, 'we might have ended up in Rimini. It sounds rather nice actually.'

'And you wouldn't have got your watch back,' added Victoria as, some way before the point where the road began to rise, they came within sight of the stone gateposts.

'Oh, that. I'm not all that bothered about it, really.'

'What!' cried out Gareth as the car slowed.

Victoria turned with a baleful stare. 'Sophie, you're going fully dressed into the bloody swimming pool as soon as we arrive. Just you see!'

'And I'll hold her head under the water for at least ten minutes,' added Gareth. 'That should solve all our problems.'

The voice from the back seat was meek and barely audible. 'Only kidding – honest.'

Crunching slowly over the gravel, the car circled about and came to a halt a short distance from the main entrance. Victoria peered hard up at the windows. 'It looks deserted.'

'But then it did when we first showed up,' said Gareth.

'They probably heard our car,' added Sophie, 'took one look and said, "Oh, bloody hell, it's them again, we'll pretend we're out." '

'I wouldn't bet too much on that theory,' said Victoria. 'The door is part open. Someone must be at home.'

'So it is,' said Gareth. 'Then I think we should all go.'

'I'll bring the carrier bag with their pressies,' added Sophie, struggling out of the car.

Gareth tugged the bell-pull and the three waited. No one

appeared. Gareth pulled a second time. Over a minute passed. At last he looked about and said, 'Perhaps the bell isn't working. I mean, you can't hear anything can you? Maybe I'll stick my head inside and shout.'

'If you want,' said Victoria, 'but I'm going to look around the back. I don't think we should poke our noses into someone else's house like that.' She set off along the front of the house and disappeared around the corner. Another minute had passed when Gareth glanced about again and said to Sophie, 'Look, we can't hang around forever. There must be someone inside. You wait here.' With that, he stepped up to the opened half of the heavy door and pushed it slowly inwards.

After the bright daylight, the entrance hall seemed dark at first. Gareth moved a little further in as his eyes became accustomed to the low light, then stopped, waited and listened. For a time there was only silence. To one side something moved. An amorphous shadow descended the stairs. Above it a figure appeared in a long black gown, hand upon the stout bannister, walking none too easily in high-heel shoes. Gareth's eyes were sufficiently adjusted by now to recognise the shoulder-length blond hair of Gemma. He stepped forwards. 'Hello! Sorry to barge in . . .'

He had not intended to startle her but she glanced at him in wide-eyed horror and at once turned to hasten clumsily back up the stairs. In that brief moment of confrontation he had seen why she did not, could not, speak and his mind was a riot of confusion. He glanced quickly at the empty stairs and hurried the few steps back to the door. As he emerged into the outside glare, two figures in long black dresses confronted him on the step. Close behind stood Victoria and Sophie. Having no time for self composure, he blurted out, 'Oh, er, sorry. I just stuck my head inside to – to, er shout. The bell – I didn't think the bell was working!' It was quite impossible to conceal his reddening face. He hoped they did not realise what he had seen for the image still hung in his mind, clear and bright as the sun.

Elaine regarded him coolly. 'The bell only sounds near

the kitchen and on the landing. That's why you couldn't hear it. People usually wait.'

Barbara's green eyes were upon him too, but the merest shade of a smile passed across her face and she said in a clear, soft voice, 'Perhaps the three of you would like to come inside.'

'We've brought something for you from Siena,' put in Sophie, jerking up the olive green carrier bag.

Victoria eyed her sharply, 'Let it wait a minute, Sophie. Give them a chance to get through the door!'

Sophie grinned sheepishly and, with Gareth and Victoria, followed Barbara and Elaine into the house. Gareth was now convinced that they must know what he had seen. He felt more at ease, nevertheless, in the entrance hall for the subdued light would render his embarrassment less obvious. As for the stairs where he had seen Gemma, Gareth deliberately positioned himself so that his eyes might not fall in that direction. But as Victoria and Sophie renewed acquaintances with the sisters, he was aware of Barbara's gaze upon him and aware, too, that his very manner, his caution and occasional inept comment must serve only to reinforce her suspicions, or worse, confirm her conclusions.

'So what do you think?' Victoria's sudden question interrupted his train of thought.

'Sorry – what?'

'About us all staying on here for the evening again of course. I think it's awfully kind of Barbara and Elaine.'

'Sounds a brilliant idea to me,' added Sophie.

'He is daydreaming,' smiled Barbara. 'The house affects people that way – some more than others.'

Gareth forced a smile. 'I appreciate the offer, but we don't want to be in anybody's way.'

'If we thought that,' put in Elaine, 'we wouldn't have suggested it. Apart from anything else, this place could do with more life – it feels a bit deserted sometimes, even creepy, especially at night.'

'And you will never find a hotel vacancy near Florence,' said Barbara. 'Everyone wants to go there, though personally I find it rather noisy and tiring.'

Wondering now if the image of Gemma could have been an illusion, Gareth's attention was becoming wholly taken by that of Barbara and Elaine. Both, especially Elaine, held a dark fascination for him. 'I think we ought to talk it over and, well – if we all think –'

'Basically,' cut in Victoria, 'we have to be sure we compensate you for all the trouble.'

'Yes,' agreed Sophie, 'we'll have to chip in.'

It seemed to Gareth that the deal was being carried through whether he liked it or not, especially when Barbara said, 'I can assure you that there is not a problem, you are no longer strangers to us. We are happy to have your company.'

The look on Sophie's face was one of unambiguous delight and she at last relieved herself of the carrier bag by handing it to Elaine. Gareth found himself inwardly glad at having, apparently, been overruled.

'So,' continued Barbara, 'there is no reason why you cannot relax for the remainder of the afternoon. You know where the pool is. Sebastiano keeps it in good order always. Or you may wish to go for a walk. The vineyards are quite extensive and you have already seen how attractive our countryside is. I think it will be a more pleasant prospect than hurrying back to Florence – and oh, yes, Sophie – you will find your watch by the bed in the room you used last time. You may go up as soon as you wish.'

'That was really weird,' remarked Sophie, floating on her back in the crystal water and shading her eyes against the sun. 'I mean, the whole point in our returning wasn't to ponce off them again but to get my watch, and what happens – I'd almost forgotten about it and we're signed up for another evening!'

'Quite,' said Victoria bobbing up and down a short distance away. 'I think they caught us a bit off guard you know. It's as though they'd already planned on us staying before we got here. Sounds silly doesn't it? And what about the hotel near Viareggio? Won't they be wondering where you are?'

'I don't know,' replied Sophie. 'Don't really care any more to tell the truth.' She watched Victoria pull herself up to the poolside in a sun-shimmering cascade, her nipples dark and hard, her small swimslip a deeper blue even than the sky above. 'I hope they don't mind us being at the pool like this,' she continued, 'they seem a bit straight-laced in some ways if you ask me. I can't see either of them sunbathing at all.' At the same time she wondered about their connection with the room in the tower and concluded that there might be none other than the fact that it came with the house.

'Yes,' replied Victoria, 'I suppose we ought to have asked, but there's no one around, is there, not even Amber and Gemma, though I don't suppose they'd be bothered. Come to think about it, where did he go?'

'Who, Gareth?'

'No, dear, the man in the moon. Have you seen him since we came back down? I haven't.'

'He said he was going for a walk, that's all I remember. Perhaps he's trying his luck with the maids. We both know what he's like.'

'Don't we just,' muttered Victoria, closing her eyes and relaxing in the poolside chair to bask in the late afternoon sun.

He could have taken the path which led across the vineyard and was, he guessed from the patterns in the ground, used by a tractor. But that went in the direction of a group of stone buildings and sheds, part of which he assumed must be the estate manager's residence. To the left, the land rose and became wooded, and beyond that must be the road where they had run out of petrol on that day which seemed an age ago. From the hill there ought to be a fine view of the house and surrounding area and Gareth wanted to explore.

The going was not difficult though he noted there was no evidence that anyone ever came this way. It was not until he was among the trees, where it was noticeably cooler, that he found a building, though as he approached, he realised that what he saw was a ruin of considerable age, an ancient chapel which must have stood proudly on the hill before the trees enveloped it. Gareth approached closer, then stopped. There were voices. First a man's voice, then a female, laughing. The sounds came from within the walls, rising and falling for a time, then becoming less audible. Gareth moved from tree to tree, ever closer, until he found himself hard against a stone wall and close to an arched doorway from which hung the rotted remains of an iron studded door. He glanced quickly around and at once saw three figures, huddled together on a grassy rise by the far wall. What they were doing was perfectly visible, for the ruin was completely open to the sky.

They were all but partly clothed. The girl, her face hidden, lay in the arms of one of the two men. His shirt was cast aside on the grass, his trousers opened and pulled, with his briefs, part way down to his knees. His penis, in full erection, was held in her hand, and they writhed on the ground, lips fused together in passion. She wore a deep mauve, sleeveless top but was devoid of any other item of clothing. Between her legs was thrust the hand of her companion and it was obvious that she was much aroused by this attention, for this kissing was interrupted frequently by a short cry. The other, younger male, was hastily pulling off his trousers and shoes; his shirt hung from the branch of a nearby tree.

The girl, though much preoccupied, was aware of his presence for as he knelt down, her hand arose from its first charge in order to close about the younger man's throbbing member. Gareth was still unable to see her features for she let her head fall back to the ground as the first man struggled up on his knees beside her to face the second. His penis was not to be abandoned for long, however, for her free hand closed quickly upon it whilst she spread her legs lewdly. Some brief conversation took place between her two companions. It was at this point Gareth recognised the first man as the one who had been sent to procure petrol for them after the night of their first visit: the estate manager, Sebastiano.

But the group, now relatively static as the girl worked the two shafts simultaneously with her hands, was not to remain in that situation for long. The second man pulled away and sidled about to position himself between her widespread legs where he fell down, sphinx-like. The girl was almost obscured by his body but the position he occupied and the rising sound of her moans gave no doubt as to the use to which his tongue was being put. In her own excitement she began to work Sebastiano more vigorously and it was obvious that for two of the participants at least, the crisis must be close.

Then as quickly as it had formed, the tableau began to reassemble, though Sebastiano moved very little. The girl twisted up and, resting on all fours before him, promptly opened wide her mouth to engulf the engorged penis. The second man positioned himself at her rear and, without further ado, entered her well-lubricated sex to the hilt. Both men began rapid pelvic movements, the younger man gripping her thighs as Sebastiano grasped the sides of her head in his hands.

With beating heart, Gareth had for the first time seen all three faces clearly. At last he recognised who was playing hostess to both organs of lust at once, for there was no mistaking the shining copper hair: Amber! Nor was she under any form of compulsion, for her enthusiasm seemed to equal if not exceed that shown by the two men. Her moans, despite the pumping shaft within her mouth, grew ever louder and there was no mistaking that it was she who was drawn first into the whirlpool of orgasm. But her companions in passion were not to be left far behind. As the younger man threw back his head and groaned loudly, Sebastiano arched his back as though about to take a final lunge, his pelvis jerking vigorously as he ejaculated hard into her mouth.

The small group appeared to deflate slowly, like a hot air balloon settling to the ground. Both men withdrew from Amber and eased back as she lowered herself and turned over. During the performance, Gareth had dared not move a muscle but now felt strongly that his presence should be maintained no longer. With barely a sound, he left the ruined chapel and retraced his steps down the wooded slope, keeping low in case any of the three might emerge before dressing to witness his hasty retreat.

'They go with the room perfectly,' smiled Barbara, regarding the pair of coiled brass candlesticks positioned in the middle of the old table, 'but you really shouldn't have spent your money on us. It was not expected.'

'No,' agreed Elaine, 'this place is full of antiques of one sort or another, though I must say we never turned up any candlesticks.'

'Bet it's all worth a bomb!' exclaimed Sophie.

'Angelo has an inventory,' said Barbara. 'It was he who pulled everything together after the accident. Without his help, Wallace's affairs would have been a shambles.'

'I can well imagine,' said Victoria. 'Especially in a part of the world with different rules and legal structure.'

'Yes,' added Gareth, 'I reckon the sharks really would have closed in, same as back home.'

'Well, you two should know,' put in Sophie, smiling at Gareth and Victoria.

'Not all solicitors are unscrupulous,' replied Victoria, regarding Sophie with a look of impending retribution. Barbara regarded her with quiet amusement. At that point, Amber and Gemma entered the vaulted dining room, wheeling the trolley of food, wine and other essentials for what promised to be an excellent meal. Gareth felt the blood rush to his face and was again silently thankful for the dim lighting. Should he ignore Gemma? If so he must also ignore Amber. At least in her case there was no reason for embarrassment for she could not know what he had seen. The moments flew by in confusion, then he steeled himself and acted, allowing both girls a meek smile and a soft 'Hello,' to complement the more overt greetings of Victoria and Sophie.

With fleeting smiles and glances, Gemma said, 'Hello,' to all three at once. Amber managed a more outgoing, 'Nice to see you all again!' Neither girl showed the least sign of discomfort. Their dresses, as Gareth quickly noted, were plain and tight-fitting: Amber's white and Gemma's pale emerald. He was aware that he must not allow himself too long a preoccupation with their slim figures; even so, as he looked away, he was immediately conscious of Barbara's eyes upon him. Her gaze was cool, unblinking, knowing. Victoria and Sophie were chatting to Elaine. He needed a break. Unexpectedly it came from Amber, who was arranging the dishes before Barbara. She smiled directly at him and said, 'I like the candlesticks you brought back, Gareth.'

At last he had the excuse he needed, and smiled at her. Amber narrowed her eyes and continued, 'Just what this old room needed!' The wink was unmistakable. It said, 'I want to get to know you.'

Gareth returned what he hoped would be at least a smile of acknowledgement, at best one which told her how strong was his desire to know her intimately. A return wink would have been too much of a risk, for although Barbara appeared occupied, Elaine's eyes were certainly fixed upon him for the moment and there was at least one glance from Victoria. It might have been another awkward episode for Gareth but Sophie, swirling red wine around in a half-filled glass, chirped in enthusiastically, 'I bet they had lots of parties here didn't they?'

Her question had the effect of distracting Elaine who answered, 'Parties? Oh, yes. It seems they had plenty of parties all right.'

'Indeed they did,' added Barbara with an eye on Sophie. 'Wallace's friends and business associates came from all over Europe, and further afield. He certainly knew how to entertain.'

'You can say that again,' remarked Amber in a low voice as she and Gemma made a few last adjustments to the table spread and prepared to leave the room. Barbara did not respond to her remark, but appeared lost in thought for some considerable time after she had gone, oblivious to the conversation around her.

* * *

'The house,' he said, with an elegant sweep of the hand, 'has a long history, much of it undocumented, unfortunately. When Signor Devereaux, saw it, there was much neglect and the estate, it was not well managed. But he fell in love with it at once and it is the good fortune of the house that he was able to restore and modernise it at the same time.'

'It certainly is a beautiful house, Signor Manfredi,' said Barbara, as she and Elaine gazed about the entrance hall.

It had been a tedious journey. Their flight from London had been delayed and then there had been the long drive from Pisa airport, far longer than they had expected. And now, the day was waning.

'Quite charming,' said Elaine. 'Wallace kept it a secret as far as we were concerned. We had no idea that he owned such a place.'

'Perhaps Signor Manfredi will show us quickly around,' said Barbara. 'My enthusiasm was beginning to flag a little earlier; but now we're here –'

'Please ladies, you must call me Angelo. I have known your uncle for many years and we were good friends. I am here to help in legal matters, I know, but I am your friend, too.'

'Of course,' replied Barbara, 'you can blame it on our British conservatism.'

The elegant face creased into a smile. Had Barbara and Elaine only seen a photograph of him, they might have considered Angelo to be of north European origin. His neat, well kept fair hair, and slim, manicured fingers gave nothing away, though the elegant bearing and occasional gestures might have suggested a Latin quality even before he spoke.

'I just can't wait to see everything,' added Elaine. 'You say there are maids here as well?'

'Yes,' he answered, 'but these I have sent away for the afternoon so that we will be free to talk about things you may not understand.'

'Things we may not understand?' queried Barbara.

'More legal matters?' asked Elaine.

Angelo glanced uneasily from Elaine to Barbara. 'No, not legal matters. Matters of – perhaps we should discuss these things in the comfort of the main room. And I think perhaps we shall have a drink first, if you will allow me.'

'I see,' said Barbara. 'It's hardly surprising Wallace saw fit to exercise a little discretion.'

'Naughty old Wallace,' mused Elaine.

'I can arrange, of course, to have everything removed from these rooms before you go into the tower, but only with your permission. All of this is in your joint names as you already know. And there is the question of the missing key to the second room. The girls do not know where it was kept.'

'I don't think we need concern ourselves with any of it now,' said Barbara, once more meeting Angelo's eye.

'No,' agreed Elaine, 'I'm sure a few days, or a few weeks for that matter isn't going to make any difference. And to tell the truth, I really don't think either of us cares much at the moment.'

'We should have kept moving,' said Barbara. 'Now we're sat down, I do not think I want to get up.'

'Then I shall go and let you rest,' smiled Angelo. 'I know both you ladies must be tired and I have still some work to do. But for you, everything is in order: water, electricity, all are working and your rooms are prepared by the girls. If you choose to sleep for the afternoon, they will not disturb you.'

All three stood and Angelo picked up his small black briefcase. With the merest hint of a bow, he took Elaine and Barbara's hands in turn. Barbara's he held a little longer. Both returned to the easy chairs but neither spoke until the heavy thud of the front door confirmed Angelo's departure. Then Elaine remarked, 'Well, we've only been here five minutes and you seem to have an admirer. I saw the way he looked at you.'

'He's a charming man,' said Barbara with a smile. 'Not at all what I expected.'

'Life's full of surprises,' replied Elaine. 'We've known

Wallace on and off all our lives and you wouldn't have thought butter would melt in his mouth – now this. Now Angelo's gone, perhaps I might have a nose around after all. He said he'd left everything unlocked for us didn't he?'

'I believe he did. And I'm coming with you. I think it might not be a bad idea if we see what we have to see before the maids return.'

They hesitated part way up the narrow stone steps and stood between the heavy, encroaching walls to take in the stillness and solitude. In the room to which access was possible, they remained silent for some time, eyes and fingers examining the items and devices of punishment and restraint. The question as to whether Barbara and Elaine considered herself knowledgeable or sympathetic towards the purpose of the room and its contents was not raised. Each had spent her adult life largely separate from the other, though Barbara knew about a few of Elaine's previous affairs and Elaine, naturally, was aware of Barbara's marriage and recent divorce. Each wondered, of course, what the other thought, but in those long, pensive minutes, minutes which became a half hour and more, each was consciously aware that no hint of condemnation or disapproval had been expressed by the other. Had Angelo accompanied them to this bizarre chamber and asked for their opinions openly, neither could have been sure that she would not have voiced what most might consider the expected degree of repudiation. That, in turn, would have implied a foreknowledge of Angelo's opinions and Angelo they hardly knew at all.

It was Barbara who opened the large cupboard and Elaine, seeing her occupied within, joined her to become co-discoverer of the sinister contents. The doors were closed slowly, for they knew any sharp sound would echo about the stone walls. It was as though they wished to avoid attracting attention – but whose attention? Perhaps spirits of the past still lingered; perhaps the sighs and cries of those who once revelled here had left a presence which fluttered about the dark crevices in the stone walls.

At last Elaine said, 'I don't know about you, but I think we should leave all of this just as it is.'

'Yes,' Barbara answered softly. 'Perhaps we will – just as it is.'

Barbara's thoughts were dispelled by the reappearance of Amber and Gemma, who both smiled at the guests and inquired if anything else might be needed at the table. Once again, Gareth's thoughts turned to Amber, though what he had furtively observed earlier on that day had seldom been out of his mind for more than a few minutes at a time. And when it was absent, its place was occupied by the image of Gemma as she had hurried away up the stairs to avoid his gaze. When the time was appropriate, that little secret, at least, he might impart to Victoria, if not to Sophie as well. But when they returned to clear away the main dishes he realised that out of the two, it was Amber for whom he had developed the stronger fascination. Nevertheless, in trying to maintain a degree of indifference he found himself deliberately ignoring her presence even when, from the corner of his eye, he observed her to occasionally glance at him. He was not unaware either, of Barbara's unblinking eyes upon him and at once wondered if his avoidance of Amber was not overplayed. Accordingly, as she shifted to a point at the table opposite his seat, Gareth smiled at her. Amber, placing dishes on to the trolley, immediately smiled back. 'Did you enjoy the dinner?'

It was obvious that her question was aimed solely at Gareth. 'Oh, marvellous,' he answered.

'That's what we like to hear,' she responded and, turning to leave, with her back almost to Barbara and Elaine, gave what he could have sworn was a discreet wiggle of her behind. He hoped that his polite but broadening smile might serve as due acknowledgement. Had Amber felt his heartbeat, she would have known. Gareth felt himself not simply aroused by her brief attentions, but satisfied in another way; as the only male present at the table he had from time to time found himself excluded from the general conversation. The term 'being on the same wavelength' seemed to apply very much to Elaine and Victoria, though both, and Elaine in particular, ensured that Sophie was not excluded. Barbara, preoccupied in thought much of the time, spoke but occasionally.

Elaine offered the bottle around the table asking, 'Who would like a drop more wine?'

'God, I feel sozzled!' exclaimed Sophie, though Victoria noticed it was her empty glass which slid forwards almost before the question was finished.

'Never mind,' said Elaine, 'you're on holiday.'

'No, she's the same at home,' remarked Victoria. 'She helped reduce the European wine lake all by herself.'

An aroma of coffee drifted into the room, followed by Amber and Gemma, one bearing a cafetière, the other a tray of small cups.

'We don't deserve to be spoilt like this,' commented Victoria.

'No,' agreed Gareth, without too much conviction.

'Everyone should be spoilt now and then,' said Barbara. 'I don't think it does any harm.'

'I agree,' chimed in Sophie. 'People aren't spoilt enough, especially art students. Not back home they aren't anyway!'

At least the subject offered a topic of conversation for the next ten minutes or so, during which time Gareth also made small talk with Amber. 'You must be spoilt working here. I bet you don't need a holiday at all, do you?'

'Oh, absolutely not,' responded Amber, glancing aside at Gemma. 'Life is one long holiday.'

'It certainly is,' agreed Gemma, looking at Gareth directly for the first time that evening. She was not smiling and her expression seemed to say, 'I don't care what you saw earlier on – you can damn well think what you like!'

The evening ended sooner than it ought, or so Gareth considered. By the time he had finished in the spare bathroom and returned to his room, he wondered if this small household was in the habit of retiring early every night, for there was not a sound to be heard. He, however, had no wish to sleep.

5

A Sip from the Chalice

'Consider yourself lucky,' remarked Victoria. 'If you'd left it in that hotel in Siena we wouldn't have dared go near the place.'

'No,' mused Sophie, laying the watch down carefully on the bedside cabinet. 'I suppose they'd have kept it in payment against their stupid old bed. Shouldn't expect people to sleep on a thing like that anyway – it's dangerous.'

'We weren't sleeping on it were we,' replied Victoria, laying aside her clothes, 'we were screwing Gareth. I'm sure you haven't forgotten.'

'Forgotten? Me? Oh, no Vicky, I hadn't forgotten. I, er – I didn't want to bring the subject up again in case you – well, you know what I mean.'

'Yes, dear, you're touchingly considerate. Why, after all this time, I have no idea. I'll shower now shall I, since you aren't undressed yet?'

'I'm not bothered,' answered Sophie, pulling open the lid of her small suitcase. 'I had mine before dinner.'

Victoria moved towards the bathroom door and Sophie looked up. 'Er, Vicky . . .'

Victoria hesitated. 'Yes?'

Sophie clasped her fingers together on her lap. 'I was thinking – they, Barbara and Elaine, that is, probably wouldn't mind if I had Gareth's room then you and he could – well they wouldn't would they?'

Victoria considered the proposition. 'No, they've never asked as far as I'm aware. Mind you, it's not always possible to tell if people are going to be prudish. On the other hand I don't think I'd want to risk upsetting them. Anyway, it's only one night. I'm sure his lordship will survive on his own.'

The image of the room in the tower flashed through Sophie's mind as Victoria opened the bathroom door. 'Er, Vicky . . .'

Again Victoria turned and Sophie continued. 'Actually, Vicky, there's something you don't know about.'

'Well what is it? I keep trying to have my shower!'

'Well, I think they may not be prudish in the least – not really.'

'What are you talking about?'

Sophie felt the tide of words about to well forth. A tide carrying dark images: narrow steps leading upwards in blackness to a gallery with small, high windows and iron-banded doors, heavy and forbidding; the strap-hung wooden cross set within the sinister stone-walled chamber. Then she realised that she might be about to reveal the second secret liaison between herself and Gareth. The tide ebbed. 'Er, well that's what I think – not prudish, that's all.'

Victoria glanced at the ceiling, tutted loudly with exasperation and disappeared into the bathroom. Left alone, Sophie pulled a few things from the case, laying blue pyjamas in readiness on the bed. For a time her eyes rested on the spot where the pyjamas had been, then moved to the bathroom door which stood slightly ajar and from whence came the sound of running water.

Gareth sat next to the bed, browsing idly through a magazine acquired at the airport. What the article in front of him was about, he had little idea. He had switched off the air conditioning vent and opened a window to let in the warm evening air and hear the chirp of insects. Eleven o'clock was hardly late and he began to wonder, hopefully, if Amber might still be up, working in the kitchen, perhaps. Her image and the way she had looked at him, played on his mind and refused to go away. And why not? Or was he reading too much into her signals? He thought not and scoured his mind in desperation for some reason to be out and about in case she should still be around the house. Putting the magazine aside, Gareth made his way to the bedroom door. No one would question his visiting the bathroom, or better still, he might simply gaze through one of the landing windows for a time and watch the evening sky.

A light shone from under the door to Victoria and Sophie's room; there was a sound of voices but the landing was deserted. Gareth hesitated by the window, pulled aside the brown velvet curtain and peered out into the night. A full moon hung in the sky to the west, its reflection glimmering in the silent pool at the side of the house. The landscape appeared still and quite magical and after a minute he considered opening this window, too. His fingers had barely touched the iron handle when a voice said, 'It's a lovely evening isn't it?'

Hearing the very voice he wanted but hardly dared expect to hear, Gareth was at the same time gladdened and bewildered. For a moment, he looked upon her face, at the fringe of copper hair and smiling brown eyes.

'I didn't mean to creep up on you. Blame the thick carpets.'

'Oh, that's okay. I didn't realise anyone would still be up and about.'

Amber still had on the white dress she had worn in the vaulted dining room and, without the need for caution, Gareth could fully appreciate how it moulded to her lithe and curvaceous form.

'Can't you sleep?' she asked.

'No, I'm not really tired. It's always the same when I'm away anywhere.'

'I see.' She smiled. 'Then why not go for a walk around the gardens? I've just been out myself. It's a beautiful night.'

'Well I was wondering about it, in fact. What about you – have you finished for the evening? What I mean is, d'you fancy a moonlight stroll?'

Amber folded her arms and tilted her head a little. 'I might, Gareth, yes. I've got a few things to do first though, if you don't mind hanging around. It could be half an hour.'

'No, I don't mind. I'll wait down by the pool, shall I?'

'Why not,' she replied, softly. 'Though if you carry on past the pool, there's the summer house. It's nice and peaceful in there.'

'I'll do just that and see you later then,' he said, as she walked on towards her room.

Gareth watched the door close and whispered 'wow,' before re-entering his own room. Maybe half an hour, she'd said. He could stay where he was for a while.

On the landing, another door quietly opened. Elaine appeared, glanced about and headed towards the stairs.

'So that's it,' said Barbara, leaning back into the chair behind the office desk. 'I wondered why you wanted to talk to me in here.'

'Well, the point is,' continued Elaine, 'I'm convinced that little bitch has been plotting this ever since they arrived back. I wondered why she was to-ing and fro-ing like that upstairs. She obviously planned to be there when he went to use the bathroom. That's why I waited in my room.'

'Interesting, I must say. I did notice the way she kept looking at him over dinner. He was perfectly aware of it, too, but tried to act as though he wasn't. Neither of them appear to have mastered the art of subtlety to any meaningful degree.'

'Are we going to take advantage of this?' asked Elaine. 'They're handing it to us on a plate if you ask me.'

'Oh, yes, it could be just the opportunity we need, given time, it really could.'

'Given time? But they intend leaving tomorrow.'

'Well, that is their plan of course. But you know as well as I, they do not have a fixed itinerary. They just arrive at a place when and where they please, hoping to find a hotel. Things could turn out a little differently, could they not?'

'They could well do so,' agreed Elaine, as if reading her sister's thoughts.

'But meanwhile, I wonder if we might not make things a little difficult for our would-be lovers, more of a challenge, if you see what I mean. What if she was to play the damsel in distress? It might serve to dig them in a little deeper.'

Elaine considered the matter. 'All right, but we'll need to involve Gemma and I think we should talk the rest of this through quickly ourselves before we go any further. We have a few minutes, that's all.'

When Victoria stepped into the bedroom, Sophie, in pyjamas, sat on the edge of the bed with her suitcase lid still gaping open.

'You look a picture of indecision, dear, or have you lost something else?'

Sophie glanced up absent-mindedly. 'Lost something? Oh no, not really.'

'I'll switch off the main light then, shall I? When you feel you're ready, that is.'

'Yes,' mumbled Sophie, 'better had.'

Victoria did so and approached the bed but Sophie remained by the open case, rearranging that which did not need rearranging. Very faintly, voices could be heard outside on the landing, one of them being Gareth's. Victoria chose to ignore them. Sophie appeared not to have noticed anything. The room now was illuminated only dimly by one of two small, mauve-shaded bedside lamps. Sitting down beside Sophie, Victoria said, 'You're in a very odd frame of mind aren't you? Is something the matter?'

Sophie pulled an unread book out of her case, just as quickly replaced it, and without as much as a glance at Victoria replied, 'Nothing. There's nothing the matter.'

'Then we'll get into bed shall we, dear?' said Victoria, folding her arms and waiting patiently.

Sophie's eyes were suddenly upon her. 'Vicky, how d'you feel? I mean, are you tired, or anything like that?'

'How do I feel,' replied Victoria, pausing a few moments to consider the question. 'Well, a bit pissed after all that wine, but I wouldn't say I was suffering unduly.' She placed an arm about Sophie's shoulder. 'Come on, out with it. You can tell me.'

Sophie smiled weakly and gazed down at her hands. 'You know what you said in the hotel at Siena? Remember, when we were waiting for Gareth?'

A smile touched Victoria's face. Her lips brushed Sopie's cheek like a candle flame. 'Of course I remember! Why shouldn't I?'

Sophie turned and kissed her on the lips. 'Well I thought – if you fancy the idea, that is – I thought we could . . .'

Victoria squeezed her hand. 'Are you going to fish it out or do we sit here all night?'

'Are you sure?' asked Sophie, but her hand was already pushing down into the suitcase to close upon the cool, smooth form.

'Of course I am, you silly girl. It was my idea wasn't it?'

'I suppose it was,' smiled Sophie, holding the pink vibrator out between them.

Victoria placed a hand on each side of her face and pulled her forwards until their lips were once more warmly joined. This was a lingering and passionate kiss which stirred Sophie deeply. Sophie, with eyes still shut tight, felt the vibrator taken from her hand, then fingers brush the top button of her pyjamas. Sophie's fingers entered the play but Victoria pushed them lightly aside and whispered, 'Your treat first, dear. Just relax.'

Sophie let her head fall on to Victoria's shoulder as first the pyjama top, then the elasticated band at her waist loosened. With a hand on her thigh, Victoria helped Sophie up from the bed, and silently slipped the pyjamas from her. Sophie was intent on kissing again and Victoria allowed this, whilst cupping one of the exposed breasts in her hand and squeezing an already hard and reddened nipple. A sigh told Victoria all she needed to know as arms curled warmly about her neck. Victoria, an arm clasped about Sophie's waist, slipped cool, exploratory fingers down her stomach to the lips of her sex, dallying voluptuously at the gates, where admission was already assured.

But Victoria's hands moved from her to take up the object which had been placed close to the bedside lamp. She eased Sophie down on to the bed where she sat for a moment, expecting her to take up a position on her back so that the game might continue as intended. Victoria knelt on the bed beside her but Sophie twisted about, kissed her and pulled herself up to her knees. There was a question hovering behind the hazel eyes, a question Victoria knew she was afraid to form into words but a question which needed to be expressed. 'Vicky, does it matter how we –?'

'Any way you like,' smiled Victoria, brushing a whisp of soft hair from Sophie's forehead. 'As I said, it's your treat.'

Sophie turned about to face the top of the bed and dropped forwards. Hair cascaded over her cheeks, obscuring her face and falling about the brightly coloured bedspread. Victoria understood. Her fingers twisted the knurled end of the vibrator until it hummed into life.

Sophie's most intimate places were perfectly accessible in this position. Victoria, kneeling close by, placed a leg each side of her left thigh and, with a hand resting upon the base of her spine, brought the penis shaped object beneath the uplifted behind. The vibrator found its target and Victoria felt Sophie stiffen and sigh as the head coursed and furrowed between her glistening sex lips. Victoria would play her as an instrument and make her body sing. It would begin slowly, perhaps slowly enough to torment, but eventually sweeping her up to the summit of passion she so obviously craved.

The vibrator entered deeper from time to time only to be part withdrawn in case the singing within Sophie's body too soon became a drumbeat. Sophie lowered her head until her face was pressed into the pillow and wriggled her thighs further apart. After a while, Victoria knew Sophie ought to be approaching the point of complete abandon, but she was not. Instead, each time the instrument was part withdrawn, she jerked her behind higher, only to pull it down just as quickly, almost as though she wished to expel the vibrator altogether. With a spark of intuition, Victoria withdrew it glistening and warm from the vagina, only to stroke and press the head against Sophie's anus. The effect was instantaneous. Sophie let out a sharp moan and at once pushed back against it in a manner which could leave no doubt as to the nature of her desires. The vibrator was amply lubricated by Sophie's own excitement and Victoria, whilst passing a free hand beneath her stomach to engage her sex from that direction, found the head of the instrument slipped easily through the ring of muscles at her rear passage, which relaxed to accept it. Sophie's arousal at once intensified and she began to moan softly. The vibrator eased firmly onward to penetrate her rectum, until the flared rim denied further entry. A fascinated Victoria realised what degree of control she now possessed and, given by some means the opportunity to exercise more, would have gladly done so.

The vibrator could be left to do its work and Victoria's fingers concentrated in playing with Sophie's clitoris, squeezing and caressing, feeling Sophie hot and inflamed as her body, in the grasp of Victoria's other arm, continued to shake and squirm, fingers clutching the edges of the pillow as if to grind it out of existence. Victoria marvelled at the way Sophie's pelvic muscles tensed repeatedly, as though striving for deeper penetration, but was thankful that much of the sound issuing from her was absorbed by the pillow. The muffled cries increased until they became loud, uncontrollable gasps of delight. Victoria's finger entered her sex to the hilt whilst the fingers of her other hand fell upon the protruding base of the vibrator, pressing hard and rotating it furiously. Sophie trembled violently and all but screamed into the compressed pillow as the raging tide of orgasm burst over to sweep her along in a cascade of ecstasy.

'What does it matter where I was going?' said Amber, confronting the two figures who had entered and now stood between her and the bedroom door. The black canvas bag rested ominously on the floor between them.

'It matters at this moment,' replied Elaine, holding her gaze with sharp, accusing eyes.

'We really do not need further complications,' added Barbara. 'Just do as you're told and when they go in the morning, we'll forget about whatever it was you were up to.'

'I'm not up to anything!' protested Amber, with darting eyes. 'There's nothing wrong with me going out at night, is there? Well, tell me if it's suddenly become a crime.'

'If that's all you were doing,' said Elaine, reaching into the bag, 'then this will only be a temporary inconvenience won't it? Be quiet and get your dress off – now!'

'I bloody well won't!' shouted Amber, attempting to circle towards the door. She might have guessed what lay within the bag but what Elaine withdrew first was quite unexpected and her mouth fell open in dismay. 'Now wait. I've got my rights in this house. You'd better not use that on me – or else!'

Elaine curled the braided whip around her hands. 'Or else? Or else what, you little whore? In case you hadn't noticed, we have rights under Wallace's contract too, and that includes your instant dismissal for theft and disorderly behaviour! And instant means now – right now!'

Barbara moved forwards, her expression one of calculating coolness. 'Amber, it really would be in all our interests for you to do as you're told. It will make no difference in the long run.'

Amber ran her hands down the sides of her white dress and stared at them in astonishment. 'What d'you mean about theft? I've taken nothing of yours, so just try and prove it!'

'The watch,' said Barbara. 'All right, you handed it in to us but where did you really find it and what was your handkerchief doing behind the curtain in the tower room? Were you hiding in there?'

There was a long pause as Amber stared at the floor in awkward silence.

'Do as you are told,' continued Barbara, 'and we'll forget all about those incidents, yes?'

Elaine appeared to have made her mind up regarding the outcome of the confrontation, for she was in the process of extracting the main contents of the bag. Amber made as if to issue further protestations but turned quickly about to face the curtained window on the far side of the room. She heard the swish of leather as the garment fell open and knew they were moving quietly towards her. Amber took a deep breath as the zipper buzzed down and the dress loosened. Still she said nothing as the dress was pulled away to reveal her naked breasts. She hoped they did not infer, from the minimal design of the gossamer-fine black G-string, sheer black stockings held up by lace garter tops and stiletto heel sandals, that these were a recent addition to her apparel. Indeed, barely two minutes had elapsed since she had made the final adjustments to her stocking tops and pulled down the hem of her dress. It also occurred to the beleaguered Amber that Barbara and Elaine might question the newly applied lipstick and perfume, which neither could fail to notice. However, they did not.

The heavy leather garment, held by Elaine, fell open before Amber. She knew, of course, that she was expected to insert her arms through each end of the internal sleeve, to have them contained and folded across her middle.

'Come along now,' said Barbara, guiding her arms into the restraint. 'It's not the end of the world. And Gemma can keep you company.'

Amber glared tight-lipped at Elaine then half turned as though about to appeal to Barbara. Barbara's cool expression was of no comfort and Amber found herself complying with their wishes. With arms enclosed, she stood swaying and adjusting her stance as they pulled the straitjacket over her shoulders and about her upper body. Its rich, heavy aroma filled the air, rivalling her own perfume. The smooth, black leather gleamed with a sinister sheen as it tightened in its final embrace.

She had thought, when they began to fasten it on her, that there might be some way out. Gemma might be persuaded to undo the straitjacket and give her temporary freedom. But even this possibility was denied for, too late, Amber realised that this restraint was not equipped with a row of straps at the rear, but a heavy-duty zip fastener secured by a small padlock at the back of the neck. The straitjacket was tight and both pairs of hands were employed to raise the zip. Its ascent coincided well with Amber's rising despair. A despair which was at last punctuated by the soft, terminal click of the padlock.

Elaine offered her a sardonic smile. 'I'm sure he'll give up waiting for you after half an hour or so. I don't expect he'll be too well disposed at breakfast time either, especially after the way you led him on.'

Amber's eyes sprang wide with rage and she jerked about to face Barbara and Elaine. 'What! You mean that's why you – !' She heaved and twisted about in anger against the restraint. 'Oh! You pair of – ! What the fuck has it got to – !'

The sentence was terminated by Elaine's hand which flashed up and struck Amber's mouth with a resounding crack. 'Don't ever use that sort of language in front of either of us, you foul-mouthed little slut. Do you hear! Think yourself lucky you're not getting the good hiding you deserve!' Elaine pushed her face close to Amber's. 'I'm only glad I won't have to set eyes on you again until tomorrow. What a blessing that's going to be. Now, one more word and you'll be hooded as well!'

Barbara placed a hand on Amber's shoulder. 'I do not think she will give us any more trouble. Gemma will keep an eye on her. It will be something of a reversal of roles for them.'

'Yes, quite a novelty,' agreed Elaine, pushing the coiled whip back into the bag with exaggerated reluctance.

When they entered the lounge, an apprehensive Gemma was already standing by one of the big easy chairs. Uncertain of the reason for the summons, she had not considered it appropriate to sit down. Barbara asked her to do so. Elaine busied herself at the drinks cabinet and Barbara sat facing Gemma. 'You know little of this, I am sure, but we have a few problems in relation to our three visitors. I really do not have time to go into details at present but you will find out in due course, I promise. In the meantime, there is something we would like you to do . . .'

* * *

Amber caught sight of herself in the mirror, the wisps of hair drifting irritatingly just above her eyes. This, more than anything else emphasised her helplessness. Only a quick sweep of the fingers was needed, but she was unable to do even that. She fell hard upon the bed, jerking her imprisoned arms up and down, gasping in futile exasperation, hoping that by some miracle the straitjacket might give and enable her to shake it off. It would not, and she rolled about on the bed in frustrated anger. She was on the verge of tears when the door opened and Gemma entered the room. Amber struggled towards the edge of the bed and managed, after some further effort, to sit upright. 'You've come to keep a watch on me, I suppose.'

'I – I'm not quite sure. They said they were going to bed and I was to share your room with you.' She sat down by the small dressing table. 'It's funny isn't it? I mean, seeing you like that. It's usually me that ends up, well . . .'

Amber swung forwards and stood up. 'Yes! Bloody hilarious! Try and do something, will you! See if you can get this damned lock off. Find a small key – a hair grip – anything!'

Gemma glanced at the bedroom door. Amber took the hint and lowered her voice. 'Well, go on.'

'No, look, I daren't. If I did anything like that and they found out, we'd both be for it. You know perfectly well we would.'

'All right!' yelled Amber, jerking her upper body. 'I just want to get out of the bloody house for a while!'

'What, while you're wearing that?'

'God, what does it matter to anyone what I do!'

Gemma stood up and faced her. 'Well if it's so urgent I'll open the doors for you if you want. There's no reason why they should find out, but –'

'But what?' asked Amber, her eyes brightening with hope.

'Someone will have to let you back in. I can leave the door ajar but they might see it in the morning. How do we –?'

'Sod the door! I won't be gone all that long. Not with

100

this on I won't! Wait a couple of minutes, just in case, and if I'm not back, it's okay, you can go to bed. Someone else will close it for me, I promise you they will.'

'It sounds as if they've fallen out to me,' said Sophie, relaxing under the bedclothes.

Victoria sat before the dressing table mirror, releasing her hair from the clips to let it tumble about her shoulders. Her fingers touched the ebony brush. 'I'll go and listen outside as soon as I've done this. I'll have to switch our lights off though in case I'm seen.'

'It's probably nothing,' answered Sophie, sliding deeper under the sheets.

'Probably,' agreed Victoria, pushing her hair back behind her neck. She reached over to the small lamp, at once plunging the room into blackness. Light from the landing showed dimly under the door, giving her a sense of direction.

The bedroom door opened slightly and she peered through the narrow gap. The sound of raised voices from Amber's room had died away and there was only silence on the dimly illuminated landing. Victoria saw no light from beneath Gareth's door and remained motionless for a time, in anticipation of she knew not what. But two of the actors in the small drama were about to appear, for the door to Amber's bedroom slowly opened. Two figures emerged: one, Gemma, in the pale emerald dress of earlier that evening, the other Amber, in a blue silk dressing gown with the sleeves swinging empty at the sides. Victoria was about to close the door but something struck her as odd in the way the two moved, and Gemma appeared to steady Amber with her arm at the top of the stairs before they disappeared from view. Victoria glanced back into the darkness of their room and whispered, 'Sophie.' But there was no reply. After her voluptuous experience of a short time ago, Sophie had left the shores of consciousness and was adrift in blissful sleep. Victoria slipped through the door and closed it quietly, having given no thought to pulling on a dressing gown or slippers. She reached the top of the stairs to see Gemma open one of the main doors. The two exchanged whispers and Amber vanished from sight, leaving Gemma to watch her disappear into darkness.

How long the thought of Gareth had been in her mind, Victoria could not have said, but she had by now taken it for granted that he was involved somewhere along the line. There was Sebastiano, of course, and the young men who worked on the estate, but why leave the house now rather than at a more convenient hour?

Gemma stood motionless for a short time then appeared set to hurry back up the stairs. Victoria stepped out of sight and looked about for a convenient place of concealment. There was none. If she tried to get to the tower stairs, she could easily be seen as she crossed the landing. I'm going for a late night walk, she thought, why shouldn't I? What can she say? So Victoria turned on to the stairs fully expecting to confront Gemma, realising at the same moment that she was barefoot, still in her pyjamas and wouldn't be believed. But of Gemma, there was no sign.

As she reached the entrance hall, there were sounds: indistinct and muffled voices which drifted from the direction of the closed lounge. Victoria continued on to the main door.

The night was very still and silent, except for the whirring of insects, though the full moon cast black tendril shadows everywhere and created an atmosphere of brooding expectancy. Gareth listened for the closing of a door. For the sound of footsteps. A voice. From the summerhouse the main entrance was invisible and the path which led along the side of the house and past the pool was a confusion of shadows. Without his watch he could not say if twenty, thirty or more minutes had gone by. It seemed like more. Then something moved. The moon picked out a figure at the side of the house, flickering through the shadows along the narrow path. Gareth stood up, and sidled into the shadowed area with heart beating faster in anticipation.

The figure approached. 'Gareth?'

'Yes,' he answered moving into view. 'It's okay, I'm here.'

She hesitated at the entrance as if suddenly filled with doubt, then entered and walked up to him. 'Gareth, I'm sorry, I –'

'It's all right,' he responded, seeing the moonlight catch her hair and glint in her eyes. 'I knew you needed a bit of time.' He took her face in his hands and kissed her warm lips, at once aware of the rich aroma that mingled with her perfume and of the high collared garment which showed at the neck of the gown.

'No,' she insisted, 'I didn't mean about the time. I mean I can't – oh!' She gasped in exasperation. 'They found out I was going to meet you and tried to stop me!'

'You mean they know you're here?'

'No, they think I can't get out of the house now because of – oh, bugger!' Amber twirled around so that the empty sleeves of the gown flew outwards. 'Look what they've done to me, Gareth! Just damn well look!'

He gazed, puzzled for the moment, at the swell of her folded arms beneath the silk gown.

'We'll have to go inside,' she continued. 'I got Gemma to let me out so I could tell you. The front door is still unlocked.'

'Wait,' he said taking her by the shoulders. 'What are you saying?'

With a tug, he released the belt at her waist and pulled open the gown. A dull moonlight sheen reflected from the black cocoon about her upper body.

'And the bloody thing is locked!' said Amber. 'Locked until tomorrow morning!'

Gareth continued to stare in puzzlement, sliding a hand about the smooth leather, then a hint of amusement spread across his face. 'Well, I never – we are in a pickle aren't we? You look like you'd be better off in the tower.'

'Well, it's up to you. Shall we go back indoors?'

'Maybe we don't need to leave here just yet. I mean, we both made the effort to get out of the house tonight didn't we?'

Amber met his kisses with unmistakable enthusiasm and murmured, 'I suppose we needn't go in – if it's what you want. I really don't mind.'

'It is what I want,' he whispered, slipping the gown from her shoulders and letting it fall to the wooden floor. His fingers gripped the heavy leather, squeezed her shoulders and slipped down the cool smoothness at her back until Amber, with a slight shudder, felt them on the naked flesh below her waist and sliding under the elastic of her tiny briefs. 'I hope you're not going to take advantage of a poor helpless maiden,' she whispered.

'As if I would,' he answered as their lips met again and his fingers passed around her thigh to close upon the heat of her sex. As one finger eased into her, Amber sighed, 'Oh, you bastard,' then gently bit the side of his mouth. The perfume of her breath, the ripe odour and sight of the restraint which so frustrated her, he found intoxicating, and cared not that she was unable to play an active part in their covert sport.

Deeper he entered and the hand which played this voluptuous game and stirred her so with passion more than filled the little gossamer triangle which had fitted so snugly over the shaven sex. The other hand swept over the curve of her behind to tug down the elastic and Gareth promptly fell to his knees in order to facilitate its removal altogether. Instinctively, he found himself drawn close to her focus of pleasure so that his tongue might join in its plunder. Amber, wishing only to give easier access to the invader, leant back against one of the wooden ribs of the summer-house and raised a foot up to rest on an adjacent seat. Gareth assisted with a hand under the glassy smoothness of her stockinged thigh, tongue and finger driving coils of fire through her body. Amber responded with a trembling body and shortening breath. And when her moans of 'Oh – oh, Jesus!' reached his ears, Gareth knew how close she must be to the point of no return. Knew too, that if he did not change tactics his own needs might remain unfulfilled, for his aching erection, cloaked still in the darkness of the bathrobe, demanded to play a full and decisive role.

* * *

Victoria had been prudent. She had arrived too late to see Amber enter the summerhouse but heard voices carry on the night air and knew that if she followed the path along the side of the house, she would be visible in the bright moonlight. Instead of the direct route, she had circled through the bushes, bare feet treading cool grass, until she found herself crouched close to the summerhouse but well hidden. Their voices had carried clearly and Victoria heard every word, every sigh. Nevertheless, she had seen she could get closer still, with care, and eventually had a good view of the interior.

Despite Amber's moans, it was difficult to ascertain exactly what Gareth was doing, for he crouched low and Amber leant back in the shadows. Then he raised himself up, quickly slipped off the bathrobe to reveal his own nakedness, and pulled Amber around until both stood in full view, illuminated by the moonlight. Seeing how intent and occupied they were with each other, Victoria, knowing her face to be obscured, stood up to obtain a better view. She was in time to see Gareth position himself directly behind Amber and to ply her neck with kisses while his fingers reached around to occupy themselves between her legs. It was only now that Victoria realised Amber was wearing the straitjacket and wondered what might have given rise to such a bizarre circumstance. But this question was toppled from her thoughts by what happened next. Gareth lowered himself down on to the wooden seat and gripped Amber, who remained with her back to him, by the thighs. Her laughter trickled into the night as she spread her legs either side of his and eased herself slowly down on to the waiting shaft. Victoria held her breath as the penis head poised, ready for the final plunge. But Gareth hesitated, withdrawing as if to tease her.

'Gareth, for Christ's sake give it to me!' cried Amber. Now Gareth part entered her but there was to be no more torment, for with a soft moan, Amber slipped down to take in the full length of the ample shaft.

The view could not have been better other than in broad daylight. With Gareth working piston-like beneath, it was obvious to Victoria that Amber was shaved or depilated, the area about the vulva appearing smooth as silk. Obvious too was their total abandonment to lust, for listening to Amber's heightened moans and the hoarse gasps from Gareth, she wondered if she might not walk into the summerhouse to peer directly at them and remain quite unnoticed! Victoria found the sight oddly appealing and it began to dawn upon her that there must be a great deal more to the Villa Raffaello than had been revealed to her. What was the meaning behind Gareth's reference to the tower? She desired to know what secrets the villa held, and realised that she would probably never know, for they were to be gone in the morning.

Her misgivings were swept aside and her attentions at once drawn back to the scene by Amber's cries. She saw the girl's head roll back against Gareth's shoulder and the mouth fall open to give vent to her passions as her body was seized by the climax. Gareth, too, with eyes closed tightly, groaned aloud, thrusting rapidly and vigorously as his own release came. Victoria glanced back at the house, wondering how far the sound might carry on the night air.

There was no time to lose. She had to return before Gareth and Amber recovered their senses and realised that they, too, must hurry back.

No one had locked the main door and Victoria pushed it aside to find the entrance still deserted. She did not hesitate but slipped quickly across to the stairs and continued up to the first floor. At the bedroom she stood with a hand on the doorknob, wondering. None of what she had witnessed might ever have been known to her. What else did she not know? Had Gareth and Amber, despite the limited time and opportunity, been together before? She gazed along the landing at the dark stairs which led up to the tower. His remark about it loomed in her thoughts. Perhaps the answer might be found there.

Victoria retraced her steps in silence as far as the stairs. She glanced downwards to the main door. Any moment now they must enter that way. The door slowly began to open as she watched it. The decision was made. She carried straight on ahead, feet suddenly chilled by the cold stone of the tower steps. Disappearing from view as the ascending passage made a right-angle turn, Victoria found herself cloaked in darkness between the stone walls. Reaching out to steady herself, she began to tremble. But there was no choice. She had to go on. Somewhere in the gloom ahead, there must be a light switch.

Gareth and Amber, too, had entered the house without incident. Both, covered once more by bathrobe and silk gown, ascended the stairs; Gareth assisted with an arm about Amber's waist.

At Amber's bedroom door they hesitated and looked into each other's eyes. Because Amber was unable to let herself into the room, Gareth would have to do it for her. What if Gemma was inside? Whether he opened the door or simply knocked, Gemma would know.

'Better just open it,' whispered Amber.

Gareth did. Only the small bedside lamp was on, but a brief look around confirmed that the room was empty. 'She's supposed to stay in my room for the night,' said Amber. 'Until they take this off.'

Gareth saw Amber jerk her arms inside the restraint and placed a hand on her cheek. 'Do they often use –?'

'Not on me they don't,' replied Amber. 'This is the first time. It's usually – well, never mind, it doesn't matter does it? The three of you will be off for good in the morning so you can forget all about it.'

Gareth pulled her close to him. 'Amber, I know it's stupid under the circumstances, but I can't just walk off now and leave you. I can't.'

'You have to Gareth,' she answered, kissing him. 'I don't suppose I'll be alone for long anyway. I'm surprised she's not here, it's nearly one o'clock.'

Gareth sighed. 'I just can't imagine never seeing this house and you again. It's all going to seem a kind of –'

'Sorry to interrupt,' came a soft voice as Gemma appeared in the doorway.

Gareth released Amber at once and both stood in

silence. Gemma closed the door and turned to regard them with a bland expression. 'Will you be long?' she asked Gareth. 'I'll go away for a bit if you like.'

Gareth looked at Amber, each realising that no explanation was required. Gareth was surprised that Gemma had so readily accepted his presence without question, but simply shrugged. 'Okay, I guess that's it isn't it? I suppose I'll see you both in the morning.'

In silence they watched him open the door then part turn as if to say something further. He said nothing and was gone.

If ever he had felt himself ill at ease and confused, it was now. Opening the door to his room, his thoughts were full of foxy, hazel-eyed Amber and the passions they had shared in the night; of blonde and blue-eyed Gemma whose plight he had so unexpectedly witnessed upon their second arrival. And what of the coolly perceptive Barbara and her sharp-eyed, alluring younger sister, both unnervingly beautiful but sharing a charisma which served them as a citadel of stone? He had peered for a moment into the voluptuous and secret world of the Villa Raffaello, had tasted but a hint of its delights and, having barely lifted the cup to his lips, was about to have it snatched away forever.

In the morning he would awake and the three would be on their way in the bright Tuscan sunshine, heading for the next picturesque town where they would find another small hotel with a shaded garden in which to sit and talk over a bottle of wine. In the night Gareth might dream. Unless the dream had already begun.

6

Ritual by Candlelight

Morning sunlight filled the breakfast room, casting long shadows across the white plaster walls of the ancient iron brackets which in earlier times held candles as the only source of light. Gareth, never the most talkative when in female company, found it not altogether as difficult as he had feared to exhibit a semblance of normality.

Neither Barbara nor Elaine showed any hint of knowing about the previous evening. Nor did Amber and Gemma when they appeared at the table bearing croissants, jam and a large cafetière. Gareth glanced at both and nodded, with a polite smile. Victoria and Sophie were more forthcoming. He felt suffocated by normality.

If anything was to subject his willpower to a trial of strength it was the appearance rather than the presence of Amber and Gemma. Gareth was concerned that his gaze should not linger a split second more than necessary. But reality prevailed and he could not help other than to notice their identical attire as they moved about the table. The dresses were fashioned of some white, silken material; high-necked and sleeveless, in an oriental style, they stretched over slim, curvaceous bodies from neck to ankle with a lizard sheen. Indeed, so smooth and pliant were their forms that Gareth could not believe anything was worn under the dresses. No ridge of elastic from beneath, no clip or fastening spoiled the sensual topography.

'Gareth!'

Sophie's exclamation disturbed his reverie.

'Gareth – watch that jam!'

Sophie stared in alarm, a finger pointing directly at him. Gareth's eyes fixed upon the croissant which he had raised mechanically to his mouth and held poised there. The jam with which he had absent-mindedly overloaded the pastry was about to fall down the front of his shirt. With but an instant to spare, he moved the croissant away as the jam fell to the plate below.

Sophie, her own mouth well-filled, continued in a matter-of-fact tone. 'He can be quite disgusting at breakfast, I can tell you.' Her fingers were already breaking apart another croissant. 'I've seen him at the table when he's only half awake. Ask Vicky – it's like the chimps' tea party.'

'Lay off,' objected Gareth. 'You're not doing too badly yourself.'

All eyes were, for that moment, upon him. He caught Barbara's green-eyed gaze and noted the gentle smile on her face. He could have sworn it was a smile of triumph.

Mercifully, Elaine asked, 'Where are you three planning to go next?'

'Oh,' replied Gareth, 'we want to see Pisa and Lucca, definitely.'

'And a few other places if our money holds out,' added Victoria.

'Pisa and Lucca you should certainly not miss,' said Barbara. 'Of course, there are dozens of places in Tuscany not so well known but quite delightful in their own way – many of them within easy reach of here by car.'

'You're dead lucky living in a place like this,' declared Sophie.

'It's a lovely part of the world,' added Victoria.

'There is no reason why you should not enjoy it for longer,' said Barbara.

Her casual remark sent a tremor through the room. They waited for her to say more. Amber and Gemma had left the room but Gemma returned at that point with another plate of warm croissants.

'You should stay here for a time,' continued Barbara with a calmness which belied the import of the message.

110

'Use the Villa Raffaello as your base for touring the area. Who can say what hidden things you might discover.'

A long silence followed. Each waited for the other to speak. Then Victoria replied, 'We couldn't impose ourselves like that. It would be an invasion of your privacy.'

Sophie stopped chewing and looked at Victoria in disbelief. Gareth knew he must show no more than moderate enthusiasm and leant back in his chair.

'We'd pay for all our food and stuff,' blurted Sophie.

'You'd bankrupt us the way you eat,' responded Victoria. 'It's a lovely offer but we would have to make sure we could give enough in return to make it worth your while.'

'Perhaps I could help with a few jobs around the place,' suggested Gareth.

'We have Sebastiano for anything like that,' replied Elaine.

'We have met very few people socially since our taking over the villa,' said Barbara. 'If we regarded your presence as an intrusion we would not have suggested your staying. It might be of benefit to all of us, particularly as we seem to have got to know each other rather well, albeit through unusual circumstances.' Her gaze fell upon Gareth, though not quite long enough for him to take the remark as outright innuendo. Then she turned to Victoria. 'A day out in Florence or Vallombrosa is easy from here but we are a little far from Pisa or Lucca. Perhaps you would do well to go there first and then return to us. At least afterwards you could succumb to the charms of the Villa Raffaello, knowing that you have visited the main sights.'

Victoria smiled. 'It's a super offer; I'd love to.'

'Yes, so would I,' agreed Gareth.

Victoria eyed Sophie who was about to take another croissant. 'Sophie, what about your hostel?'

Sophie reacted as one caught in the act of trivial theft. 'The – oh, the hostel! Well, by the time I get there it'll be almost time to leave. I think I've gone off the idea – if that's all right with everyone else.'

Elaine said at once, 'You know perfectly well it is

Sophie.' And the whole thing seemed settled to everyone's satisfaction.

Amber appeared and asked if anyone would like more coffee. During the brief exchange, Elaine said to her, 'And by the way, our three guests will be returning in a few days to keep us company for a while.'

Amber smiled sweetly and regarded the three in turn, her eye resting finally on Gareth. 'Oh, that will be nice.'

It was on the stairs that he encountered her again. He had returned to the bedroom to collect his jacket. Victoria and Sophie were already at the main door with Barbara and Elaine. They almost collided at the top of the stairs and Gareth backed around on to the landing in case they should be seen. Amber stood with parted lips. 'Gareth, I'm sorry about last night, having to wear that . . .'

Gareth took her arms. 'God, that didn't matter! Well – you know what I mean.'

Amber pressed warm hands on his cheeks and kissed him, her breath a furnace of passion. 'Gareth, I'm really glad you're coming back. You don't know – this place can be like a morgue.'

'Yes, but I don't understand all this. Why go to all those lengths to keep you from seeing me then invite us back again?'

'Perhaps they thought what they'd done was enough. Perhaps they just changed their minds. What does it matter? Sometimes they do things – I don't always know why.'

Gareth kissed her. 'I'd better shift myself before some-one starts wondering where I am. See you again soon – promise!'

Amber gave him a farewell smile and an affectionate wave. Gareth hurried down the stairs. She continued along the landing, the smile still on her face.

'It's about time I had a go at driving anyway,' said Victoria, negotiating another sharp twist in the narrow road.

'I think the roads get better as we go on,' came Sophie's voice from behind the unfolded map. 'They have numbers on them – that must mean something.'

'Who'd have thought it,' mused Gareth, 'ending up in a place like that. You wouldn't have believed it possible would you?'

'Yes, who'd have thought,' murmured Victoria recalling the sight of Gareth and Amber in the summerhouse.

'You can both thank me, actually,' remarked Sophie. 'If I hadn't left my watch behind we'd never have gone near it again.'

Gareth peered behind at the blank expanse of paper. 'If we're apportioning credit then I'll grab my share for getting lost and running out of petrol.' Gareth had his recollections too, and, enjoying the luxury of idleness as a mere passenger, could indulge them to the full while appearing to admire the passing countryside. Not only did the liaison with Amber linger in his imagination, but also the occasion of their first stay at the villa when he and Sophie had visited the tower and played their voluptuous game together.

On the foundations of memory there arose a stage of fantasy. This stage he entered, leaving behind the sunlit vistas for a darker, sensual world. There was the wooden cross and there was Amber spread helpless before him. But, no, somehow that was not her place. Gemma, she was the one; Gemma, with whom he had exchanged so little dialogue but whose quiet gaze and curvaceous body had also stirred his desires. He saw her naked and mounted upon the sinister device, felt his lips upon the soft warmth of her stomach, tasted the heat and essence of her arousal, felt her body quiver and heard her cries. And Amber hovered by him, so that afterwards they might revel in each other before the eyes of their prisoner. But in the magic lantern of his mind, another picture. It was not just Amber gazing at his helpless form, but also, moving darkly, turning slowly, Barbara and Elaine, their eyes upon his naked body, witnessing his uncontrollable excitement. Again on Barbara's face, that smile of triumph.

113

'Has he gone to sleep?' blared Sophie's voice. At once there was searing blue sky, sound and movement.

'What? Er, no! Just daydreaming. Is that allowed?'

'Suppose so,' mused Sophie.

From the corner of her eye, Victoria watched him readjust his position in the seat, attempting to alleviate the growing discomfort of a trapped erection. He seemed to be having little success.

Angelo smiled and stepped into the entrance hall, taking and kissing the hand she offered as he always did. It was not an affectation even though outwardly, at least, Angelo was nothing if not a gentleman. No, it had been a gesture undertaken with good humour and intended to break the ice when Barbara had first arrived at his sombre offices in Florence. Beneath the benign façade, Barbara had sensed a shady character. Oddly, that is what had first attracted her to him. Whenever they met afterwards, Barbara held out a hand to Angelo. As the door closed, there was, too, a gentle kiss on the lips. A kiss as discreet as everything in their relationship.

They sat drinking coffee in the lounge, among the venerable lacquered and gilded furniture, geriatric clocks and time encrusted paintings of people and things which seemed no longer to matter.

'Signor Deveraux collected here many things of great value and antiquity. There can be no true price put upon them.'

'This is not a room I could become fond of,' said Barbara, smiling. 'I look at things individually and find I like them. Some of them I find quite fascinating. But taken together it's not the same. They need a museum where they can have living space. In here they are overwhelming.'

'I agree, but two people, they will not often have the same ideas on how they wish to live.'

'Nor the money,' put in Barbara.

'No, they will not have the money, but for Signor Deveraux that was not a problem. Once before I asked you about this house, if you would wish to change it. Perhaps now you would do that.'

'No, I don't think we will change too much. Somehow it would not seem fair after all the effort he put into everything.'

'And the rooms in the tower?' asked Angelo quietly.

'Yes, the tower,' murmured Barbara. 'Angelo, we know each other well enough to talk on that subject now. It's not a problem to Elaine or myself, if that is what you thought. All these things have their place, at least they do for those who can afford it.'

'They do, as you say,' replied a thoughtful Angelo.

'What is inside the other room, I have no idea. We never did locate the key.'

Angelo offered no response to her remark about the locked room but went on. 'You should know the involvement of the two girls, especially the younger one, Gemma. She was, how can I say, often the centre of attraction in an unusual way. She is very, how you say, *remissivo* –?'

'Submissive,' put in Barbara.

'Ah, yes, submissive. *Molto remissivo*. It was her role, in the things they did here and in this she was very willing. Wallace and the others, they understood.'

'I understand too. And so does Elaine. Perhaps a great deal more than you realise, Angelo.'

'I had hoped that much would become known to you in the time you have been here and, I say to myself, if problems arrive, then I am here to help because of the things I know.'

'Angelo,' said Barbara, 'I appreciate your concern but I –'

The door opened and there stood Elaine, dressed uncharacteristically in fawn trouser suit, with hair wound about and clipped up as it always was when she went on a shopping expedition. 'Sorry! I didn't mean to butt in.'

'No, please,' responded Angelo, rising from the chair. 'What I am saying is important for each of you.'

'We were discussing part of Wallace's legacy,' said Barbara. 'The tower rooms and the two girls – Gemma in particular.'

Elaine closed the door and moved over to join them. 'Well, I take it we all know what we're talking about?'

115

'I believe we do,' answered Barbara. 'Evidently, each of them was something of a celebrity.'

'Oh,' responded Elaine, seating herself close to Barbara, 'celebrities. That's what they were! And I thought they were just randy little bitches, especially the younger one. I can imagine why she was a celebrity all right!'

'I think you already know of Gemma's special needs,' said Angelo.

Elaine settled into the chair. 'Well, she's a nymphomaniac and a masochist if that's what you're waiting to hear me say.'

'And,' continued Angelo, 'she was often present in the room to which you have no key. Did you know that?'

'It's news to me,' replied Elaine.

'She has said nothing to me either,' added Barbara.

'That is good,' responded Angelo, 'for Signor Deveraux made her promise secrecy. The other signorina he would not trust so much. He used to say to me, she plays the fool.'

'Oh, her,' said Elaine. 'Well, I can't say I blame him – she's a deceitful little bitch!'

'I would agree on that point,' said Barbara, 'though she seems to be keen enough on staying here, despite one or two misadventures of late.'

'I think,' said Angelo, 'that both await the return of the house to what once it was. That is why they were here at the beginning. That is why they have the contract.'

'And when Wallace's guests were here in force,' asked Barbara, 'what was it our little Gemma did that made her presence so noteworthy?'

'Oh, *signorina!*' replied Angelo, his brow furrowed with concern. 'I am not sure that I should discuss so much with two ladies as yourselves, for it is –'

'Angelo!' interrupted Elaine. 'We've taken over lock, stock and barrel. It seems to me we've already had it ticking over and, well – there are the photographs. I don't think Babs has looked at those. And there is another matter we are in the process of dealing with. A little complication which has arisen as a result of Wallace's legacy.'

'And that is?' replied Angelo.

'All we can say for the moment,' offered Barbara in a coolly matter-of-fact manner,' is that we might revive a little of the good old days. It seems we are in the midst of a stage set and surrounded by members of the cast. We must learn our lines properly but others do not yet realise they are in it. You are having dinner with us, perhaps you would care to be *direttore* this evening and we might inaugurate new roles for ourselves.'

'As long as you understand it for what it is,' replied Angelo. 'As long as you understand that.'

'The more I look at them,' said Elaine, regarding the two candlesticks, 'the more I think how well they go with this room and this old table.'

'It was rather sweet of them, I thought,' added Barbara. 'I always felt this to be a very intimate room. With only the candles to illuminate it, I think it is even more so.'

'These young people you have here to visit,' asked Angelo, 'you say they will return to the house and stay with you once more?'

'In a few days,' answered Barbara. Soft candlelight illuminated her face, and that of Elaine, against the black dresses and stone ribs of the chamber which curved into shadowed mystery above. An exercise in chiaroscuro, thought Angelo; a composition worthy of Caravaggio, though the master could seldom have had the good fortune to encounter such beauty.

'I think we might begin now,' said Barbara, reaching back to the wall behind her chair where hung the silken cord. The cord twitched and though there was silence in the moments which followed, in her mind Barbara heard the impatient jingling of bells in the kitchen.

For a time, Angelo reminisced about the house as it was before their uncle had undertaken its refurbishment but became silent as the door slowly opened. Gemma entered, pushing the trolley before her on which rested dishes of grilled beef and mushrooms, a mixed salad and an opened

117

bottle of Chianti. Dishes rattled as Gemma eased the trolley along the uneven stone floor, bringing it to rest at the head of the table. She went about her duties in silence, not raising her eyes as each dish was lowered with apprehensive care to its table setting. From the corner of her eye, she noted the black velvet dresses of Barbara and Elaine, and the crisp, immaculate grey suit worn by Angelo over an open necked denim shirt. She hoped they were not aware of how she trembled, how the blood beat hotly through her body. But how could they not know, for their eyes watched her closely as she moved about the table, scrutinising every movement of her body so that she felt quite naked. Though fully clothed, Gemma was hardly attired in a manner to promote reassurance. The black leather choker about her neck was comfortable enough, though it could not be removed, for under the hinged black and gold oval cameo at the front, lay a small but secure lock. And if others saw her wearing it, they might wonder about the bright metal ring at the back. But she would not be leaving the house to encounter anyone else. Not in the loose-fitting, long-sleeved blouse with low-scooped, elasticated neck, for the black chiffon was so fine that even in the dimly lit vaulted chamber, her breasts and full nipples were clearly visible. Nor would she venture outdoors in the deep-waisted skirt, for immodestly short, the metallic grey latex stretched tight as a skin over the curve of her behind and gleamed dully in the candlelight. Stockings would have been out of the question but Gemma's fine black open body tights were sheer to the waist. Stiletto heel sandals clicked upon the flagstones, echoing conspicuously from the stone walls. Tiny brass locks glimmered against the black patent leather to hold thin straps secure about her ankles.

As she adjusted the large wooden spoon and fork on the salad platter, she wondered what Angelo thought of her make-up and earrings, for the latter swung as bright gold and greenstone pendants against her rouged cheeks and her lips glistened bright crimson. She knew perfectly well she appeared as a backstreet harlot, one who might be found stalking the glitzy, neon-lit and deep-shadowed enclave in many a big city.

If she was to glance at any of them, it would be Barbara, for Barbara's gaze was one of contemplation whereas Angelo's was one of studied lust. Elaine was a big cat, eyes bright with expectation, waiting for her prey to lose concentration and commit the fatal error. And Gemma sensed that Elaine must sooner or later redress the balance for the presumption she had shown that day in the office. She knew what it had done to Elaine. The immediate result had been intense and unexpected physical pleasure; the aftermath, anger. If Elaine had made her do it, it might have been different, but only might have been. Gemma's heels clicked over the stone as she moved behind Barbara and back to the empty trolley. She had taken hold of it and began to wheel the trolley towards the door when a voice cut the silence. 'Have we forgotten anything?'

For the first time she had to look directly at Elaine. When their eyes met, Gemma's heart quickened and a sudden burning filled her belly. She listened to her own voice as though disembodied. 'I'm sorry – I . . .' Her eyes darted about the table. 'Yes – of course, the wine.'

The wine. It stood in the midst of the plates and glasses, untouched. All were perfectly aware that Angelo, when dining with Barbara and Elaine, took it upon himself to pour the wine. Gemma realised it would do no good to offer that as an excuse and moved quickly back to the table with growing awareness of the ascending hem of the tight little skirt which she dared not attempt to tug down. There was no concealing the trembling hand as Gemma took up the bottle. She hoped the weight of it might dampen the shaking as she began to pour, taking care to avoid tapping against the edge of the glass.

It was with no little relief that she accomplished the task without mishap. A relief which intensified when the soft voice of Barbara welled as a cool spring in the burning desert. 'That will be all for now but have another bottle of wine ready for when I call.'

'Very well,' Gemma muttered, and pushed the rattling

trolley towards the door. She crossed the carpeted entrance hall, pausing to ease down the hem of the rubber skirt and remove the rippling creases at the front. That she felt the material to be sensual, there was no denying. It squeezed warmly about her behind and her sex as a living thing. The skirt, the blouse, everything about Gemma defined her as subservient and accessible. Exactly the way Elaine wanted to see her and have her seen by Angelo.

'Do you think she knows?' asked Angelo, holding his glass to the candle so the flame glittered red within.

'She ought to have guessed by now,' answered Elaine. 'What's the collar for, after all.'

'She was visibly shaking,' said Barbara. 'I hardly think it was entirely fear.'

'But the fear, it is important,' said Angelo. 'For her, without the fear would be no – no *eccitazione*.'

'So I've noticed,' whispered Elaine. 'And I once wondered if I wasn't too harsh at times.'

'She has never complained to me,' said Barbara.

'That, is as I said.' Angelo smiled. 'It is her virtue: *discrezione*.'

'Talking about discretion,' said Elaine, 'where's the other one? I know it's her day off, but I haven't seen her since lunch.'

'Oh, she is back,' replied Barbara. 'I told her to remain in her room and watch television until she was called.'

'Does she know any of what we do tonight?' asked Angelo.

'We haven't said anything,' replied Elaine, 'but don't be surprised if we catch sight of her creeping about on the landing. She'll know you're here as your car's outside.'

'I do not think it is important,' smiled Angelo picking up the bottle. 'There will be nothing she has not already seen.'

'I see the wine is about finished,' said Barbara. 'I'll call her back.'

Gemma sat before the small television set in the kitchen,

so absorbed as to be startled by the insistent, intrusive jangling. She arose at once and tugged on the skirt hem before taking the bottle of Chianti from on top of the refrigerator. With some alarm, she realised that she had not yet opened it and reached for the corkscrew. Naturally, for she was in a hurry, the foil cap which sealed the neck was not going to unwind the way it usually did, but only came away in thin slivers. The cork, too, proved difficult and Gemma resorted to gripping the bottle between her knees before she succeeded in extracting it. Once more she felt obliged to adjust the hem of the skirt. Touching the cameo at her throat, she proceeded from the kitchen, hesitating to glimpse herself in the large mirror by the stairs and seeing her outrageously attired image as the others were once more about to see her. Had she tarried longer, she might have noticed a shadow move across the wall at the top of the stairs.

'What took you so long?' asked Elaine with disconcerting calmness.

Gemma stood before the table with the bottle of wine held tightly to her chest.

'Well!' exclaimed Elaine, turning fully towards her. 'Have we taken a vow of silence?'

'I – I . . .' was all the trembling Gemma could manage.

'Please pour the wine,' came the voice of Barbara.

At least the impasse was broken and Gemma moved forwards. She found the lack of conversation even more unnerving than when she had brought in the dinner and the loud click of her high heels irritating because she felt it irritated the three at the table.

She was attempting to fill Angelo's glass when his fingers slipped up the inside of her thigh, causing her to gasp, lose control momentarily and spill a small quantity of wine on to the table top. It was enough. Elaine arose angrily, scraping back her chair and seizing the bottle from Gemma's shaking hand. 'You clumsy little bitch! What use are you if you can't even manage a simple job like that?'

Their eyes met and Gemma felt uncoiling within her

body those sensations which Elaine could so easily summon.

'Stand against the wall by the chest of drawers,' ordered Elaine. With not a glance at Barbara or Angelo, Gemma obeyed, moving away from the table, Elaine close behind. 'And do not turn around!'

Sensing that Barbara had left the table to join them, she was not surprised when two pairs of hands seized her wrists. A metallic rattle reached her ears and the sensation of cool steel fell upon her wrists. Smooth bands clicked shut simultaneously. But there was something connected to the swivel link between the bracelets and held by one of the hands. Her wrists were pulled upwards against her spine. Gemma attempted to turn but the grip tightened and someone took hold of the ring at the rear of the collar. Another moment and her hands were forced up between her shoulder blades. A final click and it was done. The collar and cuffs were connected by a short strap with snap hook at the neck, only tantalising centimetres from Gemma's fingertips but totally beyond her reach.

Elaine pulled an unused chair from the long table, dragged it across the flagstones and positioned it to one side of the door where it rested in full view of herself and Barbara but to one side of Angelo who would need to turn aside to observe it. As Barbara returned to her seat, Elaine called to the manacled figure, 'Over here if you please!'

Gemma turned away from the wall, candlelight glinting in timorous eyes, and began to walk about the table, clicking behind Barbara and passing close to Angelo, whose steely blue gaze followed as she went by.

'Sit here and behave until we get through the rest of the wine,' said Elaine, brusquely.

Gemma, without the use of her arms to keep a balance, leant forwards and lowered herself awkwardly into the chair, feeling cool timber against her thighs and through the latex mini-skirt. Unlike the chairs in use by the three at the table, this one had not been provided with a cushion. With Elaine moving back to her place and not watching for the moment, Gemma squirmed to adjust herself into a comfortable position. The stretching latex rippled from side to side and the hem eased upwards inexorably over glass-smooth nylon. The three at the table once more became involved in conversation and drinking, though from time to time, sharp eyes glanced Gemma's way as a reminder that her presence was not forgotten. Forgotten or not, the chair was to prove increasingly uncomfortable and Gemma needed to ease forwards to take the pressure off her tightly pinned arms. But the latex skirt had temporarily adhered to the seat and did not move with her. She knew at once that, even in the subdued light, anyone glancing her way might see that she wore nothing beneath. Accordingly, she crossed her legs.

The swish of nylon upon nylon could not have been heard above their voices, but Elaine looked at her and asked sharply, 'What are you doing?'

Barbara and Angelo turned their gaze upon her as well and all three waited in silence.

'I'm not doing anything. How can I be doing anything?'

'Uncross your legs and sit properly.' snapped Elaine.

Three pairs of eyes watched steadily as Gemma uncrossed her legs. An ominous scraping filled the room as Elaine pushed back the chair and stood up. 'You've nothing on under that skirt have you?'

Gemma's face reddened. She squeezed her legs together.

'Stand up!' ordered Elaine.

Gemma struggled from the chair and Elaine said, 'Just look at the little slut!'

'Quite shameless,' whispered Barbara.

'*Disgustoso!*' agreed Angelo with a gesture of his hand, though the expression on his face by no means registered the stern disapproval effected by Elaine. Did the apprehensive Gemma note a flicker of amusement in his eyes? It would not be the first time. She pushed against the rough wall in an attempt to ease down the hem of the tiny skirt, but Elaine called out, 'Stop that at once! You'll damage the material!' Her eyes darted from Gemma to Angelo and to Barbara. 'I think we've seen enough, don't you? I'm perfectly happy to deal with her here rather than have us go all the way upstairs.'

'Whatever you say, *signorina*,' agreed Angelo. 'Either way she is to be punished I think.'

'We will stay where we are,' said Barbara. It was always she who would have the final say.

Elaine returned to the chest, stooped and wrenched open the lowest and deepest of the three drawers. Gemma was quite aware that Elaine had made deliberate preparations for her humiliation but did not care to think what those preparations might be. In churning expectation, she wondered for a moment what other excuse might have been seized upon had Angelo not made her spill the wine. Elaine was moving towards her with something in her hand.

Gemma gasped open-mouthed and tugged on the restraint as Elaine placed the short, black braided whip close by on the table. Barbara had arisen and both were at Gemma's side in an instant. Gemma gave a little cry as Barbara lifted her chin and, with her other hand, raised the hair from the rear of her neck. She did not see Elaine bring up the pink rubber ball until it was thrust into her mouth to hold it agape. Fingers worked deftly at the rear to thread and tighten the thin leather strap until it pressed into the soft flesh of her cheeks. When the hands left her, Angelo, too, had arisen. Their eyes met as he regarded Gemma's full red lips, now making an almost perfect circle about the ball. She wondered if Angelo might use her as he had in the past. She would not object to that in the least, but she did not think her pleasure was uppermost in Elaine's mind and she did not wish to be compromised before Barbara, who she had always thought of as being above such matters. But speculation was wasted, for Elaine, having returned to the chest, now grasped that which caused Gemma to stare in consternation and emit a long but incoherent protest from her plugged mouth.

Elaine placed the white ceramic chamber pot between the table and the wall. Gemma tottered back, twisted and strained against the manacles but succeeded only in having the skirt ride up until it concealed nothing and she was open to view by all. Elaine made no attempt for the moment to pull her back, but occupied herself in easing and snapping on a pair of pink latex gloves. It was but a short respite for Gemma, for Elaine was with her in a moment, one hand on her waist and the other tugging down the zip fastener at the rear of the skirt. Gemma saw little to be gained in resisting the removal of that which no longer served any purpose.

The next move she did resist, for Elaine, with Barbara's assistance, attempted to propel her towards the ominous receptacle on the floor. So much did Gemma struggle that both held her against the stone wall while Elaine slapped her hard, several times, about the face. Angelo had, meanwhile, turned his chair about and leant back, fingertips pressed together, to calmly watch the proceedings. Elaine's voice hissed close to Gemma's ear. 'All right you little bitch, if you're going to play at being awkward!' She reached around and seized the whip where it lay glistening, coiled and menacing by one of the candlesticks. 'Do you remember asking me if I'd whip you? Do you? Well now you're about to find out!'

A crack rang about the vaulted room. Gemma squealed through the gag as the whip stung viciously on her flesh. The next stroke fell louder still, and louder too was the cry which followed. Gemma's tears flowed copiously and all could see the inflamed weal's curve where the instrument of torment had bitten her flesh. The lash would have fallen a third time but Barbara's eye caught Elaine's and her lips spoke a silent, 'No.'

So Gemma was propelled those few steps more until she found herself with a foot either side of the pot.

'Kneel!' ordered Elaine.

Gemma, with tearful pleading eyes, glanced at Angelo and Barbara for comfort but saw no sympathy on the face of either. When two pairs of hands pushed down on her shoulders, she yielded to the inevitable and sank awkwardly to her knees, squatting on the hard floor over the waiting bowl before Angelo, with Barbara and Elaine at each side. Gemma gazed straight ahead. In the ensuing silence, time froze.

Elaine's voice pierced the silence. 'Perhaps we need a

little more encouragement! As she reached across to re-claim the whip, Gemma let out a desperate groan, nodded her head from side to side and squatted lower still until the hard rim of the pot pressed into her thighs. It was done as much to avoid further retribution as it was to reassure them of any effort she might be about to make. It did not work.

'Up we get,' said Elaine coldly, and grasped the connect-ing strap at the rear of the collar with one hand, while raising the whip with the other.

From the corner of a terrified eye, Gemma saw the whip about to fall. It was enough. What she had been unable to deliver in the face of shame was once again released by fear. The flow began copiously, hissing and splashing about the pot as Gemma, with eyes shut tight, exuded a long sigh around the gag. She appeared to relax, as though the act of urination also relieved the burden of fear.

She knew it was Elaine who stooped to dry her intimate-ly with the table napkin even though her eyes remained closed. No one else would have done it. Gemma did not open her eyes until she felt herself lifted away from the part-filled bowl and waited unsteadily on shaking legs. Elaine switched around the two chairs to Angelo's left, forming a kind of continuous seat. That done, she moved the chamber pot into the corner and pulled into its place a chair, which Barbara took without comment. The trussed and gagged Gemma saw no point in anything but total compliance as Elaine manoeuvred her around to sit in the middle of the three chairs, next to a coolly attentive Angelo. Elaine took her place at the other side of Gemma and remarked, 'What I like about her Angelo, what I really like about this little slut, is that she's like a musical instrument. You can use her any way you want if you have the skill. But I expect you probably know that already.'

Angelo glanced uncertainly at Barbara. Elaine reached for Gemma's black chiffon blouse as though to undo the top button, but instead, wrenched suddenly downwards to rip the fabric from neck to waist, pulling each side away to reveal fully the rounded breasts and hard, reddened nipples. 'Squeeze them *signore*; play with them and make them harder!'

Angelo glanced again at Barbara, who nodded almost imperceptibly. He raised a hand to Gemma's breast and rolled the nipple between finger and thumb, as did Elaine with the other. Gemma closed her eyes.

'See, we play her as we wish. One minute, *con forza*, the next, *quasi amoroso*.' So saying, Elaine slipped rubber gloved fingers down Gemma's stomach, over the hairless *mons veneris* to push between the lips of her sex. Gemma stiffened and let out a sharp moan. Elaine with the other arm about her neck, was not surprised to see Gemma part her legs. Angelo, with one arm across the back of Gemma's chair, lifted her stockinged knee and placed it over his leg. Elaine did likewise, spreading Gemma wide. 'See! In spite of the ordeal, see how aroused she is! Would you have expected that?'

The finger entered her easily and found the hidden pearl nestled within nectared heat. With no little bravura, Elaine incited the flames of lust within Gemma and set them free to course through every nerve and vessel. Her breath shortened and rasped about the gag. Elaine whispered into her ear and slipped deeper into her sex. Barbara watched impassively as Gemma's moans became louder and more urgent, and saliva traced glistening rivulets down her chin. The finger quickened its rhythm and Gemma, pushing her legs out wider still, began to shake her head from side to side. Elaine felt the vaginal muscles tighten as Gemma's moans became muffled shouts. In their arms, her body quivered as a beaten drumskin.

They sat alone. The air in the room was motionless and heavy with the scent of burning candles. Gemma, still denied freedom of limb or voice, lay across Elaine's shoulder. Elaine's arms circled and supported her and her lips moved consolingly over Gemma's tearful eyes and cheek, kissing the gag as fingers caressed dishevelled hair. 'Oh, what a wicked little angel you have been. I'm going to have to keep a much closer eye on you aren't I? Much closer. Especially when our three visitors return.'

127

She gazed into Gemma's blue eyes and ran fingertips slowly over the strap and rubber ball. 'That young man saw you wearing this, didn't he? I know he did. I know it even though he played the innocent with us. I wonder what he would think of you now. I think he would be fascinated. He was when he saw the other one – when we let her out to visit him in the dead of night. And so was the one who hid and watched them. Oh, yes, I saw it all. It will bring them back to us soon.'

Elaine lifted Gemma's chin. 'And the other day – you served me so well, so very well. Yet it surprised me and I didn't care for that. It should be a part of your duties. I think that's what we'll make it shall we – a part of your duties? Though control will need to be vey strict.' Her fingers fell upon the short strap which held Gemma's arms trussed up her back. The candles were burning low and one of them flared up as liquid wax breached the crater edge and sped down the side, pooling out on the rim of the candlestick and oozing over the edge to form a translucent, dripping stalactite.

'You are going to be free in a moment,' whispered Elaine, easing Gemma away. 'And this room – I'll be down early in the morning to look at it. And when I do, I'll want to see it as though we'd never been here tonight. Do you understand?'

Gemma closed her eyes with an imperceptible nod of her head.

'Ah, your sister,' came his voice in the darkness, 'there was one here like her before. She too was – was –'

'Sadistic, Angelo,' murmured Barbara, close by his side. Their fingers entwined beneath the bedclothes.

'Yes, sadistic,' he answered quietly. 'Her true name, it was *un segreto*. Everyone, they call her the Priestess. In the morning I will tell you more of this woman. They are much the same, I think. Perhaps it is the house.'

'I'm not sure with Elaine. She was always possessed of a forceful streak, even when we were children. Perhaps being a younger sister meant she needed to assert herself more; I don't know. The way she treats Gemma made me wonder at first. But I can see now what it does for them both. It makes a kind of sense.'

'This same relationship, it was established long ago with the Priestess,' answered Angelo. 'After the accident with the boat, Gemma, she turns to Amber, and Amber takes advantage over her. But it was not the same, for always Amber has the mischief and likes to play the fool. In Elaine, she sees another Priestess, and your sister understands this, too.'

'Perhaps you are right after all, perhaps this house and those things in the tower have awakened something more in Elaine. In both of us.'

Angelo placed a hand on her cheek. 'The Priestess, she defies everyone in the end. All were found after the accident and buried. All but her. She was lost to the sea forever.'

Barbara kissed him, her perfumed breath rippling secret fire through his body. 'Perhaps her spirit has returned to the Villa Raffaello.'

'Oh, madonna,' he whispered, 'do not say that. Everything is yours. Even sometimes I think I am yours.'

Barbara's hand slipped down over his naked body. 'Tonight, *signore*, you are.'

7

The Secret Chamber

Victoria lowered her suitcase to the pavement before the
rustic stone entrance. 'This is it – Hotel Mercurio.'

The ancient red brick façade was awash with afternoon
sunlight. Sophie peered through into the darkened hallway.
'Are you sure it's all right, Vicky?'

'Whether it is or it isn't, I doubt if there's anywhere else
in Lucca with a vacancy. Our room is a cancellation.'

'Come on,' said Gareth. 'If Vicky's seen it, I'm sure it's
okay.'

A cry of '*Ah! Buongiorno!*' greeted them from behind the
small reception desk. The smiling, conspicuously rotund
figure with tightly permed black hair, shoe-horned her way
through the hatch in the counter and stood beaming with
hands clasped under jutting chins.

Victoria smiled and announced, '*Le presento Gareth e
Sophie,*' then turned about. 'This is Signora Portinari; her
family owns the hotel.'

Signora Portinari beamed ever wider an exuberant,
'*Molto piacere! Si, molto piacere!*'

Through a doorway behind the reception could be seen
the equally generous proportions of a male figure, recum-
bent in an arm chair. The head was not visible but in both
hands was held an open newspaper and about the unmov-
ing form there drifted a thick haze of cigarette smoke.
Signora Portinari shouted through the doorway in a rising
tide of Italian, the word '*Inglese,*' occurring several times.
A hand left the newspaper to sway lazily about in the
smoke filled air and a disembodied voice called, '*Ciao!*'

Signora Portinari turned and announced with pride, '*Mio marito, Massimo!*' She took Victoria by the arm and moved her along the hallway towards the stairs, chattering continuously as they went. Victoria grinned and nodded with scant hope of verbal response other than the occasional, '*Si, signora – si!*'

Gareth smiled to himself whilst Sophie shivered with silent laughter. At the end of the hallway, they stopped abruptly. Signora Portinari peered through the open door of what proved to be the small dining room and, without warning, let out a piercing screech of 'Maria!'

Gareth gritted his teeth, Sophie pressed a hand over her mouth, but Victoria appeared unmoved by the extreme volume. So, evidently, was Maria, who failed to materialise. At the first door on the small landing, Victoria, still assailed by a verbal barrage, entered behind Gareth and Sophie. Signora Portinari halted only to peer inside with a cackle of laughter and a demonstrative '*Ciao!*' before vanishing.

'Christ,' gasped Sophie, 'what was she going on about?'

'I couldn't understand half of it. She was talking too fast. I gather her daughter wants to go to London to study and that the couch over there will be made up as a bed for Gareth later on.'

'Can't see the point,' mused Sophie, eyeing the double bed.

In the intimate privacy of the shower, Victoria wondered about her relationship with Gareth. Neither had expressed a commitment to the other and it was far from her nature to accept things only on his terms. Sophie was far more malleable. Then there was the Villa Raffaello. Once back within those darker walls, for darker they surely were, Gareth would be free to indulge himself as before. And the Villa Raffaello held a deep fascination. Outwardly, Sophie had shown enough enthusiasm for all three of them but Victoria felt the place appealed to Gareth far more than he cared to admit. Perhaps it appealed to Victoria in ways she was only now beginning to understand.

Dried and dressed in denim shirt and white slacks, Victoria found herself with little to do. Gareth and Sophie still had to get changed so she said, 'Look, there are a few things we want from the pharmacy and supermarket. What say I get off now and we can go for a drink afterwards?'

'I want to do some postcards,' replied Sophie.

'I ought to as well,' added Gareth.

'I'm not bothering till later,' said Victoria, flicking through the guide book to locate a map of the town. 'In that case I might as well do some shopping for myself.' She picked up her brown leather shoulder bag from the bed. 'If you want to come and track me down, it's the Via Fillungo. Start with the shoe shops.'

The thoughts of what had happened last time she had left Gareth and Sophie to their own devices passed through Victoria's mind as she descended the stairs, though she couldn't convince herself it was any longer that important. She had passed down the hallway only as far as the reception when the voice rang out, '*Ah, Signorina Vittoria!*'

Victoria turned, glancing through the doorway at the back of the reception where Signor Portinari still occupied the arm chair. Emerging from the dining room was the rotund form of Signora Portinari. A plump arm gestured rapidly. '*Signorina! Per favore! Per favore!*'

Victoria was on the point of refusing the invitation but relented and walked towards the insistent figure. It was Victoria's misfortune to possess a working knowledge of Italian, for without it, Signora Portinari would surely never have issued the summons. She was led through the dining room, past the kitchen and into a heavily furnished lounge. This was evidently the Portinari's private domain for about the walls and dark wooden mantelpiece could be seen photographs of individuals who, apart from those of the reigning pope, must all have been members of the family. Victoria was ushered over to the mantelpiece where pride of place was given to a group of wedding photographs, one of which, even without benefit of the chattering commentary and gesturing hands, was obviously a younger and considerably slimmer Signora Portinari on the steps of an ancient church, with an equally lithe and immaculately suited Massimo. Victoria leant forwards to gaze upon the features of the young Signor Portinari.

From the unstoppable stream of Signora Portinari's dialogue the word '*caffè*', emerged. The signora gestured towards a chair, set before the dining table. Upon it, as if by divine machination, a large, white photograph album had appeared. Signora Portinari beamed and lifted the embossed front cover. The shops on the Via Fillungo were to profit nothing by Victoria that day.

'You're still not dressed,' said Gareth, emerging in his towel robe from the bathroom and seeing Sophie likewise attired.

'I've only just finished my nails. Anyhow, Vicky will be gone for ages.'

Gareth watched her reflection as she sat before the dressing table mirror, running the brush through her hair and watching him in turn. 'What about you? Are you going to write your cards?'

Gareth sat on the edge of the bed. 'No – can't be bothered. I'm going to wait till we get back to the villa.'

'Then so will I. I was going to copy what you and Vicky wrote, anyway, to save a bit of time.'

'You lazy cow!' Gareth grinned, leaning back on out-stretched arms.

Sophie poked a tongue out at him through the mirror and narrowed her eyes. Gareth arose from the bed and stepped over, placing his hands on her shoulders and stooping to kiss the back of her neck. 'Then maybe we can do something else.'

'Gareth,' she asked in a softer voice, 'do you think it's a good idea? I mean, last time –'

'Last time the door was unlocked. This time it isn't.'

Sophie was reassured by the sight of the room key resting on the bedside cupboard. She was on her feet and facing him, a thick strand of hair swept across her face and held provocatively between her teeth. He kissed her at once with quickening heartbeat and an unmistakable stirring beneath the bathrobe. She would have responded, but Gareth moved aside and pulled the chair away from the dressing table, swivelling it to face outwards. He positioned himself there and took Sophie's hand. 'Come on, be my guest!'

Sophie sat down upon his lap with an arm about his shoulder. His arm slipped about her slim waist, their lips met and Gareth's free hand pushed beneath the edge of her bathrobe. Fingers brushed like hot feathers along her thigh. Sophie parted her legs and pressed fingernails into the back of his neck as he closed upon her sex, his finger stroking and spreading the moist lips until a sigh confirmed her response. His free hand engaged in pulling away the belt and parting the front of the bathrobe so that he might cup and squeeze her breast. Sophie felt the growing hardness beneath and whispered, 'Gareth, let's get these things off.'

Gareth released her for the moment and Sophie quickly arose to help tug away his belt, opening the bathrobe wide to free a flushed and eager erection. She would have slipped her own robe from her body but Gareth said, 'Sophie – no, just in case.'

Sophie hesitated and knelt down before him to take the burning shaft in cool fingers. It was Gareth's turn to sigh, and with eyes lightly closed, he relaxed in the chair, allowing Sophie to push between his legs. For a time, her fingers worked the soft skin beneath the penis head with exquisite slowness. When her soft lips closed over him and her fingers slipped beneath his testicles, Gareth's pelvis jerked involuntarily and a mournful groan reached Sophie's ears. All his thoughts, all the currents in his body concentrated themselves on that one place. Sophie took the ample shaft ever deeper until the constraints of human anatomy would allow no further penetration.

But in this intimate theatre of passion, the first act was quickly running its course and neither wished it to become the finale. Gareth reached out to help Sophie rise from her knees, his yearning regret at her withdrawing the glistening lance surpassed only by anticipation of the next move.

Sophie would have positioned herself astride him, face to face, for her need was as urgent as his own. Gareth, however, pulled her around to face outwards, recalling his act of lust with Amber in the summerhouse. With her legs astride his own, Gareth raised the bathrobe up about her waist to admire for a moment the curve of her behind and widespread thighs. Sophie eased herself down until the penis head butted impatiently against her sex, coursing between the lips and entering but a little. Delightful though the teasing was, neither had the willpower to sustain it, and as Gareth's grip lessened, Sophie lowered quickly down to take the fullness of the shaft into her body.

With Gareth's fingers fully occupied about her breasts and vulva, Sophie moved to a heartbeat rhythm, alternatively tightening and loosening her muscles about the voluptuous invader, judging the time to be not far away when both must reach fulfilment. But in Gareth's mind there stirred a memory which had stalked him ever since their first intimacy, one which might have asserted itself in the tower at the Villa Raffaello had not other distractions been present.

Sophie felt the grip on her waist as his arms pushed upwards. 'Gareth – no. What's the matter?'

'Remember in Arezzo? Remember what you said you'd like to do?'

'Yes,' she sighed. 'I remember.'

He continued to raise her until the glistening penis was withdrawn. Sophie showed no reluctance as he eased her forwards, letting her down again until the wet penis head butted like a hot electrode against the sensitive muscle of her anus. Gareth knew he must let her take the lead in this final act, for the benefit of experience was not his. The heat of her behind enclosed him and he felt Sophie relax as her weight began to tell. At first there was resistance, but the nectar-flow of her own excitement played its part. He felt the head ease tightly into this unfamiliar passage as she moaned softly, 'Christ, Gareth, you're a big boy.'

But the rod moved slowly up, firm and insistent, pushing into the rectum until it was sheathed tightly to the hilt in darkest sensuality. Gareth's fingers were free to enter its former abode, energising further the plumes of lust which uncoiled to devour her body.

The photograph album was opened and it was obvious that only a major earthquake or conflagration might save Victoria from being party to the entire family history.

But fate was to prove compassionate without the intervention of disaster. Victoria had arrived only at the fifth page to see when Signora Portinari smiled in school attire and Massimo stood to blank-faced attention in naval uniform when a voice chimed, 'Mamma.'

She was slim, seventeen at the most, large gypsy eyes framed by a cascade of obsidian hair. She wore a plain purple cotton dress and in her arms clutched folded white bed linen. From one finger hung a bunch of keys. Signora Portinari siezed the girl and propelled her towards Victoria, who promptly stood up. The signora beamed with pride, '*Per piacere, signorina – mia figlia, Maria!*'

Victoria smiled and brushed Maria's cheek with a kiss. A kiss given as much in gratitude as in greeting, for it transpired that Maria was to take extra bedding up to their room to prepare the couch for sleeping. Victoria at once declared her intention to assist Maria in that homely task. Unfortunately, so did Signora Portinari.

Sophie hovered in a spread of golden light, with eyes tightly shut and breath coming in short gasps. The finger which stroked like fire within her sex and the lance which impaled voluptuously at her rear had banished all self-control. Gareth knew she was approaching climax. Her gasps were becoming short, sharp moans and her body began to quiver as her muscles tightened upon him. That Sophie's release was to be a little way ahead of his seemed not to matter, and when she began to shake and cry out in the throes of orgasm, he held her tightly about the waist and began to work his pelvis beneath. A final, long moan signalled her fulfilment and Gareth knew his own was close.

At that point, outside the door, was heard the chattering of Signora Portinari. Gareth exclaimed, 'Oh, Christ!' and attempted to lift Sophie. He expected she would at once allow him to withdraw and envisaged himself gaining the bathroom with moments to spare. But Sophie, still basking in the afterglow of the climax, did not move and only became aware of impending discovery when keys rattled in the door. 'Oh shit,' she groaned, and pulled the bathrobe about her body, twisting the ends of the belt together in frantic haste. Gareth pulled his robe about himself, fastening the belt and tucking the lower part in desperation beneath Sophie's thighs as she brought her legs together in a belated attempt to contrive some normality of appearance.

Victoria's initial surprise went unnoticed by Signora Portinari. She proceeded with chuckling exuberance to introduce a smiling Maria to Gareth and Sophie, who understood little and cared even less about what was said. Signora and daughter began to pull out the couch and arrange the bedding upon it, the unceasing chatter of the mother being ladled out in equal proportion to Victoria and Maria, with frequent glances at the other two. Gareth's face was a mask of disbelief verging on panic.

'She thinks it's funny you two sitting like that,' said Victoria, whose smiling eyes confirmed that she knew. 'Actually, she might want you to get up and move in a minute.'

'No,' hissed Gareth. 'We don't want to. No!'

Sophie maintained a silent, waxworks smile as signora and signorina bustled about the couch. Gareth hoped his erection might diminish to the point where he could withdraw from Sophie and surreptitiously pull the gown about himself as she got up. This possibility evaporated when he realised that Sophie was tightening her muscles and flexing her pelvis deliberately to maintain his arousal. As Victoria looked away, Gareth hissed into her ear, 'Stop it you little cow! Stop it!'

Sophie grinned at him and began to flex more rapidly. Gareth dug his fingers into her waist to no avail, and was aware, too, of occasional glances from Maria as her mother and Victoria remained locked in conversation. The couch was all but made up when Sophie's name occurred in the conversation. All three turned smiling towards her.

'I was just telling Signora Portinari,' said Victoria, 'what a sweet little girl you are in that picture you carry about with you. She insists on seeing it. She's going to wait for you to get it out of your case.'

Gareth gazed up at the light fitting with a soft groan. Sophie managed a demure smile and said, 'Actually Vicky, you bitch, it's with the road maps in the back of the car, so as I'm not dressed, you can go and get it.'

Gareth breathed a sigh of relief, which flew from his expression as Sophie renewed her efforts to stimulate his penis with anal and pelvic muscles, an endeavour in which she was proving altogether too successful and which tendered little doubt as to the result. Molten lust pushed up through his loins and Gareth, hanging on the slippery edge of self-control, felt himself about to lose his grip.

'Then perhaps,' smiled Victoria, 'I'll offer these ladies a cup of coffee. I'll tell them you're going to put our kettle on while I go down to the car.'

'Oh, Christ,' groaned Gareth, gripping the sides of the chair as Maria's amused eyes fixed upon him. But he was beyond caring for lust had taken control and, held back for too long, plunged straight into the fast lane. Gareth caught his breath as if about to choke and began to ejaculate hard, his body quivering helplessly. Sophie clasped a hand to her stomach, looked up at the ceiling and cleared her throat. Signora Portinari peered at the red-faced Gareth with grave countenance. '*Cosa c'è?*'

Victoria smiled. '*L'indigestione!*'

Suddenly, Signora Portinari noticed the time on the bedside clock, threw up her arms and addressed first Maria then Victoria in quickening and rising tones. Mother rushed daughter towards the door and both departed the room. As Signora Portinari's voice diminished along the corridor, Victoria said, 'What a shame! She forgot to fetch Massimo's pants from the dry cleaners and they're about to close.' Then, to Sophie's astonishment, her bathrobe fell open and Victoria at once perceived the manner in which she was impaled. A smile brushed her face as she viewed this bizarre union. She moved away, sat on a nearby chair and watched quietly as Sophie eased herself up, allowing a mortified Gareth to withdraw the flushed shaft from her rear.

Victoria wondered if their return to the Villa Raffaello might herald a time of reckoning.

Two days had passed and Angelo had returned. They occupied their former places in the vaulted room and, as well as the candles on the long table, the lamp hanging from the ceiling boss cast a warm glow about the stone walls. The absence of Gemma was contrived out of deference to the humiliation she had experienced, though the consideration had been Barbara's. Elaine would have had her in attendance without a second thought. Barbara had maintained that Gemma's punishments and humiliation must never become too frequent, and certainly not routine, as this would devalue the ritual and sense of occasion.

Amber served at the table, her eyes beneath long lashes lingering from time to time on the sculpted features of Angelo. His relationship with Barbara took him altogether out of Amber's reach, of course, and rendered him all the more an object of fascination and secret desire. But Angelo, ever courteous, ever the gentleman, had shown no outward interest in Amber, not even in Wallace's day. Amber saw little reason to give up trying.

'The people who came here on those special occasions,' said Barbara, 'they cannot all have been anonymous. Would we know any of them by sight?'

'I do not think so,' replied Angelo. 'They were not people on the television or in the popular newspapers. I think maybe they are people who have power and money. Some would always be, how you say – *anonimo*.'

'Oh,' replied Elaine. 'The grey people who move in financial circles.'

'That is so,' answered Angelo.

'Presumably, they have now gone elsewhere for their fun and games,' added Barbara.

'Perhaps. Some do not wish to believe Signor Deveraux and the others died but I know this was so. Only for the Priestess is the fate a mystery.'

Elaine picked up her wine glass and let it rest between the palms of her hands. 'I don't imagine for a moment that it harmed his financial situation.'

Angelo smiled shrewdly, steel blue eyes reflecting the candlelight. 'They did not come to this house for nothing. From it he made much money and he can call upon many people for the *favore*. This for him was good in his business.'

'We've talked further about bringing it all back,' said Elaine. 'Everything seems to be in place and waiting.'

Angelo leant back in the chair. 'Well, this is so. But still, you have not the missing key to the room in the tower. There are things to learn before you know enough of this house to have once more the guests. Remember, they come here to know their fantasies.'

Amber remained in silence by the door but Angelo's remark about the key glowed in her mind like a hot wire. It ignited the memory of a casual event which seemed of no importance at the time, but which now burned bright as a flame.

'But if you are serious, *signorina*,' continued Angelo in a voice of cool enthusiasm, 'perhaps a few of these people might visit the house again and make the – what do you say – *conoscenza?*'

'Acquaintance,' said Barbara with a smile.

'Yes, acquaintance. Then we will talk more of it, for Signor Deveraux's records are as he left them and all those people we can find again.'

They might almost have forgotten about Amber, and it suited her to be a party to this particular conversation. But in her mind were being replayed the events of several days ago.

It was early on the day when the three travellers would arrive. She had been for a morning stroll and, nearing the house, had seen Sebastiano enter the garage. Amber had walked casually up to the part-opened door and followed inside, curious to see what he was up to. The swarthy Sebastiano, always glad of her company for reasons they both well understood, greeted her with a wide smile and a knowing 'Buongiorno, signorina!'

Sebastiano's grasp of English was as modest as Amber's of Italian, though verbal communication was not always a priority. They kissed almost at once. Sebastiano could be very passionate and was not inclined to let such an opportunity pass. Amber was not surprised when he slipped a rough hand up her skirt but declined his advances, for she was expected back at the house. She had, however, appreciated Sebastiano's urgent need and little time had elapsed before her hand unzipped and entered his trousers to squeeze the bulging penis contained within white cotton briefs. Without further ado she pushed her fingers down the front of his briefs, which stretched out to accommodate her hand as it closed about the hot and stirring organ. Even in the confined space, she found herself able to work it vigorously whilst looking about for some receptacle into which he might be relieved. Too vigorously as it had transpired, for she had spotted nothing of convenience when Sebastiano's hand suddenly tightened hard on her arm. Perhaps he had expected her to hesitate, but she did not. His mouth at once dropped open with a cry of 'Ah, Gesu!' and his hand fell quickly in an attempt to stay hers. Too late! Though her hand withdrew, Sebastiano ejaculated with rapidity into his briefs whilst Amber looked on innocently. 'Oh, dear, we've had a little accident! Ever so sorry!'

She turned to go, leaving a bewildered Sebastiano standing in half-lowered trousers and saturated underwear. It was then she spotted it. On a tool rack fixed to the wall, there hung amongst the usual array of items, a large iron key. It was an ornate key, a venerable and important key. Amber noted its fine covering of rust and would have asked Sebastiano if he knew what it was for if she had felt the occasion more appropriate.

Sebastiano had little access to the house and had never

been a party to Wallace's private entertainments. Only Wallace's immediate circle might have known the whereabouts of the key, but to Sebastiano it would mean nothing. Barbara and Elaine never went into the workshop, nor in the usual run of things would Gemma or herself. The key must have remained untouched and unnoticed for months. Could it be –? But with the arrival of the three travellers later that day, as well as other diversions occurring since, the matter had quite slipped her mind. Until that evening.

Elaine's icy voice blew away her thoughts. 'I don't know why you're hovering in that corner but since you are, you may as well start clearing the table.'

Amber obeyed with uncharacteristic promptness and began to load plates and cutlery on to the trolley. Barbara and Elaine wondered quietly about her new-found diligence. But she was soon finished and was on the point of asking if she might be needed again when Barbara said, 'You can wipe over the table when you come down in the morning. That will be all for tonight.'

When Amber had left, Barbara remarked, 'I'd almost forgotten she was standing there,'

'She's being nosy because Angelo's here,' remarked Elaine. 'She wants to know what's going on, as usual.'

'You must understand,' said Angelo. 'She was a part of the household and the *divertimenti* before you came – she and Gemma. Not always did they just work in the kitchen and keep the house clean. What we do with Gemma in here before today, that was –'

'Angelo,' cut in Elaine, 'believe me, I'd be surprised if there's anything they haven't done between the two of them – Gemma in particular!'

'Ah, well,' smiled Barbara. 'Enthusiasm for one's work is considered an asset in most quarters. But I appreciate, Amber and Gemma may feel that we tell them too little, even when there is little to tell.'

'Apart from financial affairs,' said Angelo, 'what we decide to do, we must tell them also. Always we should.'

* * *

'What's the hurry?' asked Gemma, watching Amber load the dishwasher.

'Guess,' replied Amber, clattering plates into the racks.

Gemma turned from wiping down the cooker. 'Guess what? I don't know, do I?'

Amber stood up, eyes narrowed. 'I think I might have found the key.'

'Key? What key? You don't mean the key to the other –?'

'I wouldn't be surprised. D'you want to come with me and find out? It's hanging in the workshop.'

Gemma considered for a moment. 'It's going to look a bit funny if we both leave the house. What if they want one of us?'

'Okay, I'll shoot off through the courtyard and around the side. They won't see me and I'm not going to be more than a few minutes.' Amber reached into the wall cupboard for the torch and workshop keys. 'You don't know where I am – right!'

Inside the workshop was pitch black though she dared not switch on the lights. In the still air hung a faint odour of oil and wood shavings. The torch guided her onwards and there, above a recently tidied workbench, was the rack of tools. She did not recall seeing so many things hanging on it. The light reflected from wooden handles, metal blades and serrated edges. But the key was not to be seen. Amber felt awash with disappointment and she sighed with frustration. She was on the point of leaving, but on an impulse, reached up and pushed aside a broad-bladed saw.

There it was, glowing softly in the torchlight. The key.

'And now what?' asked Gemma. 'Now you've got it, what are you going to do?'

Amber's eyes narrowed. 'What the hell do you think? I'm going up there to try it! I take it you are coming. Look, I know how good you are at keeping things secret, and that's fine by me. But we both know that you went in there when that – when the Priestess was here. It's me they kept out; probably just as well, too. I don't know any more about it than the two old maids so why shouldn't we –'

'Amber! You shouldn't talk about them like that – okay? They aren't old maids – far from it as far as I'm concerned. And I don't think we should do things behind their back.'

'For Christ's sake, I'm not doing anything wrong! If the bloody key doesn't fit, I'll put it back tomorrow. If it does, we'll have a quick poke around and then – promise – I'll say where I found it and give it to them! It's no big deal is it? Look, let's have a glass or two of sherry first, shall we?'

'Oh, all right, I'll come with you if it makes you feel better. If they find out you've been in, you'll be the one to really suffer. I don't care any more. And yes, I'll have a drink.'

'Doesn't it give you the creeps?' whispered Amber as their eyes adjusted to the dim light on the gallery. 'God, that bloody sherry's gone to my head!'

'Well it was your idea,' replied Gemma, 'so stop complaining.'

At the second door they hesitated as Amber retrieved the heavy iron key from the pocket of her dress. Gemma hiccuped and muttered, 'Christ, I feel pissed as well.'

Amber stooped and inserted the key cautiously into the lock. Gemma hissed, 'Get on with it – we'll be here all night!'

Amber laughed softly and the key turned with silent and surprising ease. 'It feels like breaking into a church,' she whispered, as the handle squeaked and a black gap appeared.

'The light switch is on the right,' said Gemma.

When the wall lamps lit up, they moved inside. Amber pushed the door shut, taking care to relock it. Her impression was that the heavily beamed chamber might be a little wider than the one next door. The first thing to attract Amber's attention stood against the wall to their right, the soft glow reflecting on polished steel bars. 'A cage,' she said, walking towards it. 'It's got things hanging inside – God! Talk about security! Well, are we getting a guided tour?'

144

Gemma regarded her for a moment. 'I think it's best if you walk around and see for yourself. You'll find most of it is pretty obvious. And if it isn't, well, I'm sure you'll figure it out with a bit of effort.'

Amber squeezed her hand. 'Oh, all right then, if you'll come with me.'

Opposite the cage was a fitted cupboard, then an expanse of mirrored wall similar to that in the first room, continuing to more fitted cupboards at the end of the chamber. Opposite the mirror but a short way past the cage, something large and oddly shaped stood shrouded under a black nylon dust cover. Amber stepped over and lifted the cover slightly. The rich odour of leather seeped out to greet her. 'What's this?

'Have a good look – you'll see,' answered Gemma.

Amber lifted the cover back without removing it entirely. 'Christ! Whatever –' She ran her fingers carefully over the smooth, black leather, touched the bright chrome levers and fittings, and gazed with growing recognition at the extension bars, tucked close to the sides of the chair but intended to protrude out and support the legs on padded leather rests. She wondered, too, at the numerous leather straps, the cut-away seat and the fitted toilet bowl with chrome lever taps situated directly beneath it. 'Well,' she whispered, releasing the dust cover and stepping back. 'I'm not going to stand near that thing too long in case it grabs hold of me.' She turned to Gemma. 'Maybe I shouldn't ask, but did they –?'

'That's right, you shouldn't ask. No one was ever to discuss what happened in these rooms, so if you open your mouth about this you'll probably find out the hard way.'

The screened-off washbasin, toilet and shower cubicle in the corner were familiar from the first room. But in between this and the cupboards on the opposite wall, stood two widely spaced chrome bars, springing from floor to ceiling, each equipped at head height by a leather cuff on a short strap. Standing between but a little ahead of the bars, a short, strap-hung leather platform was hinged down almost vertically on a steel post. Amber realised at

145

once that when a person was fixed to this, it would be tilted and locked in place horizontally so that the legs might be pulled wide apart and well back for attachment to the hanging cuffs.

She wondered about those who once gathered here and about the victims who must have been held in restraint and displayed with their most intimate places in full view and open to their lustful attentions.

Gemma's blue eyes were fixed upon her as though reading her thoughts. 'Have you seen enough?'

'Not yet,' answered Amber quietly.

They proceeded to the nearest cupboards and in a moment, Amber had the doors pulled wide, eager eyes surveying the interior. The heavy, sensual aroma of latex, as well as the familiar leather, emerged from the dark enclosure and enveloped them as a shifting, invisible ectoplasm. Hanging on racks appeared to be mainly clothes, but as Amber moved fingers over the cool, sheened smoothness, she touched upon laces, eyelets and numerous buckles. A few of the garments she was familiar with, though others began to reveal their sinister purpose only after a few moments scrutiny. The purpose of some defied interpretation and their fascination for Amber increased accordingly.

On pegs above the clothes hung an array of masks and helmets, some with and some without apertures, two with rubber bulbs at the end of short tubes protruding from where the mouth ought to be. Farther along, a glint of metal revealed an assortment of bars, chains and cuffs and devices of varying complexity. Here too, were instruments of chastisement: thin black rods, whips of several types and a handle from which hung a bunch of thongs. These were not at all to Amber's taste when she considered the affliction they might visit upon her own flesh. At the far end hung surgical aprons and masks in white rubber, together with an ominous pink rubber bottle and spiral of clear plastic tubing. Amber, aware of Gemma waiting patiently behind, smiled to herself and turned. 'Well, you certainly kept all this a secret! I wonder what else is waiting to come out.'

146

No reply came. Amber moved close, took Gemma's hands in hers and kissed her on the lips with the touch of a gentle flame. 'You're not the only one with secrets,' you know.'

Gemma returned her kiss. 'No, I don't suppose I am.'

Amber slipped an arm about her waist and their lips met with tingling softness. 'The Priestess – tell me about her and I'll tell you something Barbara and Elaine know nothing about.' She felt Gemma's hand on her waist and continued. 'Something I saw the first time those three came here.'

'You mean you spied on them?'

'Well, let's say I was curious. After all, they shouldn't have sneaked up into the tower, should they? I was just keeping an eye on things.'

'I'll tell you about the Priestess when Barbara and Elaine know but not until then. And I really don't care what those three did. I've told you before, I don't care what anybody does.'

'Oh, well,' murmured Amber, 'no matter.' Their lips met and stayed together a while longer before Amber said, 'We might as well make the most of it while we're up here mightn't we.'

It was a statement rather than a question. Gemma asked, 'What d'you mean?' But fingers were already pulling away the buttons at the top of her white cotton dress. 'Look I'm not sure we ought to –' Amber's lips curtailed her speech. The fingers continued down, over the softness of her stomach and between her legs until the dress was undone.

'Don't worry,' whispered Amber, 'no one is going to know.'

'You're a bitch,' returned Gemma as the dress was pulled away and her breasts freed to Amber's caress.

'I am, aren't I. They're always telling me that.'

'I don't know why . . .' began Gemma, as tentacle fingers slipped between the smooth, hairless skin and puckered elastic top of the little blue nylon briefs.

'Because you're always horny and we love each other,' whispered Amber.

'No,' sighed Gemma as the finger spread and stroked into her sex, 'it's because you're just a bitch and I . . .'

Amber felt the heat of her arousal and the quiver of her body, and let the play go a while longer before saying, 'Let's have a game with something inside the cupboard.'

She released Gemma, who gasped, 'No – please! We shouldn't touch anything in there!'

Amber stepped back to the cupboard and reached inside. 'Dead simple!' She laughed, and a metallic rattle ensued as she withdrew something, turned and stood before Gemma, raising the object in her hand with a look of mischievous intent.

Gemma gasped. 'Look – I don't think –!'

'It's only a bit of fun,' insisted Amber. 'Just for a few minutes.'

Gemma regarded her with misgiving but the effects of the sherry encouraged compliance rather than resolution. Neither spoke as Amber placed the softly lined, hinged steel collar about her neck. It closed snugly with a gentle click. From either side of the collar there protruded a short steel bar ending in a smooth, gleaming cuff, also lined and hinged. Gemma appeared as if to speak and half-resisted as her right arm was pulled up. Amber held her eyes, fitted the cuff about her wrist, and snapped it shut. For the left arm, there was no resistance at all, and Gemma found herself enslaved by this simple yet totally secure device. Amber kissed her then stepped back to admire the result of her efforts. Gemma, with arms held raised as in capitulation, said, 'Okay, you've had your way. I only hope the key's there or we're both for it.'

'I'd better check, hadn't I?' said Amber, turning back to the cupboard. 'Oh, yes, here it is.'

But it was not the key with which she confronted Gemma when she spun about. A smile flashed over her face. Gemma's eyes widened and she backed away, tugging and twisting vainly on the bar cuffs. 'Oh, you cow!' she gasped.

'Mm,' replied Amber, pulling open the aperture at the neck of the gleaming black latex helmet, 'a cow as well as a bitch. I'll be an entire menagerie by the time we've finished!'

She faced Gemma and lifted up the hood. Gemma shut her eyes and mouth tightly as though expecting a dash of cold water and Amber stretched the soft, glass-smooth material over her head. Amber pulled hard on the helmet until it was over Gemma's eyes where, suddenly, it overcame the resistance of her facial contours and slipped quickly down to her neck. The helmet was, apart from a cluster of small holes about the nose and mouth, blank and featureless, giving the enclosed head an appearance of polished diorite. Amber ran fingers over the silken sheen and said, 'Now then, the other cupboard – do I look inside that as well? Am I going to find even more surprises?'

'It's only clothes and stuff,' came the muffled answer.

'Oh, I see,' replied Amber, slipping arms about Gemma's waist. 'And now we've a bit of fun to have. That's what we came up here for. You knew that all along, didn't you?' She slipped her hands lower and pushed thumbs under the elastic of Gemma's briefs, tugging on them until they slid down the thighs and to the ankles, where Amber knelt in order to remove them completely. Amber stood up, turned Gemma about and began to propel her the few steps towards the tilted leather platform, warm light from the wall-mounted lamps glowing in her mischievous eyes. Near the small table, she turned Gemma around and moved to examine the rear of the device.

'Amber, what are you doing?' came the voice.

'Wait,' came the reply, but after a few seconds she was back before Gemma and, with a hand grasping the bars either side of the steel collar, was manoeuvring her backwards.

A staggering Gemma gasped, 'Oh!' as her naked behind came into contact with the lower edge of the table. Amber pushed hard and Gemma cried out again, feeling her back against the cool leather surface. She attempted to pull away but Amber quickly reached down at either side and seized two of the straps which in but a moment were fitted about her waist and securely buckled. Two more sets of straps completed the task. One about her neck and the other, with soft rubber padding, would have obscured her eyes had not the helmet been in place.

Gemma had not spoken for some time, the only sounds being an occasional gasp to express surprise or alarm. It must, thought Amber, be obvious to her by now where she was and what was likely to happen, so the silence could only be one of resignation. Amber loosened the lever. The small table needed little effort to pivot into a horizontal position and, as it swung back, Gemma drew up her legs rather than have them dangle awkwardly over the edge. Still no word emerged from Gemma as the lever was tightened. Amber took one of her legs and, pulling firmly by the ankle, lifted it up and back until it was close enough to the metal post for her to grasp the cuff with her free hand. Gemma's other leg swayed like a broken bough in a breeze, but not for long. It too was gripped and pulled back towards the opposite post, where it was secured, like its companion, by a leather cuff.

Gemma lay spread wide and totally helpless, as indeed she had earlier, in Amber's imagination. Amber ran a hand softly down the inside of the outspread thigh, feeling Gemma tense as the fingers returned to continue the game which earlier they had barely started. But Gemma's expectations were premature for the hand was withdrawn and she sighed, 'What are you doing?'

'I'm looking at you,' replied Amber. 'I'm looking before I decide what to do because I like looking. I wonder what Elaine or Barbara might think, or those other three if they found you like this. I bet he'd enjoy himself. Oh, yes – wouldn't he just!'

Amber walked slowly around the bound form. 'But now it's just me and I can do anything I want. I bet Elaine does too when she sends me away. I've seen those marks on your arse. She's going to love all this once they know about it.'

Gemma sensed her moving away and called, 'Please, don't go.'

'I'm not going far,' answered Amber.

The two minutes she was alone seemed an age to Gemma. Amber placed what she had brought from the cupboard down upon the floor, except for the translucent pink latex gloves which she proceeded to ease on to her hands, flexing fingers and snapping the material into place. Below the small table lay the three-tailed strap, a small jar of clear jelly and the main weapon in this small armoury of lust, an ample and realistic male organ in flesh-coloured latex. But it was more than just that, for, reproducing its form in slightly lesser dimensions, a companion sprang out parallel from the same base, to ensure not one voluptuous intrusion but two.

Amber unscrewed the cap from the jar and inserted the middle finger of her left hand. With the right, she replaced the cap, then took hold of the three-tailed strap. For a time, she allowed the jelly to rest glistening on her fingers as she dangled the strap above Gemma's widespread thighs and slowly lowered it. Gemma gave a little cry and squirmed against the restraints as cool leather touched between the cheeks of her behind. Slowly, Amber drew the hanging strap towards her stomach, watching Gemma stiffen as the ends passed with exquisite delicacy over the puckered muscle of the anus. The strap continued like a fluttering moth, over the shaven skin of her sex and on to her stomach. Then it was drawn back to begin the journey again. Five times Amber tormented her this way, watching the body stiffen and relax, hearing her breath catch each time in blind anticipation. After the fifth time, Amber reached down between Gemma's legs and brought the jelly into contact with her groin, the finger slipping easily between the folds of her already inflamed sex, then down a little to push a short way into her anus, making Gemma gasp and tense once more. Then she raised the strap high and muttered, 'Rough with the smooth, precious. Rough with the smooth.'

A sharp crack, the prelude to many, echoed about the stone walls of the secret room. But beyond the walls, the protestations and pleading could not be heard. Nor, later, could the fervent cries of passion as Gemma's body, burning from the attentions of the strap, was consumed again in the fires of orgasm.

From a window on the landing, she watched headlamps blaze across the gardens and driveway as Angelo's car moved off into the night. Her watch said one-thirty in the morning. There were voices as she moved in silence down the stairs. At the bottom she could see the lounge door standing ajar and the lights on. She crossed the hall and knocked.

Elaine was in one of the heavy old chairs when Amber entered. Barbara turned aside from the window to regard their unexpected visitor. 'What are you doing up at this time?'

Amber pushed a hand into her pocket. 'I heard Angelo mention the missing key. I remembered seeing this in the workshop a while back when Sebastiano was tidying the place up. I went out and got it after dinner but I didn't want to interrupt.'

'That is considerate of you,' remarked Elaine with the merest hint of sarcasm.

Amber offered the key to the outstretched hand. Elaine held it before Barbara. 'I certainly haven't seen this before, have you?'

'No, it's quite unlike the key to the first room.' She fixed green eyes coolly on Amber. 'You never know, do you, it could be the very one.'

There ensued an awkward silence. At last Amber said, 'Right, I'll get off to bed, shall I?'

'I think so,' answered Barbara. 'We'll see if this fits after breakfast tomorrow.'

Turning to leave, Amber saw a momentary widening of Elaine's eyes. As the door closed, Elaine said, 'Surely you don't want to leave this until tomorrow. God! I can't wait!'

'Of course not but I think just the two of us should see it first, don't you? Give her a minute or so to get to her room.'

'Well, would you have believed it?' whispered Elaine, throwing open the cupboard doors at the far end of the chamber.

'Knowing what we know about dear old Wallace,' replied Barbara, examining the chrome posts and tilted leather table, 'I think I might.'

'Yes,' said Elaine, pushing aside the array of sinister garments, 'but I can quite understand why he hid the key in the workshop. God, some of the things in here! It makes me wonder if –'

'What's the matter?'

Elaine withdrew her hand, examined it for a moment, and reached back inside. 'Well that is strange, isn't it?' She retrieved from the darkness a pink latex glove and held it close to her eyes. 'This glove! Someone has washed it recently, look! It's been powdered but there are droplets of water around the opening.'

Barbara studied the glove in silence, then walked over to the opposite corner where stood the enclosed toilet area. Elaine followed. Running a finger over the inside of the sink, Barbara said, 'Yes, this is wet, too.'

Elaine's eyes narrowed. 'That deceitful little bugger's been up here already! Who else would –'

'Perhaps both of them,' put in Barbara. 'But I'm sure we know who will have instigated it. Gemma would have handed the key in straight away.'

'I agree. What are we going to do about it?'

Barbara reflected on the question. 'For now, nothing. I suggest we wait for our three guests to return and see how things develop. I'm sure you won't mind giving it some consideration in the meantime.'

8

Black Stockings

Under a seamless blue sky, they found themselves drawn into the mêlée of tourists on the Piazza dei Miracoli. High above, surrounded by an expanse of green lawn, rose the white marble splendour of Pisa cathedral with its domed baptistry and tilted bell tower.

'I prefer it here,' said Sophie. 'It's more lively and open.'

'And more touristy,' added Victoria. 'Still, let's get a drink of something cool and then Gareth can tell us the history of the place in not more than ten minutes.'

'He'll need to talk like Mrs Portinari,' answered Sophie. At the first souvenir stall, a leaning tower in coral pink attracted Sophie's eye. Seeing Victoria move on, she reached out to stroke the side of it, nudging Gareth. 'Just look at this – aren't you jealous?'

'You're getting worse. I know just the place for you when we get home.'

'Home?' she said, looking at him quizzically. 'You mean the villa?'

'Yes, the villa. Just a slip of the tongue.'

'I phoned Angelo about the key, first thing,' said Barbara. 'He was rather concerned over what we might have found up there.'

'He's not becoming prudish about it is he?' asked Elaine, seated by the large mirror on the office wall.

Barbara leant back into the swivel chair behind the desk. Each wore her black dress, cut low at the breast. Elaine's hair was bunched up at the back and Barbara's clipped at

154

the sides. Both might have stepped down from a Renaissance portrait.

'Prudish?' replied Barbara. 'No, of course not, though I believe he knows more than he has ever told us. He is concerned that we find things out our own way.'

'He didn't bat an eyelid the other evening when we had Gemma fettered and pissing in front of us, did he?'

'No, he didn't, even if it was as much your doing as his. None of it is new to him. We all realise that, and Gemma more so. It's strange, is it not, how some people thrive on such treatment; how they achieve ecstasy through bondage and humiliation. You have quite endeared yourself to her, I have seen it developing ever since we arrived.'

'Oh, she achieves ecstasy all right,' murmured Elaine. 'The stricter I am, the more intense is her orgasm. Yet at the prospect of real punishment as compared with mere physical chastisement, she professes terror. I showed her the means the other week and she threatened to turn to you. I'm not sure what the results might have been had I gone on.'

'What do you mean?'

'The long whip.'

'You would like to use that, wouldn't you,'

Elaine breathed in slowly. 'It has a certain fascination.'

'And what about Amber? You seem not to have achieved quite the same degree of understanding there.'

'No, not with the other one I haven't. She's a scheming little slut. There's a rumour around the estate that she's screwing Sebastiano and at least two of the others, as well as carrying on with Gemma. The restraint didn't stop her from getting out when those three were here.'

'But I think it had the desired effect. Don't you?'

Elaine considered the question. 'Yes, I do.'

'I think it stirred him deeply. I doubt if the distractions of Victoria and Sophie will have driven the memory of that evening from his mind. I could tell before they left, even though he tried so hard to be normal. I sense there is a side to Gareth which is waiting to be brought out.'

'I don't doubt that,' agreed Elaine. 'And the two girls?'

'It is strange. When I think of Victoria, I think of you. It isn't just her eyes – they are lively eyes, like your own – there is something else. Perhaps her thoughts tread the same path as yours but have not fully begun to appreciate the scenery. As for Sophie, I feel she may follow in the footsteps of Gemma, though at some distance behind.'

'I think we ought to discuss this further with our two as soon as possible.'

'We could talk to Amber now,' said Barbara. 'She was by the pool not so long ago. Gemma is about her duties. I rather think one at a time would be better, anyway.'

Her eyes were closed against the bright morning sun, her thoughts detached and focused nowhere in particular. The breeze, ruffling her copper hair lightly, was no more than a pleasant distraction. She savoured the sun upon her body, her only covering a small G-string slip, the merest concession to modesty which gave her as much pleasure to wear as it might give to the eye of the beholder. When a voice from the pathway by the house called her name she looked up at once. Elaine, though some distance away, was still a commanding presence.

'Oh, Christ, now what,' Amber muttered, easing herself from the reclining chair and picking up her beach dress.

She entered the office with a nonchalance which belied her real caution. Elaine gestured to an empty chair and bade her sit down, but it was Barbara who held her attention with eyes which seemed to say, 'I know your very thoughts.'

Amber folded her arms, leant back in the chair and crossed her legs under the dress.

'You may think you are clever,' said Barbara, calmly, 'but I'm afraid you are really quite transparent at times and give away a lot more than you imagine.'

'God! Now what have I done?'

'What you have done is not the reason we called you in here, but –' she glanced at Elaine. 'We know about your visit to the tower,' said Elaine, 'before you handed over the key.'

156

Amber's eyes narrowed and she sat upright. 'Did that little –'

'No,' interrupted Elaine. 'She did not. You were careless, as usual. And if you don't believe me, let's go back further still. Try and remember where you last saw your monogrammed handkerchief.'

Amber let her gaze drop to the carpet.

'However,' continued Barbara, 'in spite of your behaviour, we do respect the fact that you were at the house over a year before our arrival, you and Gemma, and that you were here for a reason. We know how you both miss the glamour and the diversions, and I assure you, Amber, that we are fully aware as to the nature of your involvement.' Barbara hesitated but no reaction was forthcoming. 'You will be interested to know that, with the help of Signor Manfredi, we intend to establish contact with many of the people whom our dear uncle once entertained. We understand from Angelo that some of the visitors became rather involved with yourself and Gemma and that your private finances benefited too. It would be no concern of ours if that situation resumed.'

'Well I never,' muttered Amber.

'What about a proper answer?' put in Elaine.

Amber looked from one to the other. 'Well it's fine by me. Neither of us came here just to cook dinners and hoover bedrooms, that's for sure.'

'Talking of which,' responded Barbara, 'those rooms in the converted stables around the courtyard – they will need going over. Both of you had better see to it that everything is put in order over the next few weeks.'

'And don't forget our three guests will be back in a day or so,' added Elaine.

'Yes, our three guests,' continued Barbara, her eyes fixed on Amber's and demanding unqualified attention. 'I will be frank with you, Amber, it is necessary for all our sakes that they are made to feel compromised. When they leave us for the last time, they should do so not wishing to tell the outside world about this place. You began the process the night before they went.'

'What!' said Amber. 'You mean you were –?'

'Use your wits,' interrupted Elaine. 'You must have wondered afterwards why Gemma was so willing to let you out of the house!'

Amber's gasp was as much out of exasperation as of recognition.

'I am sure the two of you won't find it in the least difficult,' said Barbara.

'About as difficult as ducks taking to the water, I imagine,' added Elaine.

'What d'you want us to do, exactly?' asked Amber, with increasing confidence.

'I was rather hoping we might leave that to you,' answered Barbara.

'Yes,' agreed Elaine. 'Just be your sweet and charming selves. I'm sure it will work out one way or another.'

Barbara relaxed in the chair. 'As for the rest of our plans, we will make sure that both of you are kept informed as things are arranged. Meanwhile, whether she has finished her work or not, I think we should talk to Gemma now. Please send her in.'

A nervous tapping announced Gemma's arrival. When she entered, her eyes met Elaine's and a shiver passed through her belly. She sat down stiffly with fingers tightly clenched. 'What is the matter?' asked Elaine with apparent concern.

'You – you wanted to see me.' Gemma trembled.

'Only to discuss something,' said Barbara. 'You look as if you've been caught with your fingers in the till. What did Amber say to you?'

'That I was in for it good and proper.'

'For Christ's sake,' said Elaine with a smile, 'you of all people ought to know her by now.'

Eventually, Gemma proved as agreeable to Barbara and Elaine's propositions as Amber had been. But when the ground had been covered, a question was asked for which she was ill-prepared.

'Tell us about the Priestess,' Barbara asked softly. Gemma seemed unable to reply, so Barbara continued. 'There is no clue to her identity amongst Wallace's papers. I wonder why that is when so many others are recorded.'

'She wished us to know nothing about her,' said Gemma at last. 'I don't think even Mr Deveraux knew all that much. Everything was kept secret.'

'How melodramatic,' remarked Elaine.

'She was known as the Priestess because of her role,' Gemma continued. 'She would sometimes come here to hold rituals in the tower. She was always masked. No one saw her face as far as I know. She had an attendant, half African. He never spoke and we never knew his name either. They always arrived and went at night.' Gemma looked up suddenly. 'I think that when certain people were to come to the house, she knew. She would call Mr Deveraux from England then fly over and stay, never more than three nights. Mr Deveraux thought she had an organisation of her own and close contacts in Westminster. That's all I know, apart from what she – what she –'

'Well, I don't suppose it matters for now,' said Barbara. 'We have other things to consider in the short term.'

'Yes,' added Elaine. 'Our three guests leave Pisa tomorrow and return via Florence. They should arrive here later in the afternoon.' She looked at Gemma in a way only Gemma understood. Gemma felt the stirrings in her innards once more and Elaine said, 'There are a couple of things I'll talk to you about after lunch.'

'I don't care if it is the home of the Renaissance,' shrugged Sophie, 'and I'm not saying I'm not impressed by it – it's just too noisy and crowded.'

'I agree, I wouldn't want to live in Florence,' said Victoria, 'but I still say it's unmissable.'

They took in the chic boutiques of the Via de' Tornabuoni and Via della Vigna Nuova. Victoria said, 'Some of the prices are incredible. Even if we do have a bit extra to spend now I really don't think –'

'Let's try along one of these side streets,' interrupted Sophie.

'What are you looking for?' asked Gareth.

'Sophie and I are going to treat ourselves to some Italian lingerie,' answered Victoria. 'You can wait outside if you feel shy.'

Down the narrow, curving back street, shaded from the midday sun by overhanging balconies, they were clear of the turmoil on the main thoroughfare. The shop enticed them with sensual images: images designed for seduction and intrigue; styles in sheerest shadow nylon and frivolous lace; styles designed to emphasise what they scarcely covered and tease the eye with promise. Victoria held the door ajar as Sophie passed through and Gareth hovered at the portal. 'Coming in dear?'

Gareth answered dryly, 'Might as well, for a few minutes.'

Victoria smiled to herself and followed Sophie to a cluster of seductively posed mannequins halfway down the narrow shop, which went further back than might have been expected, and grew darker away from the windows. A girl appeared and asked, 'You are English, yes?'

She was in her mid to late twenties, slim and attractive, but heavily made up and with blue-grey mascara. Her fair hair was swept back into a pony tail and though the faded blue jeans showed off the curves of her figure well enough, the loose white blouse with wide ribbon bow at the neck showed the outline of larger than average breasts. Her heavy perfume suffused the shop.

'English, yes,' replied Victoria. 'May we look around?'

'But of course,' smiled the girl, moving behind a small counter. 'Please, you must take your time.'

Gareth stood quietly by the mannequins, gazing at the sheer black stockings with seams, pinstripes or delicate lace patterns, suspender belts and waist-constricting basques in satin, leather and lace. A quarter-cup brassière, holding out the breasts as an offering, caught his eye, and in his mind the image of the mannequin and of the girl behind the counter became as one. Soon, she wore brassière, belt and stockings, to which his imagination added a pair of stiletto heel sandals from the displays nearby. Victoria and Sophie browsed, admired and touched.

'I rather like that,' whispered Victoria. 'What there is of it.'

'There's even less of this.' Sophie grinned, picking up the G-string. 'The front's as thin as the waistband. You'd have to shave.'

'I dare you to get one,' said Victoria. 'If you do, I will.'

'Oh, I'm going to anyway,' answered Sophie casually.

They moved on and Sophie picked up a bikini brief in black chiffon. 'Hey, look, I think this is men's stuff in here.'

'You're right, I bet those would fit him.'

'Let's get him some,' whispered Sophie.

'All right,' replied Victoria, glancing at Gareth who remained by the mannequins with a blank expression. She knew the ferment of his mind, surrounded by a dream world of voluptuous imagery. In those self-indulgent moments, Victoria recalled a time in London when she had begun to understand his secret fancies.

Gareth had stayed at her flat in Notting Hill a number of times after they had become acquainted. She knew well how he was affected by the way she dressed and recalled her suspicions about him trying on some of her underwear and stockings while she was out. Victoria was, to some extent, a creature of habit and always placed things in drawers in a certain way. She had discovered briefs pushed into spaces rather than lain carefully, stockings snagged which she thought were not snagged before. She had once joked about wanting him to try on some of her things but Gareth had turned almost beetroot red and objected rather too adamantly. Victoria, however, quite fancied the idea.

One evening, not long before their leaving for Italy, she had readied herself for his arrival. Gareth had been delayed at the office so she had found plenty of time to shower and prepare a light meal, with a bottle of wine, and was sat in a black nylon dressing gown when he arrived.

She had noticed how he looked at her black patent high-heel shoes, but he said nothing. Gareth had showered, put on his own dressing gown and joined her at the table. They engaged in small talk, listened to the jazz station,

161

finished their meal then retired to the settee to continue chatting until the wine was finished. The lights had already been turned down low, so that under the circumstances, there was no question other than that they must soon incline to the pleasures of the flesh.

They kissed with increasing passion and the inevitable wanderings of Gareth's hands led to his fingers slipping under her dressing gown and closing upon her thigh. Victoria waited until the belt about her waist was loosened before pushing up from the settee. He looked surprised, thinking that something must be wrong. Slowly, she let the dressing gown slip and watched his eyes widen in astonishment as her slim and curvaceous form revealed itself.

It seemed she had chosen well. The black lace-trimmed platform bra was enough to lift and slightly separate her already firm and well-proportioned breasts without covering the prominent red nipples. From the matching lace garter-belt stretched four elasticated suspenders to hold up the sheerest of seamed black stockings which reflected the light as polished glass. The shoes matched perfectly. The lace G-string adorned her sex like a gossamer feather.

At once he loosened his own gown and slid from the settee, revealing an ample erection flushed and eager. Gareth eased her back, and falling to his knees, clasped the stockinged thighs and ran ardent hands up and down the cool smoothness. His lips followed, pressing with ardour from above her knees to the lace tops and suspender clips. Only after some minutes of this pursuit did slipping the knots on her G-string become a priority, for the sight and feel of nylon-clad legs had obviously given him inordinate pleasure.

But Victoria found standing awkward and so moved around Gareth, who turned with her, still on his knees, until she was in a position to fall back on to the settee. He began again on her thighs, fingers and lips caressing as velvet upon glass, pushing her knees back towards her breasts and splaying her thighs wide apart. In this position, his tongue gained full access to her honeyed sex and entered with a passion and ardour which quickly overwhelmed Victoria in waves of golden pleasure.

Had his attentions been more leisurely, Victoria would have taken an active role, for mere passivity was not in her nature. It was too late, however, for on this occasion, the faculty of self-control fled ignominiously before the rising tide of orgasm. His tongue continued in its fiendish revelry, alternately sporting with the clitoris then pushing deep inside to squirm within the nectared sanctum. Her head fell back and her arms spread along the top of the settee, her fingers gripping the fabric like claws. Throughout the room rang gasps and cries while her body shivered and set as glass. She was on the verge of screaming!

Gareth did not enter her as she expected, but released his grip on her legs so that she might regain her senses. But Victoria recovered quickly, leant forwards to kiss Gareth, and reached down to take his erect penis in cool fingers. He caught his breath and stooped forwards to rest a hand either side of her. Victoria, knowing the powerful attraction of her stockinged legs, caressed the swollen and quivering organ against the inside of her thigh while gently working the soft skin behind the glistening head. She expected that, at any moment, they would engage in full intercourse. What happened next did so with little warning. Gareth raised his head suddenly and gasped, 'Oh, Vicky, I'm –' But it was too late. He lost control as quickly as had Victoria, his pelvis jerking wildly as he ejaculated forcefully, semen jetting copiously about her stomach and leg, running hot against flesh and pale against sheer nylon.

'Have you decided, Vicky?' Sophie's voice banished her daydreams.

'Oh yes, almost.' Some minutes before she had spotted them, close by on a wall rack. Stockings. Lots of them, in cellophane packets. 'I'll only be a moment.' Her smile was not directed at Sophie but at Gareth, who stood watching quietly. She selected three of the packets and turned to Sophie. 'Have you looked at these?'

'Oh, yes, I've already got a couple.'

Gareth's gaze was intent and Victoria was certain that his recollections were not far removed from her own.

During their time in the shop, his fantasies must have been running amok.

'Really,' said Victoria, 'I'd no idea it would be so difficult to find a place to sit and eat.

The table was tiny. All the tables in the little cafe off the Piazza della Signoria were tiny.

'Everywhere is so busy,' mused Sophie. 'You couldn't go wrong having a cafe in a place like this.'

Gareth glanced at his watch. 'We ought to think of going soon, it'll take us a while to get to the car.'

'And we'll probably get lost again if Gareth's driving,' said Sophie, skimming the plastic spoon about an almost empty bowl of ice-cream.

'Then you can drive.' Gareth smiled smugly.

'Let's be sensible dear,' said Victoria. 'We want to get there alive.' She looked from Gareth to Sophie and back again. 'And we do want to get there, don't we? We each have our reasons for wanting to go back.'

Gareth looked down at his hands without answering. Sophie licked the spoon clean and said, 'Can't wait! Are you going to get the bill, Vicky?'

Here was that fateful crossroads and, a little further along, the hill where they had run out of petrol. 'Isn't it odd,' said Victoria as the ornate iron gates came into view, 'how familiar it seems now we're back?'

'Like coming home again,' added Sophie. 'That's what Gareth said in Pisa.'

The sun was still well above the wooded hills when the Villa Raffaello appeared. Gareth glanced at Victoria. 'We were bothered about being late, before. I hope we're not too early.'

Their arrival had not gone unnoticed, for as the car crunched to a standstill on the gravel before the house, the door swung inwards and a figure in blue cotton dress appeared. Victoria opened the car door. 'Hi, Amber!'

Amber walked towards them, bright in the golden sun. 'Hello! Nice to see you all back safe and sound.' Each received a kiss, Gareth being the last; his was a kiss of promise as well as of greeting. In that brief moment, her eyes searched into his with the message, 'Later.'

In the entrance hall Barbara stood in her long black dress, her hair let loose to flow about her bare shoulders. She too offered each a kiss and her lips were cool on Gareth's cheek. How long Elaine had been there Gareth could not say for she stood a little further back in shadow. Being dressed as her sister, in black, she might have gone unnoticed had she not moved forwards. Elaine offered greetings as had Amber and Barbara. Again the favour was allocated to him last of all and Gareth, though eager to accept such an unexpected pleasantry from both sisters, expected no more than Barbara's usual superficial kiss. In duration, that is what he received, but at the warmth of her breath and the touch of her lips, the nerves throughout his body glowed with hidden light. Did she see the surprise flicker across his blue eyes? Did he imagine the hint of a smile upon her lips?

Even as he picked up two of the small suitcases to follow Amber upstairs, his mind was full of their images. Amber's kiss had spoken of carnality and lust. But Elaine's? Hers was a siren's kiss from within a dark cavern, a deep and sinister place, that overwhelmed his thoughts.

Halfway up the stairs, he heard Barbara say to Victoria and Sophie, 'Once the three of you have freshened up, you must go and sit by the pool. Gemma will bring out refreshments.'

Gareth and Amber disappeared on to the landing and Victoria had picked up the remaining case when Elaine said, 'By the way, you will find a selection of clothes in your wardrobe. You must make use of whatever you want for the evening.'

Sophie grinned with enthusiasm but Victoria said, 'Oh, look, we can't walk in and start using all your things! Really, we –'

'You do not understand,' interrupted Barbara. 'The clothes are not ours, not in the sense you mean. They are part of what was left with the house.'

'That's right,' added Elaine, 'they were kept for guests and visitors. Most people can't take an entire wardrobe with them when they travel, especially when they're touring around as you've been.'

'So you see,' continued Barbara, 'they are being offered as they were intended to be offered. If you do not find anything to your taste, no matter. We will not be offended.'

'Oh, yummy!' Sophie grinned, gazing into the opened wardrobe.

Victoria stood back a little. 'They seem to be putting us under an obligation. I wonder why.'

'Well they don't need to twist my arm,' remarked Sophie, pushing through the hanging garments to take a closer look. 'Blimey! Some of these are a bit glamorous for out here.'

'They are, aren't they,' agreed Victoria.

'Sophie giggled, extracting a silver sequinned dress part way from the rack. 'I'm not going down in this – look! It's topless!'

'So it is. Perhaps it got in there by mistake. Still, dear, you never know do you?'

'And these shoes,' continued Sophie, gazing beneath the dresses. 'They're definitely not for country walks!'

'Well, never mind all that for now. Let's unpack and get ourselves down to the pool. It's just what I need.'

A gentle breeze carried the scent of flowers. Victoria and Sophie, bikini clad, had taken to the water and sported in the glittering spray. Gareth had appeared a short time later, looking ungainly in white bathrobe and flip-flops.

His first comment on arrival, 'Looks like the grub's coming!' had brought them from the refreshing paradise of the pool. A minute later Amber and Gemma appeared in brightly patterned beach dresses, bearing trays of food and drink. Gemma's blue-eyed smile was followed by, 'Sorry I didn't come out earlier but I couldn't leave off what I was doing.'

'You three look like refugees in those bathrobes,' remarked Amber, placing two bottles of chilled white wine and five glasses upon the table.

'We didn't pack beach dresses,' said Victoria. 'We never expected anything like this.'

'Never mind,' said Amber, pulling over another table, 'we'll sort something out.'

They stood up as Gemma set down the food. She kissed Victoria first, then Gareth, both on the cheek. Sophie, she kissed on the lips and, for a moment, each gazed into the eyes of the other.

Gemma said, 'Hope you didn't mind us joining you.'

Before long, Sophie and Gemma seemed to cast themselves adrift together and Amber appeared to pay more heed to Victoria than she did to Gareth. He was aware of the summerhouse standing not far behind and recalled again their bizarre encounter. Surely things would not end there. And Elaine. What had happened in that brief moment? Why had it affected him so?

Sophie and Gemma stood up. 'We're going for a dip,' said Gemma, slipping off her beach dress.

Sophie shed her bathrobe and Gareth, already facing them, considered himself a fortunate bystander. Gemma wore a small, backless swimslip in jade green and her firm breasts were uncovered. Sophie eyed her for a moment. 'Oh, if you're going in like that then so am I.' She slipped off her bra, dropped it on the seat, then held Gemma's hand as both stepped over to the pool. It was the first time he had seen Gemma undressed. She was as slim and curvaceous as Victoria, Sophie or Amber, though somewhat too innocent in looks and manner, so he considered, for his tastes. Not a characteristic shared by Amber.

As the two slipped into the shimmering water, Victoria pushed back her chair. 'I think I'll join them for a while.'

'And me,' said Amber.

Amber's body emerged as the dress eased over her head. Gareth's eyes darted to the little swimslip: satin turquoise with diagonal white pinstripe and, as Gemma's, brief enough to confirm, if confirmation was necessary, that

167

neither had pubic hair. Victoria too released her bra and smiled down at him. 'Is it all too much for you, dear?'

'Come along,' smiled foxy-eyed Amber, pulling his arm, 'the water will cool you down.'

It was Amber who had captured most of Gareth's conversation. Her attentions were reinforced by the fact that Victoria avoided interrupting them and engaged herself mainly with Sophie and Gemma. Sophie wondered for a time if she ought not to be jealous, but the fact that she openly shared him with Victoria seemed to make Amber's intervention of less importance, especially as it was only to last a few days. Apart from that, she was beginning to feel she wanted more of Gemma's company though she knew it must not appear too obvious.

Returning to the house, Victoria found herself amused by touches of little significance. Perhaps it was the effects of the wine and strong sun. It was getting on for dusk now and she felt, somehow, there was more in the air than just the scent of flowers.

'It's good of us to let him use our bathroom isn't it,' said Sophie. 'I mean, the way he behaves!'

'It's a bit late to let that worry you, I would have thought,' replied Victoria with a mildly sardonic smile.

'No, not with us. That just happened because we're together all the time, you know that. I mean the way he was paying so much attention to Amber.'

'Oh, I'd let it run its course if I were you, dear.' Victoria turned away from the mirror. 'God, we've got stuff all over the place haven't we!' She contemplated the scattered items of make-up and clothing on the bed. 'We should use the drawers.'

'Okay by me, but what about old Mr Blue Eyes? Are we getting dressed before he comes out, or after?'

'No, he'll be out in a few minutes. Let's put our things away then decide what to wear when he's in his own room. There's plenty of time, after all.'

Next door, the shower stopped as Victoria pulled open

the top drawer of the chest. Sophie glanced up to see her motionless and staring into the drawer. 'What's up Vicky? Are there already things in there?'

'You could say that,' answered Victoria, slowly reaching inside. There followed a metallic rattling as she slowly withdrew that which had so distracted her. The light from the wall lamps by the antique mirror reflected brightly on smooth steel.

Sophie moved closer. 'Vicky – what on earth is – Oh, blimey! Why would someone want to –' She began to laugh. 'Vicky, I think it's funny – I really do!'

'I think it was meant to be found. Whether it's a joke or not I wouldn't like to say.'

'No, maybe it's been there for ages and has just been forgotten.'

'Well, whoever forgot it left this, too,' proclaimed Victoria. From the drawer she produced a ring from which glittered a small silver key.

'So,' shrugged Sophie, 'what are we supposed to do about it?'

From the bathroom came a light-hearted whistling. Flip-flops scuffled on the tiled floor. Victoria glanced towards the bathroom and, gripping the collar, shook it gently so that the two steel cuffs swayed from side to side on their short chain. Sophie splayed her fingers over her mouth. 'No, he wouldn't let us! I bet he wouldn't!'

Victoria resumed gathering her things from the bed. Sophie followed her example, finding the other drawers quite empty. Both turned around and faced the bathroom door as it swung open to reveal a smiling Gareth, adorned about the waist in a heavy white towel. 'Sorry, have I interrupted something?'

'No, dear, we were just saying, weren't we, Sophie?'

'Yes, we we're. Just saying.'

'Just saying what?' asked Gareth, puzzled.

'Just saying,' continued Victoria, 'what a good sport you've been, the way you've treated us both.'

'You're such good fun, Gareth, that's what we think.'

Gareth looked from one to the other with an uncertain smile. 'Well, thanks. I think you're both great, too.'

Victoria stepped over to him and spread her warm fingers over his cheek. 'How would you like to please us again now, dear?'

Gareth caught his breath and gazed into her eyes. Sophie appeared at Victoria's side and both kissed him on the side of the mouth. Gareth slipped an arm about their waists. 'What is lurking inside those crafty minds?'

'We'd like to play a little game,' said Victoria, coyly, returning to the chest of drawers and lifting up the steel restraint.

'Yes, we really would,' added Sophie, as Victoria rejoined them.

Gareth discerned the collar and cuffs, and promptly backed away with raised hands. 'Hey now, I'm not sure about this!'

They moved close and kissed him once more. 'Variety, dear,' smiled Victoria as their arms caressed his body, 'is supposed to be the spice of life, isn't it? Now, come along and see what a good time you'll have.'

Gareth took a deep breath as the collar embraced his neck. He felt his heart begin to pound and the blood rush to his face. A click, and Victoria's voice whispered softly in his ear. 'You can serve us much better with this on, just you see.'

Gareth stiffened as something cold touched between his shoulder blades. Victoria and Sophie reached behind and each took a wrist, bending his arms and tugging his hands higher behind his back than he would alone have been able to reach. He teetered on the verge of objection and resistance, but their smiling faces, the warmth of their bodies and the perfume of their breath on his cheeks and collared neck thwarted his resolve until it was too late. The steel bands closed and the almost simultaneous ratchet clicks confirmed how easily they had achieved their intentions. Only when Victoria and Sophie moved away did Gareth twist his shoulders and arms about in a futile effort to free himself. Only then did he realise fully the extent of his helplessness, and watched, bemused as both stepped over to the bed and sat down. They regarded the mute

Gareth in silence until Victoria said, 'You know, I think I prefer him like that,' and kissed Sophie on the lips.

Sophie kissed her in return and said, 'What shall we let him do?'

Gareth felt the blood pounding in his veins. His penis stirred and hardened uncontrollably beneath the towel. He had allowed them to enslave him with no more than a token protest.

'All that walking around Florence has made my feet ache,' said Victoria. 'How about yours?'

Sophie looked aghast. 'Oh, mine are killing me, Vicky!'

Victoria smiled at Gareth, 'Then that's where you can start. Come along! Over here!'

'Hang on, I'm not sure –'

'You said that a few minutes ago, dear, and it made no difference.' Victoria pointed to the floor in front of her. 'Do as you're told and get down here at once! Remember who has the keys. There's no way you get free until we're satisfied. No way!'

Gareth stepped forward with mouth ajar and lowered himself awkwardly to his knees. In adjusting his position, he knelt hard on the towel and felt it loosen about his waist. A foot appeared before his face and he heard Victoria's voice. 'You really are going to have to work to earn your freedom.' The foot moved closer. 'Lick!'

Gareth stared at it, then delicately licked the underside of the big toe. The skin felt cool and slightly rough.

'All of them,' demanded Victoria, shaking the foot. 'And in between! Properly!'

A hint of amused surprise crossed Sophie's face but Gareth began in earnest. His tongue pushed apart her toes in turn, darting about to kiss and suck each one with a skill and eagerness which impressed even Victoria. When the other foot was presented, Gareth continued with undiminished enthusiasm.

An attentive Sophie asked, 'Is it nice?'

Victoria, leaning back on the bed sighed, 'Ahhh – quite delightful!'

Gareth, lost in a whirl of thoughts, felt a hand on his

shoulder as Victoria said, 'Sophie's turn.' She twisted aside and took Sophie's legs, lifting them over her own knees with the feet placed close together before his face. 'There, now you can do both together.'

Gareth twisted his pinioned wrists inside the bracelets and appeared about to speak but Victoria cried, 'Well, go on!'

He obeyed, his tongue caressing and sucking upon Sophie's feet with renewed fervour until she closed her eyes and sighed, 'Ooh, that's wonderful. Don't ever, ever stop – please don't!'

The towel slipped further, but that was no bad thing for Gareth. It weighed upon his aching erection and he could only anticipate that, after all his efforts, he might gain ultimate relief with one or both of them. The thought of what they might do while he remained helpless drove him to greater effort.

'We should have this every evening at bedtime,' came Victoria's voice. 'I'll keep the restraint handy.'

His tongue was wrapped about the little toe of Sophie's left foot when the tapping came. Her foot at once withdrew and Sophie whispered, 'Oh, God! Who's that?'

A startled Gareth immediately struggled up, shedding the towel at last so the ample erection was freed to spring out in full view. Victoria arose, hand darting into her pocket. 'You answer it while I undo Gareth!' Sophie stepped towards the door. Victoria fumbled with the in-built locks at collar and cuffs, then gasped, 'Oh bugger! This key won't fit!' She glanced at a mortified Gareth and would have called, 'Wait!' but Sophie was already opening the door.

Victoria pushed Gareth and hissed, 'Sit down!' before hurrying over to join Sophie. Two people at the door, she reasoned, would block a person's view into the bedroom more effectively than one. The door opened wider. The smiling face was Amber's.

Her copper hair was pinned up in ringlets, her lips had a moist, vermilion sheen and she wore ornate gold disc earrings, each containing a small, fire-red stone. Had circumstances been different, they might well have commented on her clothes for a pale olive stretch-velvet had replaced the blue cotton. This dress was eye-catchingly short and fitted her slim body as a glove, from hem to scooped neckline, from shoulder to wrist. Braided thong sandals in gold leather bestowed high-heeled elegance on legs in shadow-black nylon. Upon the small brass tray in Amber's hands, three delicate cups each held a clear, golden liquid. 'I thought you might like a little refreshment before you came down. It's jasmine tea.'

For a moment, both were speechless. They eyed the tray, not for the sake of the three cups, but for the small silver key which rested by them.

'I see,' murmured Victoria, looking into Amber's mischievous eyes. 'You thought we might need that, did you?'

'Well, I did wonder. There's been a bit of a mix-up with some of the keys. But it might not really concern you.'

Victoria and Sophie glanced over their shoulders to see a cowering figure attempting to conceal itself by the far side of the bed. Sophie resisted a grin. Victoria said, 'I think you had better come inside.'

From by the bed came a despairing groan. 'Oh, God, you bitch!'

'Better get up dear,' called Victoria. 'We have a visitor. Think yourself lucky it isn't Mrs Portinari.'

'Bitch,' mumbled the red-faced Gareth, as three pairs of eyes fixed upon him.

'Yes,' agreed Victoria, as she and Sophie each picked up a cup, 'I quite like the idea of being one of those.' Turning to Amber she added, 'I think you should drink his tea; we don't want to waste it.'

'Thanks,' replied Amber taking the cup and putting aside the tray. She inspected the crouching and disconcerted Gareth, and noted the light catching the cuffs and chain between his shoulder blades. 'The restraint suits him rather well, don't you think?'

'That's exactly what I said a short time ago,' replied Victoria. 'Sophie will tell you, since he's been wearing it, we've discovered a hidden talent. If you didn't have those lovely shoes and stockings on, you could have a real treat.'

'Oh, he's into feet is he?' said Amber, sipping the tea.

'Very much so. You're welcome to try if there's time.'

'Wouldn't I love to,' said Amber, 'but Babs and Elaine were hoping you might be down in quarter of an hour or so.'

'God, and we're not dressed yet,' put in Sophie.

'He can't stay down there much longer,' said Victoria putting aside the cup. 'We'll need to do something quickly.' She stepped over to Gareth and took hold of the chain where it joined the collar. 'Come along, up we get!'

'Aaagh, no!' protested Gareth, but Victoria pulled hard, and as he began to rise, she was joined in the confined space by Amber, who took one of his wrists. To have resisted would have made the strain on his arms unbearable, so Gareth struggled up. But his arousal, having fallen into abeyance for a time, reasserted itself before the three girls as his penis grew to prominent rigidity. Mouth agape, he found it quite impossible to express himself verbally as Victoria and Amber pulled him on to the bed. He stared at each in turn and squirmed higher on to the pillow to relieve the weight on his trussed arms.

'Sophie, help keep him here,' said Victoria, slipping from the bed and pulling open the top drawer of the chest.

Sophie followed Amber's example and seized one of Gareth's legs, pulling it up and clutching it against her body so that he was quite unable to struggle free. His erection stood in flushed prominence, demanding attention. Amber reached out to run a finger up the twitching shaft and she winked at an amused Sophie.

Victoria clambered back on to the bed and positioned herself between Gareth's legs, arm held high. From her fingers there flowed a gossamer wisp, the sheerest of nylon stockings. Holding it by the toe, she let it drift gently from side to side just above his penis. A silence descended on the room. Slowly, Victoria lowered the stocking until it brushed delicately against the head. His penis jerked and his body stiffened as though touched by hot needles. Victoria lifted the stocking, giving it a little shake so that it fell open about the silken top.

174

Once again it descended. The grip tightened on his legs as cool nylon enveloped the bulbous head and lowered as a dark column of mist over the aching shaft. Gareth gasped and closed his eyes; the stocking gathered and piled with exquisite, tormenting sensuality about the penis base, swarming like hot, black moths to make him tense with each maddening caress. Soon, the shaft was encased in feather-touch nylon.

Gareth had barely taken a breath before Victoria's hand closed about the shaft and began the firm but gentle act of masturbation. Another gasp, and his fettered body squirmed in shameful ecstasy. Victoria's action quickened and the fingers of Amber's free hand slipped beneath his testicles, causing him to tense almost violently and exude a sharp moan. Three pairs of eyes watched, cool and intent, as Victoria's hand went about its voluptuous work. Their studied gaze did nothing to stem the approaching crisis. The rising turmoil was uncontrollable. It spread and seared within his loins until he felt about to burst. When he began to shake and twist his head from side to side, Amber's voice trickled through. 'Oh, my, what a naughty boy we are!'

But it was swamped by the raging passion of orgasm. Gareth cried out, ejaculating hard into the stocking, until it collapsed about the shaft, saturated.

The grip on his legs relaxed. Victoria, Sophie and Amber left the bed. Amber took up the brass tray and empty cups. 'I'll tell them you wont be long, shall I?'

'Not too long,' Victoria smiled as Amber pulled open the bedroom door. 'And thanks for the jasmine tea, it was really lovely.'

From the bed there came a soft groan.

9

Quicksands of Passion

A subdued and vanquished Gareth had retreated to the bathroom, where he stayed until Victoria and Sophie dressed and left to go down for dinner. Victoria's parting shot preyed on his mind. 'Better hurry up, dear, and make sure you come down looking smart!'

His arms still ached, the marks caused by the steel cuffs had not quite vanished. The way they had controlled and used him had left Gareth cloaked in uncertainty. He stared hard at his newly groomed image in the mirror and ran his fingers over a smooth chin. Should he feel aggrieved? Hardly – he had used all three women for his own satisfaction. The challenge of facing them over the dinner table had to be met.

Look smart, Victoria had said. His response was a new pair of fawn trousers, reserved for a possible special evening out, and a blue denim shirt, in reasonably good condition, over which he slipped his lightweight jacket.

At the bottom of the stairs, conversation drifted from the part-open door of the vaulted room, interspersed with Victoria and Sophie's laughter. Gareth stopped and gripped the banister rail; surely they were not discussing that? Not in front of Barbara and Elaine! Now was not the time to doubt, nor the time to peer sheepishly around the door. With an off-the-shelf smile lodged in position, he strode in. 'Hi, everyone!'

Where he had expected to see them, there were only empty chairs, though the table was set for five. Instead, they were gathered at the far end of the room before an old chest. Heads turned and Victoria said, 'Nice of you to drop by.' Sophie smiled cheekily in the intimate light of the ceiling lamp and brass candlesticks. It was she who stood out initially, with her flaxen hair falling loosely about her shoulders. The white lycra top, long sleeved and high necked, seemed moulded to her slim body and the swell of her breasts. It contrasted with the flared mini-skirt in black satin, swaying across her behind as she moved, though white was evident once more with the wedge-heel knee boots.

The other three wore dresses. Victoria's shimmered in purple lurex, long sleeved and low cut at the neck with black nylon fringe sweeping below the breasts. It allowed ample sight of her legs, in sheerest black, and her patent black court shoes with small purple bows at the toe. But Gareth well knew how glamorous Victoria could look and Sophie, though physically quite as mature, still hinted at schoolgirl frivolity.

Barbara and Elaine had, in his mind, always been synonymous with the elegant black dresses which seemed such an important part of their image so it was upon them that his gaze fell with greatest interest. Elaine stood partly obscured by her sister, whose pencil-slim dress in red, stretch-silk was sleeveless, high collared and split to the black-stockinged thigh. High-heeled sandals matched the dress in colour and, as Barbara turned, a shapely leg was revealed. Small gold discs swung and glittered below her ears and her hair was held up in elegant swirls. As the small gathering moved away from the chest, Elaine's appearance struck the *coup de grâce* to his composure and what Gareth had intended as a glance became a captivated stare.

Her body twisted around like a glittering snake, candle-light sparkling on a low scooped, long-sleeved dress of gold sequinned lycra. The dress was cut well above the knee to reveal legs in sheerest gossamer lace. Her open strapwork sandals in black patent, boasted small brass buckles at the ankle. The stiletto heels were enough to account for the fact that she appeared as tall as himself. Victoria said, 'We were just looking at some old pistols and stuff in that chest. You should go and see for yourself after dinner.'

Gareth muttered, 'Er – yes, maybe I will.'

They passed by, enveloping him in a sensual warmth and perfume. Elaine was last and Gareth felt a secret tremor as he looked upon her beauty. He dared not glance down at the low scoop of the dress though his eyes took in her full lips, burnished red as were those of the other three. She was, like her sister, transformed but there was more. In that fragment of time when he felt her breath on his cheek, she turned her eyes directly to him. It was a look of recognition. Recognition of something deep within himself. He craved to know her intimately and felt a sudden uneasiness, for he was certain she knew his desires.

Candle flames flickered as they took their places at the table, Gareth's seat facing the door. Next to him was Sophie, who in turn sat adjacent to Barbara, occupying her customary position at the head of the table. Opposite Sophie sat Victoria and facing Gareth, the sequinned, red-lipped, sharp-eyed, quite unavoidable vision of Elaine. And when his eyes were not upon her, the image persisted at centre stage and would give way to no other. It was almost a surprise when, through the mist of small talk, Victoria's voice emerged like a clear chime. 'You're awfully quiet, dear. Are you feeling under the weather?'

There was silence. All eyes were upon him. 'Quiet?' began Gareth. 'Well I suppose I –'

'It's the shock of having to turn up for dinner looking smart,' cut in Sophie. 'It's spoiling his appetite.'

Gareth glanced at her and was about to continue when the door pushed open and the velvet clad form of Amber appeared with a brass tray bearing several small, deep plates.

'This is *ribollita*,' said Barbara, 'a thick vegetable soup. I'm sure he will have no problems with it.'

'Really,' insisted Gareth, 'there's nothing wrong. I'm just . . .' His voice trailed off, for as Amber placed the dishes upon the table, another figure appeared at the door. Candlelight gleamed subtly on a black dress, if dress was

178

the appropriate term for a garment intended to arouse the senses by its style and brevity. The neckline, elasticated and trimmed with white lace, as were the little flounced sleeves, was cut so low that the total exposure of Gemma's breasts appeared imminent, being avoided only by the care with which she moved as she lowered the silver ice bucket and protruding bottle down on to the table. Amber had meanwhile moved to Gareth's side, where the soup was placed before Sophie and himself. She said not a word, though took care to ensure Gareth's attention was momentarily diverted by a discreet nudge.

'You may pour the wine,' said Barbara. Gemma, with her eyes fixed permanently upon the table, withdrew and wiped the bottle before beginning, at Elaine's side, to fill the tall-stemmed glasses with chilled Verdicchio.

Gareth's resolve not to stare dissipated in the ensuing silence as Gemma clicked from Elaine to Victoria and around to Barbara. If the dress was less than modest above the waist, it made no pretensions elsewhere either. The flared skirt, with tiny, semicircular white lace apron at its front, might have been styled for the skating rink or ballet stage, though the shadow-nylon on her legs and the impractically high stiletto heels of the black sandals were hardly suited to either.

No one spoke as Gemma moved closer and another odour mingled with that of the perfume and candles. It spiralled invisibly about his nose with tantalising sensuality. But Gareth had already recognised the sheen and smoothness of latex before Gemma filled Sophie's then his own glass. The swish of stockings, the tap of heels on stone and her breathing by his side filled the vaulted room as though his senses had become abnormally acute. He tried to remain expressionless despite the closeness of her body and the warm, sensual odour of the dress, but in the strained silence she demanded his attention. Gareth wondered if Sophie expressed any reaction but the act of turning about to observe her face would have been too deliberate. Victoria appeared almost amused. Elaine watched Gemma casually, fingers poised on her wine glass.

Gareth glanced aside to Barbara and saw that her eyes were fixed for that moment upon him. She also knew his thoughts.

They were tormenting him, playing cat-and-mouse with his desires and fantasies. Did anyone expect him to pass comment? Could any remark he might make possibly be appropriate? They had surely schemed to corner him emotionally. Why? He turned away, not too quickly he hoped, and Barbara said with a faint smile, 'I trust this wine is to your taste, Gareth.'

'Oh yes,' he grinned sheepishly. 'It's fine.'

'You haven't drunk any of it yet,' remarked Sophie.

Victoria, her own glass balanced between outstretched fingers, smiled discreetly. Gareth drank the cool liquid gratefully, not caring for the moment to look at anyone. After a time, and a little more wine, he relaxed and found himself able to indulge in something approaching normal conversation. That inevitably faltered when Amber and Gemma returned to serve the next course, accompanied by two bottles of Chianti.

Throughout dinner Gareth pondered on Barbara and Elaine's intentions. Sophie, too, became lost in thought at times and was not her usual whimsical self. Victoria, quite unperturbed, found much to discuss with the two sisters.

A bottle of Malvasia was brought in with the desserts. By now, Gareth was determined to catch Gemma's eye, if only because she took great pains to look directly at no one other than Elaine. He did not succeed until the last dishes were being cleared and she stood behind Victoria and Elaine. Gemma allowed her gaze to fall upon him and her lips parted as if to ask a question. But what question?

Amber had already left the chamber and Gemma remained by the door, waiting in silence. Elaine turned around and said, 'Switch the light off, please!'

As the iron caged lamp at the apex of the vaulted ceiling went out, shadows leapt in as though to engulf the remnants of light. The world about them shrank.

'It's so much cosier with just the candles,' remarked Elaine.

Indeed, the end of the table where they sat had become an illuminated island about the two dancing flames. The stone walls were barely discernible, though as his eyes became accustomed to the gloom beyond, Gareth saw that Gemma no longer stood by the door. He glanced about and wondered if she might be waiting somewhere in the shadows in her delightfully outrageous little dress.

There was plenty of space to stretch out at the table. The large, heavy chairs were built for room and comfort, not for portability. With the overtly erotic image of Gemma no longer a distraction, he was again preoccupied with Elaine. She held a magnetism, a power he could no more understand than deny. He was sure that Barbara held it too, but here, the gates were closed against him, whereas with Elaine, he was permitted a glimpse into another, forbidden world.

His deliberations, as well as the drink, had lulled Gareth into sprawling relaxation when something touched his senses like a dark feather. He glanced about, expecting to find that Gemma had re-entered the room unseen. The odour of latex was growing stronger by the moment.

A hand touched his knee. Gareth looked down, startled. There, dimly visible beneath the table was a pair of wide eyes and a finger, bidding silence, pressed against full red lips. He glanced up to see if this was some prank shared by the others, but no: Victoria, Elaine and Sophie all had their eyes upon Barbara who was, in her calm but commanding way, describing some of the characters about the estate and in the nearby village. Before Gareth could look down again, Gemma was forcing her way between his legs and her fingers had closed over the buckle of his trouser belt. His first reaction was to squirm upright and pull away but then she squeezed his enclosed penis and his mind spun in confusion. During those moments of indecision, her fingers had commenced their devious work with a speed and dexterity which made him realise that moving now might have far less desirable consequences than staying put. He glanced at Sophie sitting to his right. The table offered some hindrance to observation but perhaps not enough.

181

Gareth slipped a little further down into the chair and, with wine glass in one hand, attempted with the other to push Gemma away without attracting attention. It was no use, the zip fastener was whirring down and the top of his trousers already gaped wide open. Victoria's voice entered like a thunderclap. 'Gareth, you're not dozing off are you? Show Barbara that old ring you wear, the one your grandmother gave you.'

The ring was on his left hand. The hand under the table. 'No – er, I wasn't nodding off.' He grinned, withdrawing the hand for all to see. 'I'm enjoying the wine and the company in my own way – honest!' He hoped they did not see him tense in the chair, for as Barbara asked to see the ring, Gemma's fingers slipped into his trousers to enclose his trapped but swollen penis. Gareth tugged at the ring, which came off his finger only with difficulty.

Fingers coursed unimpeded over gossamer nylon, for Gareth, after his shower, had put on the diminutive briefs which Victoria had purchased for him in Florence. Gemma's fingers squeezed intimately as though nothing lay in between burning flesh and cool fingers.

Barbara, watched by everyone, held the ring close to the nearest candle and remarked, 'Mmm, it's quite old – worth a bit, too, I would think.'

Fingers eased down the elastic until it stretched tightly behind the head of the engorged penis, straining like a coiled spring close to the point of release. Barbara handed back the ring and said, 'I wouldn't leave that laying about when you're on your travels.'

Victoria stared at him as he twisted it clumsily back on to his finger. 'You look flustered, dear, are you sure there's nothing wrong?'

'No – no, I'm fine!' replied Gareth with hoarsely exaggerated confidence.

Elaine picked up the Malvasia. 'We may as well finish this off.'

At that point the elastic slipped further and his penis sprang free, feeling oddly cool as if discreet currents of air eddied beneath the table. Free, that is, until fingers closed around it, just below the head, and began their devilish work with the soft skin, sending shockwaves through his loins and stomach as he reached with trembling hand to grasp the refilled wineglass.

Mercifully, Sophie livened up and began to chatter about some of her student friends. Gareth kept the glass poised between himself and the table as if to appear occupied, intending to take just the occasional sip. As he raised the glass to his mouth, the hand which so voluptuously worked him slipped down to enclose the base of the shaft. The liquid had passed over his tongue when Gemma's fingers pushed under his testicles to entirely cup them, and her lips closed softly over the penis head. Catching his breath, Gareth barely avoided a sudden and violent fit of coughing. Gemma, holding him in a lustful and fermenting embrace from which he could not withdraw, was remorselessly stoking the flames within. She would not desist. He knew she would not, until it was too late! And though his mind shouted that it must not happen, his body refused to take heed.

Gemma began to work more vigorously with both hand and mouth. Coils of passion unwound and seized him with carnal urgency as his groin muscles tightened. The glass he set down upon the table rang like a bell and the crisis approached as an express train. His hands arose to cover his face and he breathed in deeply, hoping through the turmoil to feign a yawning tiredness. Gemma sensed the rising pressure, felt the tensing of his body and slid her lips further down the shaft.

Gareth came. Gemma's grip tightened as he quivered and spurted rapidly within the enclosing warmth. Fingers dug hard into the ridges above his eyes but he could neither suppress nor stifle a long groan, and leant forwards with elbows hard upon the table.

Sophie's voice bubbled clear through turbulent waters. 'Don't tell me you're tired already.'

'Tired?' he heard himself gasp. Gareth peered through his fingers. Victoria was talking to Barbara. Elaine glanced casually at him: a moment's glance that froze in time.

'No,' he continued, 'no – not tired. Just too much drink – that's what it is.'

The hand slipped from beneath his testicles. Slowly he was withdrawn from the unseen mouth, wet and inflamed. Then she was drying him with what felt like a serviette. Gareth forced a smile at Elaine and Victoria. 'Maybe I'll go out for a breath of fresh air in a few minutes.'

'Yes, why don't you,' murmured Elaine, 'the fresh air will cool you off a little.'

Gareth realised she knew, and wanted him to be well aware of the fact.

The hands which had so efficiently gained access to him were pulling the briefs up over the semi-erect penis, squeezing it down and fitting the elasticated nylon back into place. Fingers were soon tugging on the zip fastener and Gareth adjusted himself in the chair in order to aid her efforts. The belt seemed her only real problem, for Gemma could not pull and fasten it as tightly as it ought to be. No matter, thought Gareth with a different kind of relief.

'I think a walk around the gardens might do us all good,' said Barbara, scraping back the heavy chair. Gareth considered the timing of the remark. A few minutes earlier and he would not have dared move. Surely Barbara was not a party to this!

Victoria and Sophie, too, prepared to leave, while Gareth, desperate to appear self-possessed, arose slowly. Gemma, he knew, must still be close by and waiting in hidden silence. Elaine eased back her chair and glanced at Barbara. 'There are things I have to do. I'll see all of you later, no doubt.'

She did not rise from the table.

'Of course,' answered Barbara, turning to the others. 'Shall we go?'

They moved towards the door, their shadows dancing about the stonework in shivering candlelight. Knowing Elaine was still seated and had her back to the door, Gareth glanced back. Below the row of empty chairs, beneath the table, there was only blackness.

* * *

The night air was pleasantly cool, the moonless sky dusted with a myriad stars. As they walked by the pool, around the summerhouse and into the gardens, no one spoke until Victoria said, 'Barbara, the dinner was wonderful and, well, really special – you letting us borrow these dresses for the occasion.'

'That is what they are for,' smiled Barbara. 'They are, if you like, a kind of resource.'

'Not a resource everyone could afford,' continued Victoria. 'And you two, we've only ever seen you in black before. You both looked so –'

'Fantastic!' cut in Sophie.

'Yes, fantastic,' agreed Victoria. 'So did Amber and – well –'

Barbara stopped. 'And Gemma, I think you were about to say.'

'Yes, Gemma, I thought she looked quite the part in that little dress.'

Gareth said nothing but his attention was total.

'Oh, I wouldn't dare go about in something like that,' declared Sophie. 'It's too pervy.' She smiled at Victoria and Barbara. 'Well, not unless everyone else was –'

'You are keeping quiet on the subject,' Barbara said to Gareth.

'He feels out of his depth this evening, don't you dear,' commented Victoria.

'If I'd been wearing a tie,' offered Gareth, 'I'd have loosened it long ago. I'm only glad I don't have a coronary problem.'

They resumed walking and reached the perimeter path where the garden ended and the vineyards began. Here they turned left, for the vineyards were obscured in total darkness.

'What you saw this evening was a taste of the old Villa Raffaello, before Elaine and I came here.' Barbara stopped to face them. 'But of course you know quite a bit about that already, don't you?' Her eyes glistened in the light from the house. She was expecting a reply.

'I suppose we do,' admitted Gareth uneasily.

Sophie's eyes darted from one to the other. Victoria watched Barbara steadily. As neither Gareth nor Sophie appeared about to add anything further, she said, 'It must have been quite exciting in those days, if that's the right word.'

'Oh, yes,' replied Barbara, 'the people who came here found it very exciting indeed, otherwise they would never have taken the trouble. It is not the easiest place to get to, as you found out for yourselves.'

'If only we were all that well off,' put in Gareth.

Barbara eyed him with an expression which said he had not done too badly and that what he had done was no secret. 'You have in a short space of time become our friends,' she continued, 'and friends expect confidentiality. It works both ways, of course.'

'You've done an awful lot for us,' said Victoria. 'Confidentiality is the very least you should expect.'

'Absolutely,' agreed Gareth.

'Oh, quite definitely,' added Sophie, folding her arms to imply the irrevocable finality of the statement.

'And what you have seen,' said Barbara, softly, 'perhaps you found it disagreeable. Perhaps you found it not at all to your tastes.'

Gareth glanced at Sophie. Both turned to Victoria, whose expression hinted at amusement. 'I don't think you need have concern about any of us. We're nothing if not open minded.'

'Good,' murmured Barbara, 'then there is something I shall allow you to witness in the tower tonight which may or may not confirm the truth of what you have just said. You know perfectly well what the tower was used for; should you wish to decline, you may do so, of course.' She started slowly along the path. 'I think we might return to the house now, it is getting late.'

Elaine tugged at the strap end until she was satisfied it was tight enough. Three soft clicks followed. 'There! I think that will do.'

'It's a bit late isn't it?' asked Gemma. 'Why now? Why so late?'

'Why now – why so late!' mocked Elaine, stepping back to appraise the figure standing in the centre of the room. 'It beats me why you bother to ask.'

Gemma stood with breasts prominent, for her shoulders were pulled back and her arms all but invisible. She still wore the maid's dress, but the elasticated neck had been pulled down to expose reddened nipples and cradle the breasts from below. Two black straps emerged from beneath her armpits, crossed her bare chest and disappeared over the shoulders. Elaine walked slowly around Gemma, then stopped to pick up an object which had been placed out of sight on one of the leather chairs. She examined the silent figure from behind, the light from the wall lamps gleaming on the black leather sheath. This, kept in place by the straps, contained her arms and held them securely down her back, from the shoulder blades to where the tight pouch squeezed her hands palm to palm. From the tip of the bondage glove, beneath her fingers, hung a small steel ring. Elaine continued until she was again facing Gemma. 'Well, you gave a bloody good account of yourself down there didn't you?'

'You told me to! You said for both of us to –'

'Under the dinner table!' shouted Elaine. 'Did I tell you to do that! Did I?'

'No,' protested Gemma. 'You didn't say what to do, did you? Well, did you!'

'I didn't did I! And I should have known better shouldn't I, you little slut. I should have known you'd take it in the mouth before anywhere else.' Elaine slapped her hard across the face. 'It's a wonder you're not still a virgin down there! What if one of the others had seen you?'

'I was doing what you wanted,' cried Gemma. 'What you both expected – and now this! This is what I get for it.'

'Not quite. There's more to it than you think.'

'What do you mean?'

Elaine reached up to place a hand on the back of her neck. 'Well, you won't be using your mouth for anything else. Not until I say so.' Gemma blinked as the red rubber ball was thrust between her jaws, but knew better than to

187

struggle. The slim strap tightened about her cheeks and neck, forcing her lips into a tight circle about the embedded ball. Elaine placed a hand beneath her chin. 'Our friends were quite impressed with your appearance downstairs. And if Barbara and I have judged those three correctly, they'll be impressed again before the evening is out.'

Gemma pulled away and shook her head with a stifled, 'Mmm – mmm!'

'Oh, don't worry, my little pet, I'm not going to make you pee. Dear me, no. That might be a bit much for our two lady guests – even for him.' She placed a hand on Gemma's cheek. 'We'll have a little show, just to test the water if you like. Just enough to get them to dip their toes in. Then their feet and legs. Perhaps eventually, they'll go right under.'

A face appeared at the kitchen door, eyes squinting to compensate for the poor illumination of the entrance hall.

'Oh,' said Amber, 'I wondered where everyone had gone.'

'I thought our guests would like an evening stroll,' replied Barbara. 'Are you up for much longer?'

'No, a couple more things to do then I'm off to my room; unless you want anything else.'

'No, nothing. We'll see you at breakfast.'

Amber watched them disappear up the stairs, then waited and listened. She wondered about Elaine and Gemma, who had disappeared earlier on, and wondered, too, why Barbara had accompanied the three visitors on what can only have been a short walk around the garden. Barbara seldom went out late in the evening unless with Angelo.

At the top of the main stairs they hesitated. Barbara moved to the tower steps. 'Well, do we go on or do you wish to say goodnight?'

'Okay by me,' said Gareth, with a thin veneer of self-assurance.

188

Victoria had already begun to follow and Sophie muttered, 'I'm not being left out.'

Gareth watched Barbara's slim form as she led the way upwards, watched her nylon-shadowed leg flash from the smoothness of the split-sided dress, his mind in a turmoil of speculation as to what they might be about to witness. He wondered what Sophie must be thinking, though Victoria seemed not in the least concerned.

The globe lamps cast shadows behind as they approached the first door. Gareth expected Barbara to knock but her fingers fell upon the iron handle. The door opened smoothly. Barbara entered a short way then stood aside. Gareth followed and, with the wall lamps casting muted illumination about the sinister chamber, glanced first at the wooden cross. That instrument of restraint stood empty and waiting. What they had been brought to see lay a short distance beyond.

The door closed with a subterranean boom and Gemma's eyes darted in alarm from Gareth to Victoria and Sophie. She at once attempted to rise from the heavy wooden chair, but Elaine, standing like a sentinel behind, placed a firm hand on each of her shoulders. As the others approached, she gazed straight ahead, her legs squeezed tightly together.

'Well, aren't we the centre of attention,' said Elaine. 'What a pity you can't greet our friends – shall I do it for you?' She lowered her head close to Gemma's and smiled with mock innocence. 'Hello Vicky, hello Gareth, hello Sophie. We've been waiting for you.'

Barbara joined her sister and both pulled Gemma forcibly up from the chair, Elaine's sequinned dress shimmering in the soft light. Sophie gripped Gareth's arm and whispered, 'Oh, poor Gemma.'

Gemma was moved a short distance from the chair before stopping an arms length before the wooden cross, where a length of iron chain hung from one of the ceiling beams. At its end, less than two metres above the floor, was an open metal link. Gemma, realising the purpose of this, began to struggle, her verbal protests reduced to an incoherent moan by the rubber ball lodged in her mouth. Elaine seized the metal ring at the base of the bondage glove and lifted it as Barbara held Gemma's shoulders. As her sheathed arms were pulled higher, Gemma doubled over until her head was level with her knees. With a click, Elaine secured the ring to the hanging link. Reaching down, she picked something up from behind the cross. From both ends of the steel bar hung a short strap. It took only seconds for her to secure one end of the bar to Gemma's right ankle and only a little longer to force the legs apart enough to secure the left. Elaine had ensured that Gemma was turned with her head towards the cross so that her most intimate places, revealed by the open-bodied tights, might be on full view to all. At last she stepped back and turned to the small, silent audience. 'Now then, what do you think happens next?'

No one spoke.

'Never mind, you've probably guessed anyway.'

In this assumption Elaine was correct. Everyone had noticed what lay on the chair next to the cross. From a short black handle, thongs reached spider-like over the edge of the seat. Barbara stood some way aside, watching not Elaine, but the three guests. Elaine picked up the whip and slowly walked around Gemma, letting the thongs trail across the floor and ensuring that they passed within her vision. She lifted the hem of the latex dress and draped it over Gemma's back, exposing her rear completely. Without a word the whip was raised, to swish and fall with a crack across Gemma's behind. Her muffled cry was masked by a loud gasp from Sophie, who placed fingers prayer-like against her lips. The whip hissed again. The next crack was louder. Gareth thrust hands deep into his pockets and shuffled uneasily. Sophie looked wide-eyed from him to Victoria, who stood with arms folded in expressionless calm. A third time the whip fell and Gemma's legs jerked, feet twisting in the cuffs. All heard the stifled protest.

Victoria was surprised when, as a fourth stroke rang about the room, a voice whispered softly by her ear, 'I think you understand, Vicky, don't you.'

Victoria whispered, 'Yes Barbara, I think I do,' and a fifth crack split the air.

Noting the communication between her sister and Victoria, Elaine lowered the whip. There was barely a nod from Barbara, but at once Elaine approached and stopped before Victoria, eyed her and lifted her hand. Laying in her palm was the leather handle; swaying beneath, the black thongs. 'It's a skill you may do well to acquire.'

Victoria glanced down briefly at the whip and her sharp eyes fixed upon Elaine's. The smile which crossed Victoria's face as she grasped the handle was one of complete assurance. In contrast the smile of response on Elaine's face was tinged with surprise as she stood aside to let Victoria pass. As Victoria reached the appointed spot by the helpless Gemma, a gasp of, 'Oh, Vicky!' came from Sophie's lips as Gareth stared with mouth open.

Victoria did not hesitate, nor did she glance back towards Elaine, but raised her arm at once and brought the whip across Gemma's twitching behind with a crack which echoed about the stone walls. Sophie's gasp was followed by another stroke and a low murmur of approval from Elaine. Barbara stood in quiet contemplation. Gemma tottered on the high heels as the next stroke fell and Victoria noted the reddened weals on her behind. She counted six strokes, each followed by a shivering moan from Gemma. Each was followed by a gasp from Sophie, whose fingers remained pressed against her mouth.

Victoria showed no indecision on that sixth stroke but dropped the whip at the base of the cross, knowing well she might have been expected to hand it back to Elaine. Her action said that Gemma's punishment was ended, whether others approved or not.

As Victoria rejoined them, Elaine took hold of Gareth's arm. 'Come along! You're not going to let us ladies do all the work are you, Gareth?'

Her kiss, falling on his cheek, came as a shock. He stared at her in mute amazement, but Elaine began to pull gently and he found himself following. At the bound and bent-over figure, Gareth looked about in confusion, only to see

191

Barbara usher Victoria and Sophie over to join them. But it was Elaine who once more demanded his attention, for her arms encircled his neck and her breath fell upon his face, warm, perfumed and irresistible. Gareth trembled, imagining she was about to kiss him again, but Elaine began to push him down to the floor, saying, 'Be the gentleman, Gareth. Give the lady a little consolation in her hour of need.'

He did not see who took hold of his arms. It could have been Victoria as well as Elaine, or even Barbara, for his wrists were enclosed simultaneously in the steel cuffs. Before he could twist his head about or voice any objection, ratchet locks closed and he was held once more a prisoner. He dared not protest; he simply obeyed and sank to his knees until his face was close to that intimate part of Gemma which had so recently been subjected to Elaine and Victoria's stinging attentions. Elaine ran fingers up Gemma's nylon clad leg and over the reddened behind. 'A little comfort Gareth,' she whispered, pushing him towards it. 'Come now, don't keep her waiting.'

Between the outspread legs, two blue eyes watched him from beneath the rubber ball, wet with saliva. His lips touched the warm and inflamed flesh. Gemma tensed.

'Please her,' whispered Elaine. 'Please her the way she pleased you at the dinner table.'

Gareth's eyes widened. Elaine's fingers fell and tightened upon his neck. 'Do it, Gareth. Show her – show me how good you are.'

Suddenly there was Victoria by his other side. 'We're all waiting, Gareth.'

He breathed the heat and perfume of Gemma's sex even before his lips touched. And when they did, and his tongue entered the sanctuary of her passions, it was only to find her hot and wet with expectation, for the whip had already fired her arousal and prepared her for this next act. His lustful tongue performed well, as Victoria knew it might. It taunted and teased the clitoris, darted deeper and alternately withdrew, glistening, to probe with exquisite delicacy about the sensitive puckering of the anus. His hands pulled her cheeks further apart to give him better access and Gemma moaned through the gag as though in pain. Gareth was aware of his own arousal asserting itself for the third time that day but knew his carnal debt must be paid before he could be master of his own body.

That Gemma's threshold was low was soon evident, for as the tongue flickered and squirmed, her moans became more insistent and she began to writhe against the restraints. At a discreet gesture, Sophie accompanied Barbara to Gemma's front where both supported her by the shoulders, for it appeared that in the turmoil which was taking over her body, she might be in danger of losing balance.

Gareth cared no longer that others watched but worked upon Gemma with greater fervour, his mouth closing upon her sex to drive the approaching climax. Her cries suddenly became louder; her body set as glass, only to shudder as if stricken by convulsions as the unstoppable tide of orgasm boiled up within.

They released Gareth first and he, on a gesture from Victoria, left the room at once. He gave no thought to the fact that the heavy door was already ajar, nor did he catch sight of the fleeting shadow at the end of the gallery as he emerged from the room, distinctly ruffled.

Elaine uncoupled the bondage glove from the hanging chain and proceeded to release Gemma's legs from the spreader bar. The ball gag was also removed but Elaine laid a hand on the leather sheath and looked at Barbara. 'Perhaps she ought to keep this on until we all go to bed.'

'Please,' put in Sophie. 'I don't think she should!'

Elaine looked at her with questioning amusement. 'Oh, don't you now? And what makes you think –'

'Why not give Sophie the key?' interjected Barbara.

Elaine hesitated. 'I – yes all right, why not.' She placed the small silver key into Sophie's hand. 'Well, dear, we'll leave it to you, shall we? But make sure everything is put away properly – Gemma knows where if you haven't yet found out!'

Sophie watched Barbara, Elaine and Victoria leave the

room. When she turned, a dishevelled Gemma was staring at her. For a moment, neither spoke nor moved, then Gemma sighed and laid her head on Sophie's shoulder. 'I don't know what to say. I don't know what you must be thinking.'

Sophie placed a reassuring arm about her. 'Thinking? I don't know.' Her eyes fell upon the whip, still laying by the cross. Her other hand slipped over the leather sheath which yet held Gemma's arms tightly secured. Her heart beat hard against the naked breasts and she knew that Gemma was aware of it.

'You understand,' said Gemma. 'You do understand, don't you?'

Sophie lifted her head and looked into the wide blue eyes but did not reply, for Gemma kissed her and Sophie returned the kiss. They remained with lips sealed together as though they had waited half a lifetime for that moment.

Eventually, Sophie took up the little key and released the locks on Gemma's restraint; one at each of the shoulder straps and one which prevented the heavy zip fastener from being pulled down to open the sheath. Sophie waited and helped where she could while Gemma removed, wiped and powdered her dress.

'I'll finish in here if you want to go to bed. I'm going down to the pool,' said Gemma when she had finished.

Sophie glanced at her wristwatch. 'The pool! It's almost one-thirty.'

'It doesn't matter, I used to do it a lot. We both did when – well never mind.'

'I'll keep you company if you like. It sounds like fun.'

'I'd like that, yes,' murmured Gemma, pressing a warm hand to Sophie's cheek.

The night air was still and warm as they slipped silently into the water. Sophie drifted on her back next to Gemma, hand in hand under the stars. 'Won't they be annoyed with us if they see the pool lights on?'

'No,' answered Gemma, 'they won't bother about that.'

Gemma talked about the house and the people who used

to visit. She confirmed that her role then had been much as it appeared to be now, though Sophie was not inclined to question her on anything too intimate in spite of what had happened, except for one small exception. As they heaved themselves on to the poolside, she remarked, 'I see you're shaved. Do they make you do it? I've tried it myself a couple of times.'

'Oh, no, it's nothing to do with them. Some of the guests liked it. Amber's the same. Tell the truth, I prefer it anyway.' She squeezed Sophie's hand. 'If you want, Amber's got a tube of cream stashed away somewhere.'

'I wouldn't mind, if you remember to ask.'

'I will in the morning,' replied Gemma. 'Let's sit on the grass for a while and dry off.'

They sat close together watching moths flutter about the poolside lamps and Sophie remarked, 'You must like it an awful lot here, despite – well – you must.'

'I suppose it stops me getting bored. Amber gets bored sometimes, she misses the entertainments.'

'It's a lovely place to be,' sighed Sophie. 'I wish I was lucky enough to –'

'Don't think about it,' interrupted Gemma, kissing her cheek. 'Only think about now.'

'Yes, I'll only think about now,' answered Sophie, slipping an arm about her waist.

'Now and nothing else.' Gemma kissed her on the lips as warmly as they had kissed in the tower. Sophie bit her ear gently as Gemma's hand slipped over her thigh and between her legs. Sophie recoiled and grasped Gemma's wrist.

'No – not here! We're in full view!'

'They're all in bed,' whispered Gemma, renewing her advances.

'Oh, God!' Sophie groaned, as cool fingers pushed down and spread the lips of her sex.

'You're like me,' murmured Gemma. 'We're two of a kind. I can sense it. I know it.'

'No, you don't know anything,' protested Sophie, opening her legs a little. 'How can anyone know?'

'I just know.'

Gemma's finger stroked and caressed, entering only far enough to arouse Sophie's clitoris until her sex was moist and inflamed. Gemma knew the contest would not be difficult. She knew that for Sophie, as well as herself, the ways of Sappho would not be strewn with obstacles. And she was responding, even quicker than Gemma had hoped, for she leant back on her arms and spread herself wider, allowing Gemma to kiss her breasts and warm stomach. Gemma clambered between Sophie's legs and seized her beneath the knees, lifting her legs up and apart to pay as lustful a homage to Sophie as Gareth had paid to her. Sophie fell upon her back with a moan and Gemma forced her knees almost against her sides in order to access fully that which she most desired. As Gemma's tongue spread a feverish arousal through her body, Sophie moaned and clasped the sides of her face as though in anguish. But it was when her tongue darted about Sophie's anus that Gemma discovered her most intimate secrets for she gasped and trembled in heightened ecstasy.

When the climax arrived, Gemma's tongue pushed firmly into her rear. Sophie cried out and writhed in a frenzy, shouting her orgasm to the living night.

10

The Closing Web

'What happened to you?' asked Victoria, sitting before the dressing table mirror.

'Sorry Vicky, I couldn't tell you, not without waking you up.' Sophie sat on the edge of the bed to watch Victoria's reflection. 'We went for a swim then – well, she needed someone to talk to. In the end, it was easier for me to stay with her. Sorry if it bothered you.'

'No, dear,' replied Victoria, plying a brush through her rich, brown hair. 'What you do is your business. I was a bit concerned, that's all. Next time, I'll know.' She wound up her hair and added, 'I'm going to have my shower in a minute.'

'Yes, okay,' muttered a preoccupied Sophie. 'Vicky, has anyone actually said how long we're here for? They haven't have they?'

'No, they haven't. But Gareth and I would have left on the fourteenth. That gives us eight days.'

'But that doesn't mean we're staying until then, does it?'

'They said we could and, well – after last night we seem to be a part of one big happy family. Are you saying you want to go sooner?'

'Go sooner – me! God, Vicky, it's the last thing I want. Tell you the truth, if they needed another bloody servant I'd –'

'Yes, I've quite taken to the place myself.' Victoria turned to gaze out of the window across the vineyards and towards the sunlit hills. 'But you've already seen how they treat their servants.'

Sophie gazed down at the carpet, wondering what kind of answer to give. Her dilemma was solved by a knock on the door. Victoria crossed the room and pulled the door open to be greeted by a smiling Amber in blue cotton dress. 'Not too early with the coffee am I?'

'Oh, no,' replied Victoria, taking the brass tray. 'Come in.'

'I can't,' replied Amber, reaching into her pocket. 'I'm doing breakfast this morning. By the way' – she produced a white packet and placed it on the tray – 'Gemma asked me to give this to Sophie.'

Victoria examined the packet, which contained something the size and weight of a tube of toothpaste. 'It's all in German.'

'It's depilatory cream,' smiled Amber. 'Easy to use, if you're interested as well.'

'Oh, how long do you need to –'

'Give it ten minutes and it will last a couple of weeks. You'll be back in England before you need to bother with anything again. There's plenty there.' Her eyes narrowed, 'Get Gareth to try it!'

'I just might,' mused Victoria as Amber continued along the corridor. She took the tray to the dressing table and held the packet up before Sophie. 'And here's a present from Gemma for you, well – for both of us I suppose.'

'Oh, yes, I'll give it a try after coffee.'

As Victoria poured the coffee there was another tapping on the door.

'That'll be Lord Muck,' remarked Sophie. 'He'll be wanting to scrounge our bathroom again.'

Gareth appeared in dressing gown, a large towel draped over his arm. 'Mind if I do the usual?'

He was already halfway to the bathroom when Victoria's voice caught up with him. 'Yes, we do mind!'

'What?' said Gareth, turning abruptly.

'We do mind! After the way you behaved last night – in fact, the way you've been behaving all along.'

Gareth stared in perplexity. 'Me? But I thought – look, you can hardly blame me can you? We all went up there and – and –'

'Well, Sophie and I have discussed the matter and we've made a decision.'

'Yes, we have,' agreed Sophie, hoping that what she was agreeing with would soon become clear.

'From now on,' continued Victoria, 'all privileges have to be paid for and that includes using our bathroom.' She looked pointedly at Sophie. 'Don't you think so, dear?'

'Oh, I do. He's been getting away with murder!'

'With murder!' echoed Victoria.

Gareth shrugged, 'Okay, see if I care. I'll use the spare one instead.'

'You can't,' responded Victoria, 'there's a blockage – Amber just said. They've already phoned the plumber.'

Gareth sighed. 'Go on then; what's it costing me?'

'Catch!' called Victoria, as the white packet flew through the air.

Gareth caught it and after a moment's scrutiny, asked, 'Am I guessing or are you going to tell me?'

'It's to remove unwanted hair,' said Sophie. 'We're going to use it so you have to as well.'

'Unwanted?'

'Yes,' said Victoria, 'you know where. Just leave it on for ten minutes. You'll love it, dear. It's supposed to increase sensitivity.'

Gareth regarded them with a broadly developing smile. 'And how do we prove this contention?'

'You'll have to wait and see, dear, won't you?'

'God, did that stuff burn!' said Victoria, feeling the caress of the morning sun.

Sophie, relaxing in the shade, agreed. 'Didn't it just. And poor Gareth, I heard him going on about it ruining his sex life.'

'Burning!' exclaimed Gemma, her head appearing above the edge of the pool. 'You did read the English leaflet didn't you?'

'Leaflet?' responded Victoria. 'I didn't see any leaflet. Amber said you just leave the stuff on for ten minutes.'

'Ten!' exclaimed Gemma, rising further out of the water.

'Ten minutes! No – it's only two minutes! Anything over five and roots are killed – it's almost permanent! That's what we did a year ago!'

Victoria sat upright. 'What! She definitely said ten!'

'Oooh-er!' gasped Sophie. 'Who's going to tell Gareth?'

'Never mind that, I don't like being tricked. That little cow's gone too far!'

'I'm afraid it's her nature,' said Gemma, 'given half a chance'

Victoria thought for a moment. 'Look, no one say anything about it. If she asks you Gemma, tell her we're hanging on to it. Say we haven't decided.'

'Keep her guessing,' added Sophie, knowing well they would need to take care not to reveal at the poolside that both were quite devoid of pubic hair.

'Yes, keep her guessing,' added Victoria, 'until I catch her out. Where is she, by the way?'

'She's in the lounge chatting to Barbara and Elaine,' replied Gemma. 'It seems rather private.'

Victoria relaxed back into the chair and closed her eyes. 'I'll think about this one.'

'Better make the most of today,' came Gemma's voice. 'They say we're in for a storm tomorrow.'

Fifteen minutes passed before Gareth appeared, strolling along the side of the house in blue denim shorts, paperback in hand, towel about his neck. He slipped off his shorts to reveal the small, gold and blue striped sun slip they had acquired in Florence. The matter of the depilatory cream was not raised, though Victoria wondered if he did not feel sore in more ways than one. His quick entry into the water might have been an indication, she thought.

A minute later, Amber appeared in brightly coloured beach dress, her expression betraying not a seed of guilt. 'Vicky, I think Barbara and Elaine would like a word with you.'

Victoria suspected another trick, but said in what she hoped was a convincingly casual manner, 'Oh, okay, I'll pop inside before I take a dip.'

She entered the heavily furnished lounge, incongruously

attired in patterned beach dress and sandals. Barbara and Elaine sat by the coffee table, dressed as usual in black. Victoria felt uneasy in the staid and mildly oppressive surroundings of this room. 'Coffee?' offered Elaine.

Victoria picked up the small cup and attempted to relax in the upholstered embrace of the old chair.

'Vicky,' began Barbara, 'we have all got to know each other rather well through chance circumstances. I suppose that happens more often than people realise. However, we have plans for this house which we think – we hope – may be of interest to you.'

'You see,' said Elaine, 'when we first arrived, we envisaged living a quiet life, almost in isolation, running the estate and growing old. Neither of us really wanted that and we might have ended up selling everything if circumstances hadn't proved to be different than we first imagined.'

'You three coming here,' continued Barbara, 'has made us think; made us reach decisions we might have put off for who knows how long. You have acted as a kind of catalyst.' She paused to refill her cup from the cafetière. 'You are the strongest willed of the three, Vicky. Strongest by far. Last evening, I think you showed your natural spirit and inclinations rather well.'

'Yes, last night,' murmured Victoria. 'It isn't something I do every weekend.'

'Of course it isn't, Vicky,' smiled Elaine. 'But it's what this house was about on those special occasions. Amber and Gemma were, as you realise, left over from those days and would be more than happy to see them return. They did rather well financially out of it, so we gather. We could all do that, Vicky, if we wanted to. Do you understand?'

'So you're wondering if I'll stay,' put in Victoria, calmly.

'We would ask you to consider a number of propositions,' said Barbara. 'We know you well enough by now, I hope, to rely on your discretion.'

'Oh, I can assure you of that. I'm as keen on keeping quiet about it all as you are.' She took another sip of the coffee. 'Well, I'm listening.'

* * *

Amber and Gareth had made small talk and watched Sophie and Gemma circling and laughing in the water under the blue sky. When they had climbed from the pool and put on their beach dresses, they walked hand in hand along the path which led from the garden into the vineyards.

'They seem to have hit it off all of a sudden,' remarked Gareth.

'Best of friends, aren't they.' Amber picked up the book he had placed face down on the table. '*House of* – mmm, I see.'

Gareth shifted uneasily in the chair as she examined the paperback, opening it at random to scan several pages. 'Rather naughty, isn't it, Gareth?'

'Er, well – I grabbed it at the shop just before we left England.'

'Stay in this place for long enough,' said Amber, running a finger over his shoulder, 'and you'll have enough material to write your own.'

'Chance would be a fine thing,' he replied, grinning. With the distraction of Sophie and Gemma gone, he found Amber's presence much more compelling. Burnished copper hair fell in a fringe across almond eyes – eyes which more than once glanced down at his own minimal covering, making him all too aware of the fact that she was attired almost from neck to ankle, whilst he was virtually naked. It should not have mattered; they were by a swimming pool in broad daylight. But it did. Only one other person could have made him feel so self-conscious, but he doubted if she or her sister spent much time in the sun.

'The other evening,' said Amber, 'I hope you weren't annoyed about – well, that little trick with the key.'

Gareth felt his face burning with more than the sun. 'Didn't have much say in the matter, did I. What made you so sure anyone would – you know –'

'I wasn't sure. Like I say, it was just a little game to see if anyone grabbed the bait. But, as it happens, I rather enjoyed seeing you like that. I find it a bit of a turn-on.'

He stared at her for a moment, aware of his arousal stirring against the pouch. 'I suppose that's the kind of thing you used to get up to is it?'

'Yes, sometimes. Part of the job, as they say. But I think it's fun anyway.' She stroked his shoulder softly. 'Especially if I like someone, Gareth. Do you find it odd? How would you feel? What I mean is, just the two of us, in private?'

He gazed across the pool, seeing nothing but her face in his mind's eye. 'God, you're pretty forthright aren't you?'

'You had no problems in the summerhouse, first time around.'

'That wasn't quite so premeditated.' He turned and grasped her hand. 'Amber, you're a bitch!'

'Of course I am,' she smiled, glancing at her watch. 'Look, I've got to push off and sort out the lunches, I'm afraid.'

As she arose from the chair, Gareth said, 'Okay – er, shall we meet later on?'

Amber leant over, eyes narrowed with wanton promise. 'What about five-thirty, dearest, on the landing?'

Gareth's heart was pounding. 'Yeah, okay. Five-thirty.' He watched her lithe form stroll casually along the side of the house and vanish around the front. Letting out a long sigh he relaxed back in the chair and glanced at the unread paperback. Disinclined to embark upon the effort of reading, Gareth closed his eyes, became aware of the chirping insects and played back his conversation with Amber like a closed loop tape. But though her image remained, across it was cast the shadow of another.

How long he remained suspended in thought he had no idea, but the silence was eventually shattered by an eager shout.

'Gareth!'

His eyes opened. 'Oh, Vicky! Hi!'

'Haven't you finished that pervy book yet?' asked Victoria, regarding the monochrome dominatrix on the front cover.

'Can't concentrate in this heat.'

'Just as well, because Elaine and Barbara wish to have a word with you and you'll need to be composed.'

'You wouldn't care to tell me what's going on would you?' he asked reaching for his shorts. 'After last night I feel anything could happen.'

'I wouldn't worry about that today, dear. This could be the turning point in your life, so if I were you I'd go to your room and smarten up first.'

'Collar and tie?' He grinned, picking up the towel.

'Not quite,' answered Victoria. 'But I'd get a move on.'

'It's like being summoned by the headmistress,' he mumbled, stepping towards the path.

Victoria watched him go and whispered, 'You never know, do you, dear.'

Once clear of the garden, Gemma said, 'I want to talk to you.'

'You are talking to me,' replied Sophie.

'No, I mean seriously.'

But neither spoke again until some minutes later, when they found themselves on a gentle, grassy slope above a wooded valley and out of sight of the house.

'Let's sit and be serious in the shade by those bushes,' said Sophie.

'Yes,' murmured Gemma, 'it's so oppressive today.'

'Well?' said Sophie as they spread their beach dresses on the grass.

'Sophie, you like it here don't you? I mean, at the Villa Raffaello.'

'Of course, you know I do.'

Gemma reached up and pushed the straw blond hair from Sophie's ear. 'You know they're going to start up again the way it was when Wallace was alive? After Barbara and Elaine arrived, Amber and I thought there was nothing to stay for, but when they kept things in the tower the way they were, we hung on. Now it looks as if – well, you saw last night – that's Elaine for you. She loves it, and that's what it was often about – at least for me. Even so, I did wonder what you would think if you had the chance to work here. Sophie, I'm asking if you want to stay.'

'Gemma, I love this place, I honestly do, but I never thought – whose idea is this? Is it just yours?'

'No, but if it wasn't what I wanted, I wouldn't be talking about it, believe me. They have to take notice of us – we're part of the fittings, remember!'

Sophie gazed across the valley. 'I'll need to think it over. It would be so easy to say yes.'

Gemma kissed Sophie's neck. 'Do think about it, Sophie, please.'

Sophie returned the kiss. 'Last night you said we were two of a kind. I'm not altogether sure I understood.'

Gemma looked into her eyes. 'My role at the house was to serve. I don't mean just food and drinks either. You know by now what a submissive – what a masochist is. Well, little blue-eyed, butter-wouldn't-melt-in-the-mouth Gemma's been trussed, flogged, displayed and fucked in every way imaginable, and probably a few that aren't. If I was to take three men at once right now, it wouldn't be the first time by any means. People think Amber's a slut! God! I'd go bloody mad if it wasn't for – well never mind. After what I've said, you might be on your way first thing in the morning.' Gemma took a deep breath. 'And you know, that's the irony of it. Some of the things they've done with me – I've sworn I'd leave so many times! And they wouldn't stop me either; I can bugger off whenever I want. The trouble is, I don't want to.' She laid a head on Sophie's shoulder. 'I've never felt I could talk to anyone like this until now. Sorry if I've spoilt things.'

They propped themselves up on their elbows, faces close. Sophie said, 'No, you haven't spoilt things. We don't know what other people get up to, do we, not a fraction of it. Personally, lovey, I don't care.' An arm slipped about Gemma's waist and they kissed. Gemma sighed as a finger slipped under the elasticated triangle, stroked and entered her sex, an unexpected but welcome guest. A voice in her ear whispered, 'You gave me such pleasure last night, I wanted to scream. Now I'm going to please you.' She bit

Gemma's lip. 'I'm going to make you come so hard you'll scream your head off. See if I don't.'

From the top of the stairs he observed Barbara crossing the entrance hall and about to leave the house. Reaching the bottom, he paused before the large mirror to assess his appearance. He was satisfied with the shirt and slacks but looked about, puzzled by the disappearance of Barbara.

The lounge door was ajar. Gareth tapped and peered into the room. From the group of armchairs about the low table a voice called, 'Do come in, Gareth.'

Gareth walked towards the figure in black. 'I saw Barbara going out. I wondered if I was still expected.'

The air was heavy with perfume. Elaine stood to face him, with a swish of satin on nylon. 'Oh, you certainly are expected Gareth. Would you care for a drink? Scotch, Bourbon, vodka, gin – just name it.'

He noticed the empty glasses on the table and asked, 'What are you drinking?'

'Fino sherry.'

'That's okay by me then.'

He sat and watched her move across the room to the glass-fronted gothic cabinet and return with a clean glass and half-empty bottle. Her black satin dress, long-sleeved and high at the neck was, like Barbara's dress the other evening, split high up the side. It revealed tantalising glimpses of a shapely leg in sheerest black. Maroon, stiletto-heel leather sandals were fixed by criss-cross straps at her ankles but the heavy, oriental patterned carpet rendered her tread soundless. The dress hissed against her stockings like a snake as she sat down. 'Now,' said Elaine, filling the glasses. 'I trust you are fully recovered after yesterday evening?'

'Recovered? I suppose I am, yes. I thought I'd dreamt it for a bit.'

'Well you didn't, Gareth, and I reckon you played your part admirably.'

Gareth cleared his throat and hoped she would not notice the tremor of his hand as he picked up the glass. The confidence he usually felt in the company of Victoria and Sophie, indeed with most women, was all but neutralised before Elaine and her sister. Waiting for her to continue, he wondered if the answer might lie in their lack of vulnerability. Gareth had always considered women more or less vulnerable until now.

'Gareth, do you look forward to going back to England?'

'I don't know.' He shrugged. 'It's where I live and where my job is.'

'And what if you had a job here? What if you had a situation where you could meet a number of quite important people in the financial world?'

'Job?' he asked in near disbelief. 'What sort of a job?'

'What you're already doing in London, dear, only a bloody sight less boring. I'm sure you know what I mean.' She downed the remains of the sherry and looked at Gareth's glass which remained part full. 'We need someone to run the estate accounts, it's as simple as that. Angelo helps but he's away on business much of the time. It's difficult for us and it really isn't what we want to do. Barbara prefers to deal with the import and export people the way Wallace did and I intend to take over the management of the estate when Sebastiano clears off to Rome in September.'

Elaine lifted the sherry bottle and, without asking, refilled both glasses. 'There would be other duties of course, Gareth: secretarial, domestic. But I'm jumping ahead aren't I? You may refuse outright or you may want to think about it over the next few days. You have time, Gareth, plenty of time, and who knows . . .'

Having eaten little for breakfast, the effects of the sherry at this unaccustomed hour were undeniable. He was tempted to express a positive interest at once, but fragments of caution assembled and he said, 'Yes – yes, I will think about it.'

Elaine crossed her legs to reveal more of the stockinged thigh. All the time her eyes were upon him and because they sat for the moment in silence, his nervousness increased. He imagined himself before her, in the situation he had been in with Victoria and Sophie in their bedroom. Had she bid him kiss her feet, he might have displayed but token reluctance. He could not help wondering what she did for physical gratification. Barbara had Angelo. Elaine seemed to have no attachments.

After the interview, he had changed again into swimslip and shorts, and returned to the pool where he had thought to find Victoria. She was not to be seen, nor were Sophie and Gemma. The paperback still lay upon the table but from underneath protruded a slip of paper. The note revealed, in Victoria's handwriting: *Gone for afternoon to Florence with Barbara. Amber says lunch for you, Sophie and Gemma in fridge. Back for dinner – V.*

Sitting down, his fingers touched the book, stayed a moment, then retreated. Whatever voluptuous goings-on it might contain would not hold their own against the images of Elaine or Amber. One offered prospects of, he knew not what – the other a promise, so it had seemed, of devious and carnal indulgence.

He was already perspiring in the heat and stillness. The swimming pool was mirror-calm. Only chirping insects prevented Gareth from forming an illusion that the scene before his eyes was some great, empty stage set beneath a blue-hazed dome.

A grating sound in the distance. Another close by, and voices.

'He's waking up!'

'That's a shame,' replied Sophie dragging a chair into position on the flagstones, 'we could have had lunch and watched him twitching.'

The light was intense and Gareth held a hand above his eyes. 'God, where have you two been?'

Sophie and Gemma sat close by in their beach dresses, dishes of salad and prosciutto ham, and a basket of bread rolls on the table before them. 'We've been walkies,' answered Sophie.

'We saw the note under that rude book,' said Gemma.

'You should be ashamed of yourself leaving that kind of thing laying about where ladies might see it,' added Sophie.

'Disgusting,' added Gemma. 'By the way, your lunch is still in the fridge.'

Gareth eased himself upright with a sigh.

'Yes, it is hot isn't it,' said Gemma. 'Not the sort of day for anything energetic.'

'Shall I bring some drinks out?' offered Gareth.

'What a good idea.' Sophie smiled.

Once Gareth was beyond the pool, Sophie said excitedly, 'I'll have to talk to Barbara and Elaine this evening, won't I! I'll have to tell Vicky and Gareth! I'll have to write home, or go back first then fly back again! God, the things I'll have to do!'

'You can leave all the legal details to Angelo,' said Gemma. 'But tonight, say nothing to anyone – play the sexy maid with me. That will tell them you've accepted.'

'What! In one of those dresses?' Sophie laughed. 'Yes, all right, I will if you are. It'll be worth it to see Gareth's face, won't it?'

It was gone five-fifteen when he left the bathroom. It had been his intention to go to his room and pull on shirt and jeans. Already primed by a heady mixture of excitement and apprehension, Gareth stopped abruptly when the voice behind said, 'Enthusiasm! Now there's a virtue!'

Amber, still in blue cotton dress, leant against the door of her room, head tilted to one side. He forced a smile. 'Well, we agreed, five-thirty so I was just –'

'Just what?' she asked moving up to him.

'Er, going to get dressed?'

'Really – why?' she pouted, putting her arms loosely about his neck.

'Well, it's usually the done thing when you've arranged to meet someone.'

'But not on this occasion,' she whispered, kissing him on the lips. Her warmth and perfume whispered intimacy as surely as did her voice. His developing erection confirmed his own response as he slipped arms about her waist to return the kiss with urgent passion.

'Steady on, we have lots of time today. Not like in the summerhouse.' Her fingers kneaded the top of his neck. His spine tingled as her fingers ran down his cheeks. 'Lots of time . . .'

He stared into her eyes, waiting, for she had the advantage of him and the moves were hers. 'The end room,' she said at last. 'You've never been in there, have you? It's above the lounge, never gets the sun, and it's furnished in the same horror movie style. Would you like to see?'

'If that's what you had in mind,' he answered, glancing at the solid, deeply panelled door. 'It looks quite forbidding.'

'It's the kind of room that wants to be left alone,' she whispered, pulling out an iron key. 'Fortunately.'

As they entered, Gareth knew this was a room which did not like sound. The heavy, ornate furniture and gilded rococo mirror was impressive but he had eyes only for the brocaded four-poster. He imagined it as a bescrolled royal barge about to embark upon its stately progress but set frozen in time. Quite a contrast, he thought, with the room in the tower where he had anticipated they would go. The soft grating of the key as Amber turned it in the lock reached his ears. 'Fascinating,' he murmured. 'It's like another world.'

'That was the idea. It's a room for seclusion and privacy. A room where you can be what you want to be.' She placed a hand on his arm. 'That's why we came here.'

Within the dimly lit depths of the four-poster, for the fringed brocades were pulled aside, there were clothes, shoes and other items laid out, waiting. Amber guided him forwards and when they stopped, her breath fell softly on his neck. 'Now we're going to play our little game so you must forget the world outside. We're going to visit fantasyland.'

He glanced inside the four-poster. 'Are you going to put those on now?'

She kissed him and smiled, 'No, dear, you are.'

Gareth's eyes widened. 'What! You want me to – to –'

'You can start with this.' She reached down and, with one finger, hooked and held up before him the smallest, sheerest and lightest of bow-sided black chiffon briefs.

'You're kidding! I'll never get into –'

'You will if you try, so please, let's not argue. They should give enough and I'd like to see you under control for the time being. It's part of our little game.'

He opened his mouth to protest but Amber continued, 'The stockings are self-supporting. Pull them all the way up and they'll stay.' She placed her hands on his cheeks. 'Everything else should be easy, even the high-heel sandles. I'll leave you to get on with it.'

'Leave?' he said weakly.

'My things are in the bathroom. I'll wait in there until you're ready.'

After the bathroom door closed, he stood for an age, listening. He could go with her demands or make his exit now. But no! She had the key. There again, it was quite private. Only a bit of fun as she had said. Only the two of them. Only a game.

The bathrobe fell away and his erection sprang flushed and free. He regarded it and the G-string. 'God this is impossible.' But with some concentration it proved possible after all. Just.

When Amber reappeared, she did not enter the room but leant on the doorframe with arms folded. The fact that she had not changed went unquestioned. She appraised the figure standing silently by the four poster. The maroon satin top fitted perfectly from flounced sleeves to wide collar, from the floppy black bow at the neck to the top of the high-waisted, flared mini-skirt in shimmering black satin. She was pleased not to be able to see the garter tops of the stockings. Pleased too, that the stiletto heel sandals in patent red fitted so well and were fastened correctly at the ankle by the small brass buckles. 'Don't move yet,' she ordered, stepping into the room and turning to the low chest.

From the lower drawer, she produced a loosely permed,

short blond wig. Gareth made no attempt to prevent her from placing it over his head and adjusting it until she was satisfied with the result. 'Wonderful!' she declared, backing away. 'Now, go over to the mirror and see for yourself.'

He beheld the image, blood coursing through his veins. It was an alluring, erotic image. Had it not been for the sensual feel of nylon and satin caressing his body, the stretching gossamer which cupped his aching penis like a hand, and the faltering steps he took on the high heels, he might have denied it as his own.

Amber slipped an arm about his waist. 'Doesn't it feel sexy? It looks fantastic!'

Did she realise how much he burned inside, how much he desired sexual release? Perhaps she did, just as he knew his desires must be subject to hers, for the image he had become had not the will to initiate, to persuade or even to resist.

'Do you feel guilty?' she asked softly. 'Some people do. Guilty about admitting how exciting it feels.'

The image opened its mouth. 'Yes, I feel ashamed to admit it.'

'Then we'll take away the guilt shall we?'

What she removed from the still-open drawer was not discernable until she swung about to face him. He gave no thought to the gleam of mischief in her eye once her intentions became evident. 'Hey, now – now hang on!'

The stout leather belt swung from her hand. Even one with no experience of such things would have understood its purpose. But Amber moved behind him and whispered, 'We've gone this far, Gareth. Let's not spoil things now.'

The belt constricted about his waist, then came the soft click of brass padlocks. He allowed her to take his arm and pull it to his side, where a strong leather cuff, riveted to the belt, lay waiting. Amber did not hesitate but slipped the band about his wrist, passed the brass loop through the reinforced slot in the leather and snapped on the lock. Placing the other arm in readiness was an admission to himself as well as Amber, that there was no turning back. Gareth flexed and tugged against the cuffs to test the restraint but found it impossible to pull free.

'Is that comfortable?'

'I suppose it is,' he answered dryly.

'Comforting as well, I should have thought. No more choice. No more guilt.' She turned for the last time to the drawer, this time producing an oblong of flesh pink plastic tape. Renewed apprehension seized him as she peeled away the backing strip. The intention was obvious and now his objections surfaced. 'Look – you can't! I won't be able to –'

'It's my game, Gareth!' she interrupted. 'And the tables are turned! I'll do everything but you must do as you're told.' She raised the adhesive strip and smiled, 'Close up tight, dear – yes, that's it – don't move.' The tape fitted coolly over his mouth, then stuck fast as she smoothed it out hard with fingers and thumbs. 'Good. That will stay in place for hours.'

At her last remark, his eyes widened and a muffled. 'Mmmm!' emerged.

'Well now,' said Amber, cupping his cheeks in her hands. 'Dressed in kinky female clothes, helpless and speechless. I wonder how you feel.' She let her hands fall down to rest on his thighs, just above the hem of the skirt. 'As you can't tell me, I'd better take a look for myself.'

Anticipation stirred him as she sank slowly to her knees and lifted up the hem of the skirt. And there was the bulging organ, coiled and straining in gossamer skin. She hoped the material would keep it secure, for whatever Gareth might be thinking, release of any kind was not imminent. His body tensed as she leant forwards and lightly kissed the exposed root of the aching penis. Her lips moved down further to feel hard heat through smooth nylon. 'I see you used the cream. Perfect!' She let the skirt fall back, and raised herself up. 'Gareth dear, how are you going to reward little Amber? People used to be ever so kind to me for playing games like this.'

Folding her arms, she looked him in the eye. 'Elaine has asked you to stay on and you haven't given her a definite answer; I know that. And do you know what else I know Gareth? I know you really want to. You can't help wanting to, any more than you can help the way you are right now. They've asked Vicky as well, and Sophie. Sophie's already made her mind up but you and Victoria must make your minds up this evening. In fact, dear Gareth, this evening is going to be my reward. The rest of our game! It's a pity you can't do for us all what you did for Gemma the other night. Yes, I know, I wasn't supposed to be there. Never mind, you can't talk about it now, and when you can, it won't matter.'

Reaching into her pocket for the key, she moved towards the door. Behind, a muffled protest as the restrained figure followed with precarious steps. The key twisted in the lock. As Amber pulled the door ajar, a coquettish smile touched her features. 'And you know what I'm like with keys, don't you? I have no idea where yours are. Perhaps Elaine has them!'

For a time he stood before the gilded mirror, tugging, turning this way and that until his arms ached and he had convinced himself for the tenth time that he was not going to get free of the belt and cuffs. And if he was unable to do that, he could not remove the tape, clothes, stockings or shoes.

The painted dial on the encrusted clock told him it was six-fifteen. Once more he found himself gazing at his own bizarre image, wondering what was to befall its physical counterpart. He decided to rest until Amber returned but found only the backless seat before the mirror comfortable because of his awkwardly placed elbows. For a while he sat with eyes closed, aware of the tactile sensuality about his body. Why he opened his eyes, he did not know, for no sound tripped his senses. But in the mirror he saw the door open and what it revealed took his breath away.

There was Victoria! There was Elaine!

Their images approached his image in the crazed glass and he wondered if it might be a dreadful illusion for all was locked in silence. Then there came a fusillade of voices as he struggled from the seat.

'I hope we're ready for our duties!' said Victoria.

'Yes, good and ready,' added Elaine.

It seemed that image was all, for he faced two more, quite as bizarre as his own. Each was clad in skin of smooth and polished black. Each a supple, python-limbed fetish icon, complete with patent black knee-boots bearing lethal, steel-tipped heels. Gareth looked on in deepening despair as he perceived the riding crop each of them wore at her belt.

'We're eating at seven,' announced Elaine. 'You will attend at table and assist the girls in the dining room. Of necessity, your duties will be undemanding and you will remain as you are until they are completed to my –' she turned to Victoria with a broadening smile. 'No, to our satisfaction.'

Gareth backed away, yanked hard on the restraint, twisted about violently and almost overbalanced. Withdrawing the riding crop from her belt, Elaine pointed at the open door. He stood paralysed with indecision until she stepped forward. With a viper hiss, the crop flashed and fell to give a stinging crack across the thinly veiled behind. Gareth's eyes started wide, but he obeyed and moved towards the door, any second thoughts being quashed by the sight of a stern eyed Victoria flexing her own riding crop in both hands.

As they ushered him towards the stairs, mind and body were in conflict. The sensation of the clothes, his helpless condition, the manner of the two beautiful women who had assumed authority over him – all conspired to intensify his arousal. Yet he willed it to be a dream, urged this reality to dissolve in the face of a greater one, for if this was true, it was not just the physical restraint that mattered but the trappings of humiliation which none could ever remove.

At the top of the stairs they hesitated and he raised a high-heeled foot timorously over the drop. At the same time, a steadying, compelling hand closed on each of his arms. The descent into servitude had begun.

Dinner was, of course, no ordinary affair. He entered, or rather was propelled into the room with a determination to undergo the forthcoming ordeal with bland stoicism, looking no one in the eye, standing out of the way and in the shadows whenever possible, thankful that two candles were the only source of illumination. He dared not consider how easily such intentions might be thwarted.

Standing by the wooden chest, he could hardly fail to notice Barbara. Metallic gold flowed over her lithe body. The sleeveless dress was cut daringly low, running to a deep V under her firm breasts and filled to the neck with a panel of finest black gauze. She turned abruptly and caught his gaze, smiled lipstick bright and spoke clear as a bell. 'Oh, my! What a perfect outfit.'

The ensuing silence was total. All eyes fixed upon him as a fugitive caught in the full glare of searchlights. Amber, her copper hair tumbled in delicate disarray about the black sequins of a vest-top dress, smiled mischievously.

Sophie and Gemma stood some way from the door and it was at once obvious that their attire was exactly the same as his own, though both were free of limb and speech. Elaine and Victoria turned about on clicking heels to admiring glances from the others. Each revelled in her own dominatrix image and Gareth wondered where it might all end. Would he be released to sulk alone? Were his pent up sexual tensions to be relieved? Would he be obliged to serve the carnal fancies of another?

The swarming speculations were dispelled when Victoria presented him with a brass tray. 'Now just hold it by the edges. You can manage that.' The tray pushed against his waist belt. Restrained hands instinctively took the cool metal, their distance apart being ideally suited to fit its width. 'Now then,' said Victoria – the Victoria who was once a friend and lover – the Victoria who was as deeply involved in his enslavement as any of them. 'As things are placed on the tray, just take them to the kitchen, and when the tray is empty, bring it back and wait. So simple! Best stand by the door. Out of sight, out of mind as they say. I think you'd prefer that wouldn't you, dear?'

So saying, she guided him to his allotted position, much to the approval of Elaine, who took her place at the table where she might observe him directly. Victoria proceeded to sit by Elaine's side; two figures in candle-lit obsidian sheen, casting dark, amorphous forms on the stone vaulting above.

Yes, his tasks were simple. Made all the simpler by the fact that he was seldom called upon at all. And so the distractions pressed in. Only minor in nature was the wisp of nylon hair which hung and irritated about his right cheek. So simple an annoyance to eliminate, had he possessed the means. The other asserted itself very differently, in the form of a regenerating arousal. Unable to see if his burgeoning penis pushed out against the skirt because the tray blocked his view, he was nevertheless reassured by the nylon skin which managed, just, to contain that part of his anatomy. Alas, even that consolation was soon to be revoked.

It happened when he was returning from the kitchen, three cups and the cafetière rattling on the brass tray. The voice called, 'Wait a moment!' He hesitated, halfway across the entrance hall, expecting Amber to appear. Instead, hands alighted on his thighs from behind. 'Don't move; we need a little adjustment here and there.' Fingers sped beneath the skirt. 'Especially here!'

Realising what she was about, Gareth attempted to pull free. Too late! The bows gave, releasing the tiny pouch which she promptly tugged away. 'Better get a move on with the coffee or Elaine will be mad.' He glanced aside to see her hurry off and disappear up the stairs. Ahead, the door of the vaulted room lay open, awaiting his return. When he entered, Sophie was clearing dishes from the table and placing them on the trolley. Gemma, he knew, was in the kitchen.

'Bring that over here please,' called Elaine, eyeing Gareth and the tray.

In the short route which took him around the table, behind Barbara and to the side of Elaine and Victoria, he thought hard of anything and everything to take his mind from the situation. But the proximity of the three women, their perfume, their very appearance, the whispering caress

217

of cool, smooth satin against his developing erection – all conspired against him. Amber reappeared and stared with a whimsical grin, not towards his face, but lower, to that which he knew was becoming very obvious.

'Oh, dear,' murmured Victoria, glancing down. A nonchalant Sophie transferred cafetière and cups to the table.

'For God's sake,' murmured Elaine, looking at the protruding form which had partly lifted the front of the little skirt. Even in his shamefaced confusion he perceived the fleeting hint of a smile cross Barbara's face, though she otherwise appeared unconcerned. Elaine scraped back her chair and stood up. 'This really will not do at the dinner table!' All eyes fell upon Gareth. To one part in particular: the quivering organ which would, should the material slip aside, be totally exposed.

'Vicky!' summoned Elaine, with her most purposeful expression.

Victoria arose as Elaine moved past Gareth, clicked a short way along the table and dragged out one of the empty chairs. 'Gareth, come here, please!'

Rooted to the spot, he watched in dismay as Elaine reached to the table, where laying almost obscured in shadow, were the two riding crops. His instinct to back away was countered by Victoria, who took one of his pinioned arms and pushed him towards Elaine. She reached out to seize his other arm and Gareth, tottering on the stiletto heels, was propelled into the gap left by the chair. Whether the manoeuvre had been planned or not mattered little as he was forced down over the table. A hand snatched away the brass tray and Elaine's voice rang out. 'Amber! Do something useful for once.'

Responding immediately to her command and gesture, Amber jumped up to reach across and assist Victoria by pushing on Gareth's shoulders. His struggles and stifled protests were to no avail nor, without the use of his arms, could he resist the pressure they applied to keep him face down against the table. At that point Gemma entered. After expressing a brief, initial surprise, she joined Sophie behind Barbara's chair to witness the spectacle of the skirt being pulled briskly up and over to expose a naked, twitching behind. A burnished black Elaine contemplated her victim. Not a breath could be heard.

But it was a mere hesitation. The crop flashed up then fell with a hiss against Gareth's defenceless flesh. The muffled howl in no way deterred Elaine from applying a second stroke. Nor a third and a fourth as the vaulted chamber echoed to each crack. Sophie and Gemma stared attentively; Barbara poured the coffee and observed the proceedings with impassive calm.

A final resounding crack, a final groan of muffled outrage, and Elaine turned to Victoria. 'Has he received a thrashing before?'

'No – at least not from me.'

'Then,' said Elaine, regarding the stripe-reddened behind, 'I think ten strokes will suffice on this occasion. Perhaps next time he'll wear something to keep himself under control.'

The sequinned Amber glittered in brown-eyed innocence. 'I'm surprised, I must say. He couldn't get the rest of the stuff on quick enough. I know I left him some briefs.'

A shamed and red-faced Gareth was raised up from the table. 'Oh, dear,' said Amber, 'if looks could kill.'

Elaine glanced at Amber with thinly disguised suspicion then addressed Sophie and Gemma. 'I dare say he won't mind eating with you two so I suggest you take him to the kitchen. The keys are behind the radio.'

After the dim vaulted room, the kitchen appeared bright and clinical. They stood and regarded Gareth as he tugged on the restraints and made sounds through the tape which probably meant, 'What are you waiting for?'

'Oh, poor boy,' cooed Sophie, closing the door and stepping forwards to place her arms about his neck.

'Yes, poor boy,' agreed Gemma, joining Sophie to offer embraces of her own. 'So ill treated and not an ounce of sympathy all evening.'

'Not fair is it.' Sophie smiled, feeling the regenerating hardness against her leg. 'Not fair at all.'

Both felt him shiver as a hand slipped under the skirt and cool fingers closed about the engorged shaft. Gemma tugged on the skirt until the waistband was freed from under the security belt. The hand which so voluptuously enclosed him only released its caress for as long as it took to remove the skirt. 'I think he should sit down,' said Gemma, scraping a padded stool across the floor.

'So do I,' agreed Sophie, releasing his inflamed penis and pushing its owner backwards until he was obliged to collapse on to the seat. 'He's not lifted a bloody finger all evening and his conversation's hopeless. There's only one thing left!'

'And that's already got him into trouble,' said Gemma, viewing the organ of lust, which thrust upwards and seemed to twitch with a life of its own. 'And look at that – smooth as a party balloon!' Silent thoughts might have passed between Gemma and Sophie. Each fell to her knees either side of Gareth. Sophie slipped a hand under his testicles; Gemma slipped fingers about the base of the shaft, saying, 'Well there's plenty of life in this!' Each moved closer and pressed lips against the bulbous head. Each teased it with her tongue, moving down over the foreskin and licking until it glistened wet. Gemma said to Sophie, 'I think one of us could – I mean, are you going to . . .'

Sophie contemplated the ample penis. 'Go on, why don't you?'

'You don't mind?'

'I don't own it,' answered Sophie, 'neither does Vicky. And he won't mind.' She looked up at Gareth, whose eyes were fixed intently on Gemma. His eyes glazed over and closed slowly. A groan sounded from Gareth's taped mouth as Gemma's full, soft lips closed over his penis head and moved downwards.

Sophie placed one hand on her cheek and the other about the base of the shaft. 'Are you going to give him a blow-job?' she asked, watching the tight lips move back and forth. The muted sound emitted by Gemma might have indicated yes or no, and she continued her work. But it was no more than a prelude. After a minute, she withdrew the reddened lance and quickly rose up to tug down and shake off her skirt and briefs. Sophie, her hand resuming the work begun by Gemma, was obliged to move as Gemma, with her back to Gareth, placed legs either side of his and positioned herself over the waiting organ. Sophie clambered around to the front and, pushing herself between the two pairs of stockinged legs, took hold of the shaft once more, feeling it quiver with impatience before the haven which so eagerly awaited to receive it. But Sophie placed her other hand under Gemma's thigh and held the two apart, for her own role in this game of lust was far from ended. With lips pressed against Gemma's sex, her tongue began its revelry within, fuelling already heightened passions, while her hand worked the soft skin of the eager penis. Not too quickly, for she knew the aching tensions within Gareth's loins must remain under control.

Gemma's hands clutched the back of her head, fingers pressing into her scalp. Sophie tasted flowing nectar, saw how inflamed Gemma had become, and so shared the busy tongue with her other charge by twirling it about the penis head. But lustful desire was taking the reins. Gemma pushed down until the reddened lips of her sex were poised but a finger's breadth above the seeping lance, which chafed and fretted to gain admittance. Sophie could keep them apart no longer but guided the head to its target and released her hold. Before her eyes Gemma thrust down with a gasp, sheathing the ample penis to the very root before beginning a rapid, rhythmic jerking of her body.

Even with the two so voluptuously united, Sophie played a part, for she tongued the clitoris and base of the shaft in turn, from moment to moment. The soft, repeated cries from Gemma and the muffled groans from behind said the climax was about to seize them. Sophie felt their bodies set as crystal. Gemma moaned as though beset by torment and Gareth jerked violently beneath in ecstatic release.

Sophie rested her head against Gemma's stomach, hearing her sigh deeply.

221

11

The Climax

'No,' he insisted, 'I'm not sulking! Do I look as though I'm sulking?'

'All right,' said Victoria, leaning against the door, 'then why not come down for breakfast?'

'You know why. Okay, I fell for it. I let her set me up because I thought it was a bit of fun in private. Then I find you're all in on it. Very bloody amusing that was!'

'I thought you played the part rather well, actually.'

'Didn't have much choice did I?' he responded, throwing unfolded items of clothing into his suitcase.

'Oh, don't give me that. You could have sat down and refused to move if you'd really wanted. You only came unstuck when Elaine did her bit with the riding crop. And if I read the expressions on the faces of those two correctly when you left the room, I bet you didn't do too badly in the end, either. It's all a bloody game, Gareth. All a charade! Don't you understand? Everything here is a charade!'

'I don't give a damn,' he retorted. 'In front of all of them, in front of Barbara! That's it as far as I'm concerned!'

'You'll be leaving on your own, you know that.'

'Yep,' he replied forcing down the lid of the case until it bulged.

'Well, it's been a holiday with a difference, Gareth. I don't suppose you'll be saying a lot about this place at the office, will you? You never know what else might get about.'

'Maybe that was their idea,' he responded, struggling to close the case locks.

'Maybe it was, but you'll never forget the Villa Raffaello. Things will never be the same again.'

He did not reply, but pushed his hands into the pockets of his blue jeans and walked over to the window. The sky was overcast with an odd pallid light picking out the vineyards and wooded hills beyond. In the courtyard below, Barbara walked with Angelo. They stopped from time to time, evidently to discuss various aspects of the buildings. When Gareth turned, Victoria was gone.

Crossing the entrance hall with the suitcase he heard voices from the breakfast room but saw no one. Outside the villa the air was a warm, oppressive blanket. The sound of his footsteps on the gravel hung in the stillness and an ominous booming sounded in the distance. There was still his coat and a small bag to retrieve from the bedroom. Leaving the case by the car, he returned to the house.

On the landing drifted a perfume. It hung in the air, invisible veils, cloying and sensual. He did not recall its presence earlier. It was not Victoria's. As he passed along to reach the bedroom door, it grew stronger.

Silhouetted dark against the window was a figure. It did not stir as he entered the room, but the air was heavy and encroaching with her scent. She wore the short, gold sequinned dress which had so impressed him on the first occasion. He thought at once what an odd time of the day it was that she should wear it again.

Elaine turned to face him. 'The storm is closing in, Gareth. Do you not hear the thunder? It's not unusual this time of the year.'

'That's my problem,' he muttered, heading towards the cupboard.

Elaine splayed fingers against her thighs. 'Oh, but Gareth, it isn't that simple. Once it begins, the country lanes between here and the main road will flood. It really does become very dangerous, Gareth, and it can happen so quickly.' Her eyes were fixed intently upon him. He tried to avoid her gaze, to avoid speaking to her. Outside the window, the sky had darkened to a rolling sea of grey and a low, resonating boom sounded from below the wooded horizon. Elaine moved closer. 'You shouldn't leave the house now, Gareth.' She placed a tingling cool hand either side of his face. 'You simply shouldn't.' Her breath enveloped him as a perfumed forest and their lips met.

'Christ, what are you trying to do?' he whispered.

'Do, Gareth?' she answered softly. 'Why, I'm saving you from yourself. Saving you from making a decision you will regret. You will understand.'

Beyond the window came a sudden and vivid glare and seconds later another boom rolled over the house. Elaine took his hand and both walked to the window. The courtyard below was deserted and sombre. Large raindrops splashed casually on grey cobblestones. Elaine said, 'Your case, Gareth. You ought to hurry down and bring it indoors.'

He glanced again through the window, wishing it to appear that his decision was a result of the oncoming storm and had nothing to do with Elaine.

It was so dark by the time he reached the entrance hall that someone had switched on the wall lights. A searing glare whitened the driveway and bushes as Gareth opened the door and felt the air alive on his face. He was halfway across the gravel when a thunderclap struck so close and loud, the very ground seemed to shake. The random spattering was becoming a downpour as he hurried back towards the house, and was about to become a deluge. Another flickering but this time the door was closed before the tide of sound crashed against the walls.

The case. He could leave it by the door, but if the storm was to last, he would need some of its contents. Perhaps he should return it to his room. As he crossed to the stairs, Amber appeared from the kitchen in her blue cotton dress and called, 'Hello there!' The lights faltered momentarily.

'That was a clever little trick wasn't it,' he said, turning to face her. 'Whose the next victim? Victoria? Sophie? No, it wouldn't be would it? You were all in it weren't you?'

'Gareth,' she clutched his arm, 'it was just a game. Just a bit of fun.'

'That bloody riding crop wasn't fun,' he countered, though the thought of it stirred him oddly.

'Perhaps it wasn't fair, but I didn't lie to you altogether – really I didn't. I thought you were – look, let's talk about it later; the two of us, alone.'

'You mean like last time!' he responded. Amber eyed the rain-spattered case as he left her. On the landing, he felt his heart beating and told himself it was only because he had hurried up the stairs with the extra weight. And there was her perfume.

She was still by the window when he entered the room, watching the rain pound the courtyard and lightning lay bare the sky. He was not sure if she was aware of his presence until she spoke. 'I'm glad you're back, Gareth.' She turned and approached as he placed the wet suitcase by the end of the bed. 'You are annoyed with me, Gareth, unhappy with the way I treated you.' She slipped her arms over his shoulders. 'But now you're back and we can reach an understanding.'

His arms were about her slim waist before he realised what he had done. Her body was firm, lithe and warm. Her kiss burned through every nerve and fibre. Squeezing her tightly, his fingertips touched the zip at her back and moved up the metal pathway until they found the tab. But Elaine looked deep into his eyes. 'Oh, no, Gareth. Oh, dear me, no.' If the words had come from one with a gun at his head, they could not have been more effective.

'Then why?'

She continued to hold him. 'Some things we have to work for. It can take a long time.'

The storm was growing and the room lit up fitfully moments before each detonation.

'Work for?'

'Oh, yes, dear Gareth. We offered you a position here did we not? You walked out a short time ago, intending to leave. I wonder how far you would have got had it not been for the storm. Another little hotel? On your own with no company and hardly a word of Italian? Well the weather has saved you from that and given you the chance to think.' A lurid glare filled the room and at once the air shook with a shattering double report. Gareth looked to the window to see the hills all but obscured by the torrential downpour. Elaine appeared hardly to notice, but let her hands fall about his upper arms. 'It is an offer you may wish to reconsider, Gareth, for you will serve me personally. Do you understand?' He gazed into her eyes. The storm seemed diminished by her presence.

'You mean we – the two of us –'

'Sex, Gareth? Why don't you say the word? Christ, you've had enough of it since you arrived that first day! You've fucked both the girls even if it wasn't quite the way you usually go about it.' He did not respond. 'We all need our little diversions but mine, Gareth, are on my terms. On my terms only!' She released him and backed away. 'You're lucky, really,' she continued. 'You might find you can't leave here for days if this keeps up. You can treat it as a trial period if you have the nerve.'

'Have the nerve?'

'Yes, Gareth, the nerve. You may not be up to it in the end, and I of course may not consider you satisfactory. I assure you I can be rather demanding.'

'You mean last night – that's how you'd want me to –'

Elaine smiled, 'That all depends. Perhaps not for a while. I know you would prefer to keep that side of it discreet.'

'But Amber,' he began, 'she's the one who talked me into all the . . .' He pointed to his own body.

'Oh, her. Yes, she loves the theatricals, that's why Wallace gave her the job. But I, Gareth, demand complete obedience. Whatever means it takes to enforce it I am more than happy to use and the way the one in servitude is attired should reflect that.' She gazed about the room and up at the ceiling. 'I can't help but think this house was a godsend.' Then once more her eyes were upon him. 'Are you willing to make the commitment, Gareth, even for a few days?'

His eyes passed over the curves of her sequinned body to the shining cascade of long brown hair and a face almost stark in the pallid light. He heard a voice next to his ear. His own voice, biscuit dry. 'All right. I will.'

'You must swear Gareth. Swear on your word of honour. I think you have honour don't you?'

He could not avoid her eyes. 'If it's only ourselves, yes, I swear.' Light flickered across her face and thunder crashed as if sealing his promise in some great and secret vault.

'At least we're out of the storm in here,' said Sophie. A subdued booming could still be heard through the stone walls, but the tower rooms were windowless. Sophie adjusted herself against the upholstered rubber side of the shallow, circular well which they had referred to as the cockpit. A heavy odour of latex emanated from both this and the garment which enclosed her upper body in gleaming black. Laced through brass eyelets at the rear, it held Sophie in totally secure comfort, with arms inside and folded across her middle. Apart from the straitjacket, her attire consisted only of gossamer black stockings with lace garter tops. Her patent leather sandals had been removed and stood outside the enclosure next to an identical pair, the owner of which knelt upright close to Sophie. But Gemma's restraint was more comprehensive. Her arms were folded tightly behind her back, held in a smooth sleeve of heavy black rubber which extended from armpit to armpit to form a squared letter U and was laced securely from the elbow to the top of each arm. Of her face, only the area around the eyes showed, for her head was enclosed by a sleek helmet of the same material as the restraint. Below the cluster of breathing holes about the base of the nose protruded a short tube from which bobbed and swung a rubber inflation bulb. At first, Sophie had not understood why Gemma should be denied speech.

In the silence, she recalled clearly the events which had led up to the situation.

* * *

Victoria had approached her when they sat reading in the lounge, trying to ignore the thunderstorm which had gone on all morning and seemed as though it might never stop. She informed Gemma that Elaine wished to see her and Sophie noted the look on Gemma's face. It reminded her of her school days, when someone was ordered to the head teacher's office but not told why. Victoria sat in Gemma's place and said calmly, 'It's time to begin, Sophie. Time for you to experience one of our little rituals.'

Sophie remained silent and imagined herself as Gemma had been that previous evening so that both fear and sensuality uncoiled within. She was aware how Victoria had formed an alliance with Barbara and Elaine, just as she had become attached to Gemma. Victoria leant closer. 'You must come and join her, dear. She wants that – I know she does.'

Sophie wavered on the verge of refusal but the blood stirred in her veins as she heard herself say, 'I suppose I might, if I knew what was going to happen.'

'Now, that would spoil everything, wouldn't it?'

Other questions faltered behind Sophie's lips but she let Victoria take her to their room to shower and put on the stockings and shoes. When she left the bathroom, Elaine was there too. It was then, without a by-your-leave or a hint of concern regarding her acquiescence, that they took hold of her arms and fastened her into the restraint. Had it been only Elaine, she might have refused outright, but it was Vicky as well, and Vicky was her friend. So she had said nothing.

'Did you know I'd be here too?' asked Sophie.

The rubber bulb danced as Gemma nodded an affirmative.

'Is that why you can't speak? Is it because you know what's going to happen – because they don't want you to tell me?'

Gemma remained still and Sophie struggled up to face her. 'It's that bad is it? I mean, it's something bloody awful!'

Gemma let out a nasal 'Mmmm!' and moved closer until each could feel the warmth of the other. Sophie wanted to kiss her lips but the helmet prevented that, so her mouth fell instead to her breasts where her tongue sucked and twirled about reddening, swelling nipples. Gemma's response was a low moan and Sophie saw that her eyes were closed. This was encouragement enough and it fuelled her enthusiasm to the point where her attentions were drawn elsewhere. Neither was conscious of the opening door as Sophie's lips brushed moth-like down Gemma's stomach to find the heat of her sex.

'Well, here's a fine state of affairs!' exclaimed Elaine, yanking the three-tailed strap between black-gloved hands. 'We turn our backs for a few minutes and look what happens. We should have gagged both of them.'

Victoria also held a three-tailed strap. She grinned and followed Elaine to the edge of the cockpit. Sophie, her face a picture of dismay, and Gemma, her eyes darting from Victoria to Elaine, struggled in their restraints, trying to disengage from each other. It was the excuse Elaine needed and, standing over the cockpit, she found their naked thighs and behinds an easy target for the strap. Resounding cracks echoed, with Sophie's squeals, about the room, to cries from Elaine: 'Stand up you little sluts! Up! Both of you – up!'

Victoria studied her technique with the strap. Sharp, rapid strokes were administered to both with undeniable skill and effect, for Sophie and Gemma were soon standing and cowering together in the enclosure. And for the first time, they were able to appraise their untimely visitors. Elaine's black satin shirt top shimmered in the mellow light, as did the long, red satin pencil skirt, split up the front to expose, as she moved, a leg clad in finest black fishnet. Black, too, were her patent leather slingback shoes, poised on high stiletto heels. Earrings glittered and swayed beneath rich, flowing hair, banded at the top of her head into a long pony-tail.

Victoria's hair was clipped up in swirls. Her short tunic, like her high heels, was of blue vinyl and she wore sheer black stockings. The vinyl belt at her slim waist was white, as were the trimmings at her breast pocket and collar. Sophie wanted to ask why she had presented herself as a nurse but dared not speak. Elaine's voice cut the air as she glared at Gemma. 'Out of there – now!'

Gemma stepped over the raised rubber edge to face a stern Elaine, who pointed to a nearby chair and ordered her to sit. Her stay in the chair was brief, lasting long enough for them to fit her sandals and do up the ankle straps. Elaine made her rise and, as both proceeded to the door, Victoria turned to a dishevelled Sophie and said, 'Out you come as well, dear!'

'Vicky, why are –' Sophie began. But Victoria cut her short with a terse, 'No questions now! Just sit in the chair and we'll put your shoes on, too.'

Sophie obeyed quickly enough but continued. 'You're not the Victoria I knew. You're just not!'

Victoria stooped and proceeded to fasten the shoes. 'You hardly know me at all, Sophie, just as I didn't really know Gareth until we came to this house. I'm not even sure how well I knew myself, but I can assure you I'm certainly finding out now and so are you and he!'

'But we're all friends still, aren't we Vicky – I mean you wouldn't let them –'

'Friends? Did either of you think of that when you were giving him a blow-job in Arezzo? And what about the hotel in Lucca? I'm only gone a few minutes and there he is screwing you up the arse!' Victoria stood up and gazed down at her. 'Tell you the truth, dear, now I've had plenty of time to think about it, I've come to the conclusion that you – both of you, probably wanted to get caught. It's part of the turn-on isn't it?'

Sophie's hazel eyes widened, 'But Vicky – the three of us and you and I – we all –'

'Oh, I wouldn't dream of denying how much I enjoyed that! Yes, face-sitting and fucking each other was great fun. But it was a journey of discovery and now other doors have opened. What I see beyond them is even more satisfying.'

'How very true,' came the voice. 'It certainly makes me realise what I've been missing all these years.'

Elaine approached the chair and moved to Sophie's side. 'Well now, I think we should go and join your little friend, but first . . .' Elaine's hands moved quickly, one pushing the red rubber ball into Sophie's unsuspecting mouth, the other pressing against the back of her head. Victoria moved promptly to put her fingers in place of Elaine's upon the gag, enabling Elaine to seize the two strap ends, pull them tightly and buckle them together at the rear of Sophie's head. Two pairs of hands lifted Sophie up and to the sound of stifled protests, ushered her out through the door and into the gallery.

Lightning seared the stone walls and Sophie blinked, startled. She had all but forgotten about the storm which continued to afflict the land, though soon there would be other distractions.

On entering the second room, Sophie at once spotted Gemma, hardly three steps away. Still wearing the restraints, she was contained and held by straps within the narrow cage. Apart from the eyes which fell upon Sophie, and the shivering rubber bulb, she was quite motionless.

So engrossed was she by the sight of Gemma, Sophie only realised what lay before her when they were almost upon it. There, in sinister purposefulness, waited the chrome and leather chair. Beside it, in identical uniform to Victoria, stood Amber, wearing a devious smile. Sophie gave out a plaintive 'Mmmm!' and tried to halt any further advance but her action elicited a stinging crack across the behind as Victoria applied the strap, followed immediately by another from Elaine. Sophie jumped rather than walked the last few steps. Amber moved forward and Sophie was manipulated forward by three pairs of hands, turned about and lifted, struggling and twisting against the straitjacket, into the cool embrace of the chair. Pungent black leather slid beneath her body but there was no time to think, for scurrying hands whisked gleaming black straps about her neck, waist and enclosed arms to the swish and rattle of chrome buckles. Her flaxen hair spilt over the blackness of the headrest and straitjacket. Her legs were seized and lifted high and wide apart, only to be secured with more straps into padded U-shaped rests at the ends of the chrome bars, springing out at an angle from each side of the chair.

But only when she was secured in this voluptuous display before them did Sophie's eyes take in more of her surroundings. By the wall, watching intently but rendered indistinct in a black dress, sat Barbara. Much closer, on a bright chrome stand, was suspended a pink rubber hot water bottle from which spiralled a length of clear plastic tubing. Her eyes followed it down to see, swaying at the end, the pink plastic nozzle equipped, where it joined the pipe, with a small valve. It took little imagination on Sophie's part to comprehend its purpose, though her knowledge of such things inhabited a world of fantasies to which she would never have dared admit. Faced with the reality, Sophie appreciated ever more the futility of struggle.

It was Victoria whose hand took the pink nozzle and passed it under Sophie's upraised legs: Victoria who held it for a moment over the ceramic bowl beneath the chair and released a little of the liquid, causing small, trapped bubbles to jerk within the pipe. It was Victoria's rubber-gloved fingers which squeezed a little clear lubricant jelly from a small tube on to the tip of the nozzle.

Sophie stared, mesmerised, as the spout disappeared from view below the bulge of her folded arms, but stiffened suddenly as the cool and moistened head of the object pushed against the tightened daisy of her anus. She cried out through the ball-gag and squirmed but nothing could prevent its progress as the nozzle pushed cool and insistent into her rectum. Fingers twisted the small valve, unseen, but the effect was instantaneous and electrifying. Bubbles scurried down the shivering pipe at her side before the surge entered her body.

Elaine was framed between her legs and at her other side was Amber, who reached down to the bowl. The sound of swirling water was heard. A quiver shook her body as the

232

nozzle slowly withdrew. Throbbing drums began to beat inside her. The chair itself shook as Amber twisted a large chrome wheel at its side and Sophie felt her balance alter. She was moving forwards and tilting down. So far, in fact, that the white ceramic edge came into view just as, further back, a part of it pressed under her thighs. But the throbbing had become a whirlwind; she willed herself to contain it but to no avail, for the pressure had increased to bursting point and she was taken over by that which would have no thought for dignity or decorum. There came a long moan and Sophie's body discharged its contents forcibly into the gurgling maelstrom beneath. Shame and ecstasy mingled and she could not discern one from the other.

Sophie closed her eyes and waited. What now – release? No, for fingers were at work again, slipping with ease about her sensitive groin and spreading the lips of her sex. But attention was also paid to her rear and Sophie moaned loudly as a finger slipped without resistance up her back passage. Even the motion of the chair being tilted back to its former position hardly detracted from the voluptuous sensations spreading within. Had Sophie been of a mind to deliberate, she might have considered herself cresting the final rise before the plunge into orgasm, but the withdrawal of the fingers caused her to open her eyes.

Barbara had left the chair and moved closer to join the small group whose attention was upon the object that now rested in Elaine's hand. Sophie was also transfixed by its appearance and dark churnings of another kind stirred within her belly. The two-pronged weapon of lust glistened with lubricant. Each member, an ample and realistic penis in flesh-coloured latex, both sprang together out of the same base, from which trailed a black electric lead.

'Shall I do the honours?' asked Victoria.

'Please do,' answered Elaine as Amber once more began to rotate the wheel.

The chair shuddered backwards and when it stopped, Sophie's body was horizontal, her stiletto heels pointing up towards the ceiling. Four pairs of eyes looked down upon her helpless form as the dildo touched coolly against her sex. For a time, Victoria let the bulbous head course back and forth, lingering at the portal and teasing the clitoris while its companion stroked Sophie's sphincter with a cool, exquisite touch.

A switch clicked and both shafts began to sing like a tuning fork. Springs of shameful ardour uncoiled through her body as it simultaneously spread the engorged lips and eased coolly into her anus to begin the advance. Sophie drew breath, closed her eyes and stiffened involuntarily as both shafts pushed slowly and remorselessly inside until she was speared to the hilt. Control of her passions slipped from whatever grasp she once possessed. The vibrations passed through every nerve and vessel until her bound body sang in harmony.

Unseen hands stroked the hair away from her cheeks but it no longer mattered who was present. Sophie worked her pelvis about the double organ as another hand caused it to pump back and forth. Within her was a burning effervescence and an all-consuming lust. Her body she could not move but her head rolled from side to side and her thighs shook as the fires of orgasm took hold. Sophie's cries echoed about the chamber like the shrilling scream of a banshee.

Her body still trembled and her mind whirled as the dildo was slowly withdrawn. Then she heard Victoria's voice. 'She comes very quickly, don't you think?'

'Yes, just like our little friend over there,' replied Elaine. 'Perhaps we should give them a few toys and let them sleep together.'

'With the restraints on, of course,' remarked Victoria, as Elaine and Amber released the chair straps, 'otherwise they'd exhaust themselves and be no use for anything!'

'My, look at the time,' said Elaine, glancing at her watch. 'I really must get on with things or there'll be no afternoon left.' In parting, she offered a smile to Victoria, an expressionless glance at Amber, and a knowing look to Barbara. Victoria observed her pick up the three-tailed strap.

* * *

For the second time Gareth had found himself in that oddly subdued room where the four-poster reigned supreme. Elaine stood by the bed and whispered, 'It's a good meeting place, Gareth. Don't you agree? Quite cut off from the rest of the house – even more than the tower I always think.'

Gareth did agree and said so. With her black satin top and split red skirt, Elaine appeared quite as appealing as in the sequinned dress but rather less approachable. He decided that the skirt was worn to deliberately distract him, especially when it exposed most of her leg, sensually sheathed in fine black net, not to mention the stiletto heel sandal in which her foot was poised. The heavy brocade curtains damped the booming thunder and allowed, at the edges, only the merest flickering from the electrical display beyond the window. Much of the room was in shadow, the only light coming from a bedside lamp with fringed and embroidered shade.

'Gareth,' Elaine whispered. 'Gareth, come here.'

He approached her in a manner some might have described as hesitant. He would have called it apprehensive. Elaine raised a hand and placed her fingers upon his cheek. Her perfume was lighter and more exotic than before, the heat of her body more intense. Her kiss had brushed his lips like a feather. 'Now Gareth, forget about the world outside – the thunder, the rain. All that matters is ourselves in this locked room, a long way away from everyone else. No one knows. Not Amber, not Victoria. No one.' She plucked open the top button of his shirt. 'Gareth, take it off.'

He did as she wished, and continued to disrobe, for through barely a gesture, she bade him remove sandals and trousers which he placed over a nearby chair. As he faced her, she glanced at the fine nylon pouch which held in containment the much aroused penis but as yet gave no indication that this should also be taken off. A figure in chiaroscuro, she reached out to draw him towards the bed, her fingers with a spider touch about his arms and body, skimming, electrifying his spine and touching the thin cord about his waist. 'Time to fulfil your promise Gareth, dear. Time to push through the cobwebs and into our secret lair.'

Elaine reached into the hidden domain of the four-poster to withdraw something which glinted soft in the mellow light. It fell open in her hands, smelling oddly synthetic but sounding disturbingly familiar with the click and ping of metal buckles. He considered pulling away, but her arm passed about his neck and her lips gently brushed his ear. 'This is the path you must take, Gareth, to really find me.'

He felt his heart pounding as she placed the metallic grey vinyl over his shoulders, pushed each of his arms to cross behind his back inside the sleeve, pulled strap and buckle-hung edges about his body to join at the front and engaged the first strap at his neck. It had all been so easy, the way she had charmed him. Her perfume and warmth, her calm authority overlaying a well of sensual power – all conspired to negate his will. He let her continue, passing straps quickly through buckles, tightening and securing them down to the waist until he was encased in a tensing cocoon of gleaming vinyl.

'Oh, what a good boy we are,' she murmured, running hands over the smoothness of the steel beetle carapace. She gazed at him with a light of triumph and mastery in her eyes. 'Now you must wait until I return. You will learn patience in this room, Gareth. You have no choice.'

'Wait? What d'you mean, wait?'

Her lips brushed his cheek. 'Just for a time, Gareth. There are things I must do. You will be quite alone until I return. Quite alone.'

The sound of the key turning in the lock was still fresh in his mind although he knew from the glass-domed clock that an hour and more had passed since her departure. He had struggled, of course, twisting and heaving in the embrace of the restraint, but it was impossible to escape; his arms, folded and contained at the rear, were held fast. In the end he sat and listened to the softened, filtered boom from that other world which once had seemed so real, and considered the aching and swollen form of his contained penis, marvelling that he had let her do this to him.

A sound. The scraping of a mouse? No – a key turning in the lock. Seated on the edge of the bed, framed between hanging brocades, he watched the door open. The figure of Elaine slipped through in silence then stooped to relock it. Next to the lamp on the small semi-circular table, she laid the key and the three-tailed strap, knowing his eyes were upon it.

She stood before him but did not at first speak. Her fingers plucked and opened the satin bow at her neck. With deliberate slowness, eyes fixed upon his, she removed the black top, letting it shimmer down on to the chair by his own clothes. He gazed at her firm breasts, desperate to take them in his hands, as his penis stirred and strained for the freedom it, too, was denied.

'Get up!' she ordered at last, dragging a heavily upholstered chair to the end of the bed.

Gareth arose and watched her position the chair. Elaine turned abruptly, 'Down on your knees!'

'What?' he responded.

'You damn well heard me!' she cried and her hand flew up to catch him a resounding slap across the mouth. 'Down!'

He quaked on the verge of protest but held his breath and dropped to the floor. The warmth of her body, so very close, bathed his face, but there was not a trace of warmth in her voice. 'Very good, Gareth. Now listen to me and remember what I said earlier. I am not here for anyone's convenience, Gareth – you are! I do not expect to be offered service; I do not expect to wait until others feel inclined – no! I expect it when it suits me – on demand and on my terms. Oh, I know what you want! That is why you're wearing a restraint now and always will when we are alone together. And if it serves my purpose you will be restrained from head to foot – totally and utterly! Do you understand, Gareth?'

Gareth was at once angered and deeply aroused but

237

stayed rock-still while Elaine reached aside to pick up the strap then proceeded to the chair where she sat before him. The red skirt fell open to reveal her legs as she slowly crossed them to the whisper of satin on stocking. A stiletto-heeled foot swayed a hand's breadth from his face. 'You think the other one's a bitch, Gareth, don't you! I know you do.' He stared from her to the swinging shoe. 'She loves to fool around – loves her little tricks, loves to lead people on. Even tries it with Angelo and Christ knows who else around the estate! But I doubt you've never met a real bitch, Gareth. Until now, that is.' She yanked the strap between clenched fists and pushed the foot closer until the slender, metal-tipped heel almost touched his nose. 'Kiss it!'

Gareth blinked and focused on the patent leather. He had it in mind that unless he responded as she wished, the consequences might not be to his liking, and he was in no position to resist. Tentatively, his lips touched the glass-smooth side of her sandal.

'We're not really trying are we!' came her voice. 'And my patience is on ice today.' Elaine leant forwards and let the strap sway above her foot. 'You may choose between the two, Gareth, I'll oblige either way. Now, start at the tip and work up – with reverence. Reverence and enthusiasm, dear!'

He kissed the tip of the sandal, where her fishnet clad toes protruded, and let them push into his mouth. The thought of where it might lead drove him on and he could not deny to himself that the enthusiasm she demanded was not in part genuine. He pushed his lips between the thin straps, tasting and smelling the rich leather, until he reached her ankle, kissing and biting gently. Here, he wondered if he should go on, and might have hesitated if the leg had not pushed out further. At least, the doubt was gone. At the softer flesh higher up, fingers descended on the back of his head, nails digging into his neck, and pushing him against her warmth.

He had reached her knee and the cleft between her crossed thighs when she grasped his hair and pulled him

238

away. She arose with a satin swish and reached behind her waist. The long skirt loosened and slipped to the floor. Elaine stepped out of it and, pushing it clear with a toe, lifted that same foot and placed it on the chair with her knee by his face. Gareth's eyes followed the curve of her thigh, past the fine black net and the narrow garter tops of her stockings, to the shadow-sheer briefs fitting like a skin over her sex. He held his breath as he gazed worshipfully on the luscious prize he had longed for. Her voice cut through the haze of his reverie. 'Are we paralysed?'

He continued beneath and inside the softness of her raised thigh, fuelled by her sensual warmth and perfume, switching from leg to leg as he neared the ultimate goal. Her fingers had returned to his neck, kneading his flesh as his lips caressed the bare skin above her garter tops.

He was at the focus of her lust, mouth and nose pressed against the heat of her silky smooth vulva: a wandering soul close to sanctuary. Tonguing and probing, he attempted to pull away the tight elastic with his teeth, whilst his own organ felt about to burst from the confines of the pouch which held it cupped like a tiny hand.

Again she thrust him away, as though with utmost contempt. 'Get on the bed!'

He eyed her with surprise and began to move, but not quickly enough. Elaine seized the strap and, as he struggled from his knees, swung it hard to connect with a resounding crack across his behind. 'On that fucking bed!' she yelled as he almost lost his balance and narrowly avoided sprawling on the floor. Again the strap fell but his verbal protests only fuelled her zeal to punish. Several rapid strokes connected to his behind and thighs as he scrambled, fell and rolled into the brocaded depths of the four-poster. She was at once scrambling beside him in the confined space, seizing his ankles and hauling them upwards. Gareth felt no inclination to resist as, clasping his feet in one arm, Elaine reached quickly up into the dark canopy and pulled from its secret folds a pair of leather cuffs fixed to a black iron chain. With a speed and ease which, despite the circumstances, impressed him, she buckled the cuffs about his ankles, pulling his behind clear of the heavy bedspread, his upper body resting on his contained and folded arms.

Elaine's eyes were fixed upon him as she quickly tugged down the little briefs, cast them on to the chair and, recovered the strap. 'This bed,' she whispered, over his helpless form, 'this bed is full of little surprises. It was her bed when she stayed here – the Priestess. Her bed and her room. No wonder it's soundproofed! I can almost feel her presence. She belongs here. I know it!' With that she yanked on the hanging cords and the heavy brocades fell down to entomb them both in a voluptuous intimacy.

At once Elaine was astride him, facing the foot of the bed with one hand upon his thigh. The other swung rapidly and he jerked as the strap fell across his reddened flesh. With each stroke her body lowered a little until her sex was but a tongue's length from his face. The voice cried from above, 'Now you bastard! Now!'

With the final stroke he almost cried out but his parted lips engaged her intimately and his tongue found her hot and aroused. His task began with an urgency and zeal seldom accorded even Victoria. And the threat of the strap was not the only inducement, for all his resources were concentrated in this one place. He was a machine geared only for her satisfaction. Elaine spread herself wider and his tongue speared deeper to savour her passion, withdrawing only to tease the swollen clitoris.

And who now was in control? He was at the reins of her lust, driving her ever onward. Her body trembled, her gasps filled the crypt-like space and she twisted askew to settle down, fingers digging into his burning behind, cheek pressed against his thigh. Her control was slipping as she squirmed about and moaned ever louder, 'Ah, Christ! Ah, Christ!' She began to haul herself up about his legs, then with a final, long and despairing cry, her body was set quivering in abandoned passion. Gareth revelled in the nectar of her orgasm, all but feeling her relief within himself.

Elaine released his legs before pulling back the brocades.

She moved slowly, as though exhausted, then sat by the prostrate figure. In a low voice she said, 'Get up.'

He twisted aside and she moved to allow his legs to swing over the edge. His penis was distended, the pouch gaping and he felt it must soon burst. His breath caught as her fingers touched upon the smooth nylon skin and pushed under the taut elastic. That he could hardly feel his useless arms no longer mattered. Had she deprived him of speech, too, and he considered that she might at the merest whim, he would not have cared.

'You did rather well, Gareth,' she whispered, stroking the side of the coiled organ. 'I can't help but think that you have already had some training – at the hands of Victoria, perhaps. I see you're shaved too. Very appropriate. Who knows what else you might be taught to accomplish given the time and opportunity. Stand up!'

Gareth stood before her. His penis leapt free as she tugged the elastic and wriggled the tiny garment down his legs. She placed the G-string on the bed and picked up her own discarded briefs. Her finger ran along the engorged shaft, from the bulbous head to the root and slowly back again. She watched it quiver uncontrollably. 'I dare say you'd like to fuck me. Yes, of course you would. But that will not be for some time, Gareth, and it will mean your total restraint and compliance.' So saying, she lifted the gossamer briefs, lowered them over the glistening head, then part wrapped them about the foreskin. He groaned as her fingers closed upon him and she continued, 'The strap and the riding crop – you'll have to accept these, Gareth, and more. Do nod if you agree.' Her hand worked the shaft back and forth gently, but moving faster with each excruciating, pent-up second. Gareth closed his eyes, feeling his loins begin to burn. He nodded.

'Ah, good,' came her voice as he felt himself losing control. 'You'll thank me for it in the end. Much better than being a tax accountant, Gareth, much, much better.'

Her last remark was lost as the burning fire raged through his body. He gasped repeatedly and tensed hard against the straitjacket, loins shivering, spurting wildly and copiously into her briefs, his mind soaring like a golden bird into a sky of pure pleasure.

The nylon hung heavy and wet against his flesh. His eyes remained closed as her fingers released the straps at his front. The restraint slowly loosened. 'You'd better ensure any stains are removed from that carpet, dear, or I'll thrash your arse with much more than a school strap!'

'Yes,' he whispered at last. 'Yes, leave me alone – I'll do it.'

'And remember, before I go,' she continued, gathering the skirt about her waist, 'part of your commitment is your discretion, Gareth. Always discretion. It is what we must live by!'

'And you feel he accepts the situation?' asked Barbara.

'Ninety per cent,' answered Elaine, sipping the dry sherry. 'The rest of him will probably follow. I don't think we need concern ourselves with Victoria, judging from what has happened.'

'No, nor I. Already I find myself regarding her as belonging here. She will return to London with Gareth at the end of the month to clear up their affairs. Sophie does not wish to go back at all, despite her experience in the tower.'

'Or because of it,' offered Elaine.

Barbara smiled. 'You were always more direct than I, but I think Gemma may have something to do with her decision. Each of them derives – let us say – more than a little comfort from the other.'

'And the special dinner next weekend,' began Elaine, 'the day they would have left us – do they know?'

'I left it to Vicky to speak to them. It will be a celebration for us all and I have, of course, invited Angelo.' Barbara raised the sherry glass to her lips. 'By the way, I have made a concession to Victoria as regards Amber. It seems she went too far with one of her stupid tricks when they last returned. Victoria wished to be placed in charge of her. I thought it a good idea.'

'Yes, it's what she needs, and then we shall have a hierarchy.'

A pallid glare flickered through the lounge. 'I doubt if Amber will see things that way but I think Victoria knows how to handle her almost as well as you. And that is saying something.'

A low rumble followed by a louder detonation rolled by the windows and Elaine said, 'This storm is going to last through the night and into tomorrow. I find it almost comforting.'

'Comforting perhaps,' smiled Barbara, 'and something of a convenience, I think.'

Epilogue

'*Grazie, signorina,*' smiled Angelo as Sophie poured chilled champagne into his waiting glass. He again tasted the aroma of the little black maid's dress, stretching about her slim figure in burnished latex. An identically attired Gemma filled Barbara's glass before both girls moved down their respective sides of the table. Sophie filled Elaine's and Gareth's glass: Gemma, Victoria's and lastly, Amber's. Candle flames wavered and the iron-caged lamp threw soft light about the vaulted ceiling. Gareth might have felt ill at ease in suit and tie, but for the presence of Angelo, dressed with equal formality. Barbara and Elaine had reverted to the severe black dresses of former times, a style which for this evening Victoria had also adopted. It rendered the contrast between themselves and the revealingly clad maids all the more evident. So, too, in the case of Amber, whose situation was altogether different.

'Shall we bring in the first course now?' asked Gemma.

'Not just yet,' replied Barbara. 'I think we should first drink a toast with our new friends.'

'Does that mean I'm still left out?' asked a disgruntled Amber. 'All afternoon in this is more than enough.'

Barbara did not reply but turned her gaze to Victoria. Victoria in turn looked at Amber, sitting by her side with arms folded across her chest and securely contained within the heavy rubber straitjacket. 'More than enough?' responded Victoria. 'It certainly is not! Not after your last little trick. Sophie will feed you and you'll use the straw for your drinks. Everything else will be done for you before bedtime, dear, and I do mean everything!' Amber stared at her in disbelief as Victoria continued. 'If I feel you've gone even halfway to paying the penalty by tomorrow morning I might – only might – let you free!'

'I think you're very lenient,' commented Elaine seeing Amber's woeful expression. 'I certainly feel stricter treatment would have been in order.' Barbara noted how Gareth glanced warily at her.

'Never mind,' said Barbara, 'I suppose we could call this your first real day here Vicky, Sophie and Gareth, for you would otherwise now be on your way back to England. Sophie, Gemma, you have not poured champagne for yourselves – everyone must join in.' The two complied willingly. Barbara raised her glass and spoke gently. 'I propose a toast to our new friends, to our new future, and to this house: the Villa Raffaello!'

NEXUS BACKLIST

All books are priced £4.99 unless another price is given. If a date is supplied, the book in question will not be available until that month in 1997.

CONTEMPORARY EROTICA

AGONY AUNT	G. C. Scott	Jul
ALLISON'S AWAKENING	John Angus	Jul
BOUND TO SERVE	Amanda Ware	
BOUND TO SUBMIT	Amanda Ware	Sep
CANDIDA'S SECRET MISSION	Virginia LaSalle	
CANDY IN CAPTIVITY	Arabella Knight	
CHALICE OF DELIGHTS	Katrina Young	
THE CHASTE LEGACY	Susanna Hughes	
CHRISTINA WISHED	Gene Craven	
CONDUCT UNBECOMING	Arabella Knight	
DARK DESIRES	Maria del Rey	
DIFFERENT STROKES	Sarah Veitch	
THE DOMINO TATTOO	Cyrian Amberlake	
THE DOMINO ENIGMA	Cyrian Amberlake	
THE DOMINO QUEEN	Cyrian Amberlake	
EDEN UNVEILED	Maria del Rey	
EDUCATING ELLA	Stephen Ferris	Aug
ELAINE	Stephen Ferris	
EMMA'S SECRET WORLD	Hilary James	
EMMA ENSLAVED	Hilary James	
EMMA'S SECRET DIARIES	Hilary James	
EMMA'S SUBMISSION	Hilary James	
EMMA'S HUMILIATION	Hilary James	May
FALLEN ANGELS	Kendal Grahame	

EROTIC SCIENCE FICTION

ANCIENT & FANTASY SETTINGS

Please send me the books I have ticked above.

Name   ....

Address   ....

                ....

                ....

                .... Post code ....

Send to: **Cash Sales, Nexus Books, 332 Ladbroke Grove, London W10 5AH**

Please enclose a cheque or postal order, made payable to Virgin Publishing, to the value of the books you have ordered plus postage and packing costs as follows:

UK and BFPO – £1.00 for the first book, 50p for each subsequent book.

Overseas (including Republic of Ireland) – £2.00 for the first book, £1.00 for each subsequent book.

If you would prefer to pay by VISA or ACCESS/MASTER-CARD, please write your card number and expiry date here:

....

Please allow up to 28 days for delivery.

Signature   ....